I0691611

Sazerac, Sleuth & Slay

by

Mary Cunningham

An Andi Anna Jones Mystery

Sazerac, Sleuth & Slay

Cover Art by *The Wild Rose Press, Inc.*

The Wild Rose Press, Inc.
PO Box 708
Adams Basin, NY 14410-0708
Visit us at www.thewildrosepress.com

Publishing History
First Edition, 2023
Trade Paperback ISBN 978-1-5092-4744-8
Digital ISBN 978-1-5092-4745-5

An Andi Anna Jones Mystery
Published in the United States of America

Dedication

As always, to Ken.
Gratitude and love to my husband, Ken for his pep talks
when I'm worn down, and for keeping me focused
when I get lazy. I couldn't do this without his
unwavering support of my dreams.

Acknowledgements

I'm grateful to so many for supporting my journey. My dad, a journalist for forty-five years, introduced me to the world of writing. The words of my 3rd grade teacher, Mrs. Leffler, "Mary, whatever you do, don't stop writing," still inspires me to do what I love.

To the Carrollton Writers Guild for your gentle, but honest critiques. Yes! I do listen!

And many thanks to Val Mathews, for her encouragement and belief in Andi Anna Jones. Much appreciation to Frances Sevilla for making the editing process practically stress-free, yet, instructive. The lessons and guidelines I've received from editors during twenty-plus years, is invaluable, and I'm still learning. To artist, RJ Morris, for capturing the perfect Louisiana bayou vision, along with a healthy dose of humor. The cover exceeds expectations!

A big thanks to all cozy and suspense mystery authors and friends for their motivation, including Regan Black, Karen MacInerney, Julia Buckley, Joanna Campbell Slan, Dana Taylor, Roberta Isleib (Lucy Burdette), Carolyn Haines, and many more. To author/editor Jaden (Beth) Terrell for years of generosity and support for me and all writers lucky enough to be in her circle, and to my best friend, Diana Black, for inspiring, commiserating, supporting, and providing belly laughs when I really need them!

Finally, to my cherished, four-legged furkid, Lucy, for being my constant and trusting companion for eleven years. Run free across the Rainbow Bridge, baby girl.

Prologue

Somewhere in the Bayou

Luther woke up raring to go for a change. Wasn't sure why, 'cause he hated, hated the job! It was nasty. He stunk to high heaven by mid-morning.

Hells Bells! Sweat had already collected on strands of hair stuck to his grimy forehead. He adjusted the straps of his faded bibs so they fit snug to his shoulders. Couldn't have a strap fall down and pin his arm at the wrong time. More than once, he'd lost his catch cause of a careless slip.

He reckoned the only thing that got him up and moving, so all-fired early, was because today was Friday, and he figured on adding enough money to finally take Marlene out for a real dinner and some Zydeco music and dancing afterwards. And, no, those nasty mini lobsters he depended on for his livelihood wouldn't be on their plates—leastways, not his!

His toes squirmed in those hot rubber boots, but the alternative meant sloshing around barefoot through the rice fields bordering the briny water. He'd sooner have hot feet than grimy ones.

"Lawdy, Luther, you're all fish-smellin'," his going-on-four-years gal complained on more than one occasion. "Don't you even think 'bout walkin' 'cross my clean floor 'til you wash those feet!" The boots he

1

could just kick off outside and hose down, so he put up with the discomfort.

He carried an extra trap on this trip in case the one he'd left the night before was full.

Wishful thinkin' probly.

The fresh dry dog food he used for bait, he'd had to sneak out of Molly's bag when she wasn't looking, or she'd snap at him for stealing her dinner.

Smart dog, that one. Ornery as an old mule, though.

The darkening sky spit rain by the time he got to the lake, but the clouds didn't look angry; just mischievous enough to make the morning miserable and the swamp bank, slippery. He'd have to be careful he didn't end up in the water with the critters. Locating the trap line, he carefully tied it to a cypress tree, and pulled...and pulled. Something flashed in the sunlight, just below the surface of the water.

"Son of a biscuit eater! Must be snagged on a branch." Or maybe he'd caught the mother of all crawfish!

Sure, Luther. Dream on.

He moved sideways toward a large log, anchored his foot for leverage, and pulled again. The trap loosened and moved through the water, but something still dragged it down.

"Dadgummit!" He secured the rope and pulled off his boots. No choice but to wade in to see what was holding his "bounty" hostage.

His toes squished in soggy mud about four feet offshore. Hoped he didn't step on a sharp rock, or worse. Three months back, Luther'd almost lost a toe to an irritable snapping turtle.

2

One vicious pull and the trap sprang free. A mass of Spanish moss came with it.

"Now what? This ain't my day."

Luther would never be mistaken for a NASA engineer, but his ability to process the scene was slow, even for him. "Dammitall, dat ain't moss. Wuz a wig doin' in da lake?"

People had no sense of decency when it came to littering. *What next? A voodoo mask and top hat?* Grabbing the cage with his fingers, he gave one last tug and yelped with the same intensity as Molly that time she ran under a storage shed and met the business end of a skunk. The sight before him, bobbing with the current, sent him reeling backwards into the murky water.

He spun around and crawled up the bank fast as an alligator that'd just spied an egret preoccupied with a freshly caught fish.

How long could his heart pound at that rate before it exploded out of his chest? Forcing himself to focus on the trap, and its unanticipated cargo, confirmed he'd made no mistake about what he saw the first time.

Later, the St. Charles police bagged the body and all the evidence, including Luther's crawfish haul. About seventeen dollars, he figured. Money he'd planned to put with the eighty he'd already saved to show Marlene a good time. They'd hung together since high school, even though Luther dropped out after his sophomore year. For weeks he'd counted on finally being able to take her someplace nice. Nicer than the usual neighborhood bar. "Daggone dead body ruint my whole weekend," he grumbled.

"Did you say something, Mr. Bertrand?"

He shook his head at the officer. "Nah, I was jest sayin' a little prayer for da woman, whoever she was. Didn't deserve dat kinda endin'."

"Sorry we have to take your trap and haul, but you can pick it up when we're through removing all the evidence."

Realizing the "evidence" was the poor woman's hair and attached body stuck to the cage, Luther had a moment of remorse about blaming her for ruining his plans. *After all, her plans were ruined permanently. Still, all those mudbugs.*

"You kin keep da haul. Won't be worth nothin' 'thout bein' packed on ice."

Chapter One

I sorted through a dozen or more radio stations, one worse than the next.

"And, for only $159.99 a month for twelve months, you can enjoy your very own tanning bed."

I live in Florida. Free sun, idiot! Punch.

"Is your skin starting to resemble that of an alligator? Our gold and diamond infused face cream…"

Geesh, they should pair up with the tanning bed people. Punch.

"Are you a sinner? A lost soul in need of saving?"

Probably. No time today, though. Punch.

"Louisiana officials are stumped by four dead bodies that have turned up on the outskirts of New Orleans in the past three months. While no conclusive connection has been found among the victims, suspicions are building that a serial killer may be responsible."

"Oh, no you don't. I refuse to listen." I snapped at the car radio. "Depressing news is not how I'm starting this day." I turned on the custom-installed CD player and belted out the first tune that popped up.

Rolling down the window of the vintage Mustang, I let the wind whip my hair into a tangled mess and sang along with the Bee Gees.

So, my falsetto needs a little work. Who cares?

My dear, late mom was a true-blue groupie of the

Miami transplants, and I considered playing their old tunes an honor and a tribute.

Flamingo Drive was surprisingly empty for the eight-thirty a.m. rush-hour, which led me to believe, it was gonna be a fantastic day!

That would be my first mistake.

****

Four lines ringing! Four freakin' lines! Where the hell is Ellie?

"Graves Travel. Could you hold, please?" I pressed line three. "Hello, Mr. Connor, let me see what I can find for you. Did you want to leave out of Miami or Ft. Lauderdale? Hello, Mr. Conner? Hello?" *Crap.*

I stared at the blinking lights. Now three of them. Who was on which line? Let's see. Lucinda Minor was on two, or was that one? I took a chance and pushed number one. "Lucy?" *Oh, thank God!* "Let me get your information...You're looking at the Alaskan cruise and tour package for ten nights. Okay. Leaving out of Seattle or Vancouver? Got it. Let me see what I can do...Yes, I know. Outside cabin, only."

Like I'd forget that! Just picturing living for a week in an over-sized closet with no windows, made me light-headed. "I'll get back to you this afternoon...You have a great day, too. Bye."

Lines two and four were amazingly, still blinking. *Hmmm. What to choose. Where is Ellie?* After three years, you'd think she would've realized I couldn't handle the agency by myself. Who was I kidding? I struggled even when she was here. It was still a mystery why Parker Graves willed the travel business to me. Sure, he was Dad's best friend and our neighbor for thirty years, but still, I was shocked by the bequest.

More shocked that I agreed to take it.

"Eeeny-meeny-miney-mo." My scientific approach led to line four. Ta-da! "Sorry to keep you waiting. This is Andi. How may I help you?" Oh, no. Why did it have to be him? Of all days! "Hello Mr. Payne" *His name fits to a T!* "No, Ellie isn't here. Yes, I understand you'd rather not talk to me, but, how many times do I have to apologize for sending you to the wrong city? Yes," I sighed, "and the wrong state. In my defense, you did say clearly you wanted to fly to Dallas." I pulled the phone away from my ear. "Yes, I should've remembered your daughter lives in Dallas, *Georgia*, but...well, I did eat the cost of flying you from DFW to Atlanta." *Just keep your cool, Andi. Let him rant for the umpteenth time about this one tiny mistake.* Still amazed me how anyone with half a brain wouldn't know before takeoff where their flight was headed.

As I recall, he'd fumed, "I was late getting to the gate, thanks to those gol-darned inefficient TSA people, so I just handed the attendant my ticket and took my seat! Besides, I figured you knew what you were doing, so I didn't have to. I'll never make that mistake, again."

I should've let well-enough-alone and let him rant. Instead, I asked if, by any chance, he had heard the pilot or flight attendants mention the destination.

"I never listen to those idiotic messages. They're for people who don't know which end's up!"

Oh, like you?

When would I learn it never paid to argue with warped logic? "Look, why don't I have Ellie call when she gets in. Yes, I'll give her the message the minute she walks through the door." Click.

One down, one to go. Oops. None to go because

whoever was on line two hung up as I cow-towed to crotchety Mr. Payne. Might as well find something constructive to do until my tardy employee arrives. *Let's see. Alaskan Cruises.* An online search presented a number of options for Lucy. We also had brochures lying around here somewhere I could have ready when she came in, except I had no clue where Ellie put the latest ones she'd unpacked. I walked to the front rack. *Ah, here they are. Go figure. Right where they should be.*

Don't forget to have Ellie call Mr. Payne!

"I was in a good mood when I got here this morning," I grumbled to no one in particular. Pulling out a couple of cruise flyers, I shifted to more pleasant thoughts. *Sheriff Manual Rodriquez*; the one positive affair (pun intended) that sprang from my relationship with my dad's widow, Ruby, and her "mishap" in Cancun. Never could I have expected to meet such a hunk. And, I certainly didn't suspect he was a Florida native, too.

Our week together, when he flew to Miami, had been way too short. Between his family and professional obligations, we'd had one glorious night together. Nothing like the embarrassing evening in Cancun. Yes, I admit, singing with a Mariachi band was not one of my finer moments. A flush crept up my neck to my cheeks.

My attention shifted from the heat my body had involuntarily built, to the sound of screeching tires in the agency parking lot. A '91 faded orange Camaro flew into an empty parking space; one wheel climbing halfway up the tire abutment before thudding back to the pavement. The driver applied mascara as the car came to a stop. Ripping off her T-Shirt, she tugged at her bra, and grabbed something from the back seat. Slipping a sundress over her head, she sprang from the driver's seat. A vigorous yank, on the hem of the dress that had caught in her waistband, allowed its fall to the appropriate place six inches above the knee.

Ellie. It always amazed me how she could roll out of bed and be at work in twenty minutes, especially when she lived fifteen minutes away. Snatching her purse off the passenger seat, she slammed the car door. Reopened the car door. Grabbed a gigantic gas station soda. Repeated the slamming process.

Watching her barrel through the front door of the agency with the same gusto she'd parked the car, I braced for another dramatic entrance. "Hey, Jonesy. Sorry I'm late," she announced between slurps on the straw of the Big Gulp, "but I had a night you wouldn't believe!"

I braced again; this time for a thirty-minute account of hers and Rodney's latest exploits. Did they prompt another visit from the fire department after setting on fire the top of another palmetto tree in a futile attempt to "burn out" the nasty black bugs that nested in the top fronds? Perhaps sink another paddle boat in the middle of the man-made lake bordering their Florida ranch?

Leaning back in my chair, I refocused my attention on her nasal twang as she yacked about Wan and Chantelle, their neighbors, whose arguments, according to Ellie, were legendary. Wan, swearing in high-pitched Chinese-English, and Chantelle threatening, in sing-song Jamaican, to lay a curse on every single one of his body parts.

"I swear, Jonesy, when we were at their place for

dinner last night, I made the mistake of lifting the lid off a pot boiling on the stove. A goat head stared back at me! That was enough to convince me she could cook up some nasty curses on just about anybody." Ellie plopped down in front of a computer and quickly logged on while continuing her narrative. "One thing for sure, if Wan ever disappears, ain't no way I'm looking in any of her pots!" She jumped up and headed to the back. "Can you hold the fort while I brush my teeth and spray some deodorant under my arms?"

I've been holding it down for the past hour-and-a-half! "Sure, no problem. The customers and I will appreciate your efforts."

She popped her head back around the corner. "Did you make coffee? I like to gargle with it to get that awful toothpaste taste out of my mouth."

Well, that's a new one. "Careful. It's hot," was all I managed to say.

Ellie and her preoccupation with magic. She'd always had an active imagination when it came to curses and witchcraft, especially after she found out her fourth great-grandmother was rumored to have dabbled in voodoo in Louisiana.

Speaking of curses, I'll have a big one put on me if I forget to tell Ellie to call Mr. Payne.

Chapter Two

I stood in the break room and stirred stevia and a splash of half and half in my *Dolphin's* coffee mug. I used the term "break room" loosely when "glorified closet"—with a small water heater and furnace that ran less than a dozen times since I took over the suite in the Miami Lakes Plaza—was a more appropriate description. A mini sink and ultra-mini fridge in the corner left room for one occupant at a time. I'd bartered for the work with the strip center landlord. Six hours work for two round-trip airline tickets to Las Vegas. He'd wanted me to throw in a weekend stay at the Mandalay Bay Resort and Casino. When I balked, he still did the job, pouting the entire time.

The convenience of making a couple pots of coffee in the morning was crucial to my sanity. I'd also vowed to take my lunch to work until the business broke even. Three years later and I still packed my lunch. But, I reasoned, the savings to my pocketbook and my waistline had been well worth the effort. Fortunately, my speedy metabolism helped with the waistline, too. God forbid I'd have to exercise!

I took a sip of the medium roast, chicory brew, and had the sudden urge for a latte, or as it was known in South Florida, *Cafe con Leche*. Too bad it was Monday because Thursday through Saturday, the *Miami Espresso Machine* coffee wagon parked at the farmer's

11

market a couple of miles away. The money I saved on lunch and coffee, most of the week, was gladly allotted to Bruce Lindner, owner-brew master, for the special drink named after *yours truly*. The *Andi Dandi*—perfect for the Florida heat—consisted of iced espresso with a shot of half and half, dark chocolate, salted caramel, and topped with a light dusting of cinnamon. Each time I groaned at the cost of one of his golden brews, he'd retort, "You're meaner 'n ten snakes without my special coffee, Andi. Think how much I save you in court costs." I'm sure many would have agreed with him. *Yeah, yeah, whatever.*

Ah, but today I'd just have to make do with my New Orleans blend. Not a bad substitute, although I'd never say that to Bruce! I'd started toward the front room when a voice stopped me in my tracks.

"You mean that boss of yours didn't tell you I called?"

Crap! I jumped back into the break room and squeezed behind the door. Thank God the lights were off!

"Uh, oh, sure…sure she did. I have the note right here," Ellie scrambled. "Yep, call Mr. Payne, ASAP, exclamation point."

Whew, thanks for covering, El. You are hereby exonerated for being late this morning. Wonder why I forgot to tell her? *Must be some type of Freudian slip on my part*, or, *I can't tolerate that man.* Intimidating, demanding, and obnoxious, to boot. And those were his good qualities. I tiptoed from the break room into my office so I could eavesdrop on their conversation. Please, Ellie, take care of him by yourself and I'll owe you a huge raise. Make that a small raise.

Ellie addressed the sour, impatient client. "So, what can I do for you, Mr. Payne?"

"Nothing for me. It's for my wife. She's going to some hair-brained convention in New Orleans next week and expects me to make last minute arrangements for her."

Hmmm, the Big Easy. Strange how Ellie's mysterious Louisiana ancestor had popped into my head this morning, and soon after, a request for reservations in New Orleans. The computer keyboard hummed with the high speed tapping of my assistant's fingers.

The tapping stopped. "Is the convention being held near one of the hotels?"

"Oh, hell, I guess so. She mentioned they were all gathering somewhere on Canal Street. Tell the truth, I wasn't paying much attention to her yammering."

Nice guy, huh?

Tap, tap, tap, ratta-tap-tap. "The Sheraton is on Canal. Would you like me to check on a room there?"

"I better call her." He punched in a number and cleared his throat. "Yeah, Grace. I'm here at the travel agency trying to book you a room. Where, exactly, is this convention?" He listened to her reply and huffed, "Well, if it's at the Sheraton, why don't you want to *stay* at the Sheraton? You'll be on the premises and won't need a car to get back and forth. Staying in the French Quarter, miles away, is just plain asinine! I know you want to experience the flavor of the city, but…"

Hmm. I'm not the only one on the wrong side of his foul moods.

"Do you know what could happen to you there? I

just heard about a string of unsolved murders around that city. Four women found strangled in the swamps! " His voice expressed annoyance while Grace, apparently, argued on the other end. "Well, you better hope to find a way to get back and forth because it'll be too far for you to hoof it. Especially with those bunions of yours. Okay, whatever." He disconnected and sighed so loud I pictured Ellie's platinum-streaked hair in the center of a hurricane wind tunnel. I listened for another explosion, but his composure surprised me. "Seems she insists on staying in the Quarter. See what kinda 'fancy-schmancy' place you can find."

The tapping commenced. "Here's a quaint little place, not too pricey and the reviews are pretty decent, too. Here, take a look. It's the Chateau Maison on Toulouse Street."

"Yeah, looks okay to me. How much? Can I get a senior discount?"

"I don't think the AARP rate will make any difference, Mr. Payne, but here's the price per night. There is a slight discount if you book three nights in a row."

He roared. "Geeze-oh-pete! Highway robbery! One night is about as much as the round-trip airline ticket!"

I feared the conversation was getting out of hand. Set to spring from my chair, I heard Ellie calmly state, "Mr. Payne. I'm only the messenger, not the hotel proprietor. If you want me to look for something outside the Quarter, but within walking distance, I will, but please don't yell. I'd certainly understand if you tried another agency."

He slammed his hand on the desk. "Are you refusing my business?"

That's it! I sprinted to the front. "Mr. Payne, Ellie is just doing her job. Now, please calm yourself while she finds something both you and Mrs. Payne can accept." I forced myself to include him in the decision although I wanted to snap, *Grace is a competent, grown woman! It's none of your damn business where she stays!*

He glared. "I'd be better off never stepping foot in here again! That hotel is probably a flea bag. Oh, hell, what's the use? Stubborn women," he mumbled. "Just book the damned thing, but my wife better be happy with it, or I'm suing!"

You don't give a rat's behind whether your wife is happy, or not, ya big blowhard!

Ellie looked up from the computer screen; her face a picture of calm and professionalism. "How would you prefer to pay?"

God, she's smooth. Fascinated with curses, goat head-cooking neighbors, more often late, than not. *Who cares?* I needed Ellie more than she needed me. And, she knew it.

He pulled out his wallet and threw down a credit card. "Put it on this."

I stood close by while Ellie finalized the reservation, my knees visibly knocking. "Here's Mrs. Payne's confirmation," Ellie concluded. "All the information is on this sheet about check-in and checkout times, amenities, and so forth. If *she* has any questions, *she* can call anytime."

He snatched the paper from Ellie's hand and stormed out the door. "It's her damned money, anyway. Let her waste it."

"Whew. For a minute there, thought I'd have to

arm wrestle the old buzzard," Ellie smirked. "And, speaking of buzzards, his breath was enough to kill a whole flock in full flight." She faked a gag. "Oh, but thanks for eventually coming out of hiding. You'll be happy to know Mr. P-A-I-N is taken care of. Grace's trip is booked and paid for."

"You checked everything? I don't even want to think about his coming back in here!" After the Texas Georgia fiasco, he'd sue me for sure with another screw-up.

Ellie spun the computer screen around for my viewing. "She's booked, roundtrip, to Louis Armstrong New Orleans International Airport with reservations for four nights in the Quarter."

"And you're sure of the dates?"

"Yes, Jonesy, I double-checked." She let out a purposeful sigh directed at yours truly.

"Sorry, but after last time…well, you know. That mistake cost me over a thousand dollars, and it wasn't even my fault."

"I know," she snickered. "Dallas, Texas-Dallas, Georgia. One and the same."

I ignored the dig. "Anyway, Now that my heart stopped pounding, if you're happy with the reservation, I'm happy. After I finish my research for Lucy, I'm going to run some errands." I stepped into my office, grabbed my coffee mug, and scurried back to the break room wondering why I couldn't shake the foreboding something, *something,* was very wrong.

Chapter Three

Besides putting the finishing touches on Lucy's itinerary, the rest of the week was fairly quiet, with one major exception.

Oh, please no. A brand new, crimson red, convertible lurched into one of the handicapped parking spaces in front of the agency.

The car died, mercifully, before it lunged through the plate glass window. A somewhat frazzled red-haired senior citizen crawled from behind the steering wheel, kicked the door shut, pulled down a skin-tight skirt, and adjusted five-inch, sling-back heels. Not as creative as Ellie's entrance earlier in the week, but I'd give it a seven out of ten.

Uh-oh. I'd seen that indignant look on Ruby's face many times before.

I grudgingly acknowledged my ex-stepmother since she was married for five years to my deceased father, Andrew Anderson Jones, Jr.—a fact I couldn't change no matter how much I resented their marriage.

"I swear." She huffed. "I don't know why Dougie would buy me a car that's impossible to drive! 'Put one foot on the brake, the other on the clutch, move the brake foot to the gas pedal, and try to keep from slamming into something.' Land Sakes! I worked up a sweat just driving over here."

Only Ruby can knock the gift of a new car.

"That's awful! If I were you, I'd tell him to send a wrecker to pick up that piece of trash." *Or, better yet. Leave it and I'll dispose of the clunker, myself.* My sarcasm fell on deaf ears, or rather, *dense* ears.

"You are so right, Andi Anna. That's just what I'm going to do. Well, after I drive to that new boutique at Lakeside Mall, and to my nail appointment. And, of course I can't miss my weekly trip to Bayside. But, after that, you can bet I'll give him *what for*!"

Attempting to play with Ruby's head had grown way too tiresome to continue.

"So, why did you drive over here? A phone call would've been sufficient," I mumbled.

"What? Did you say something?"

I waited to answer until she'd finished reapplying her lip gloss. "Now that you're safely here, makeup intact," I mocked, "what can I do for you?"

She pursed her lips, checked her teeth for smudges and snapped her compact shut. "Now, Andi Anna, those frown lines on your face will be permanent if you're not careful. You need to smile more. Besides, it'd be good for business."

"My business is just peachy, thank you, and, it might interest you to know, wrinkles add character." Besides, I could always check out that zillion dollar anti-alligator-skin face cream I heard about on the way to work the other day. Instead, I plopped down at my computer.

Undeterred, she sat in the chair across from me. "I'm here as a client, so you have to treat me like one."

I wanted to smack the smug look off her face but, instead, I gave her my best "The customer is always right" smile. "So, Ms. Jones, how may I help you?"

18

"That's better, but you know I prefer *Mrs.* Jones. Oh, I still miss my sweet Drew." She dug a hankie out of her purse and dabbed at invisible tears in the corners of her eyes. "Oh, dear," she sighed. "I just never know when unbearable grief is going to hit." She pretended to blow her nose. "There, all done. Now, I need a reservation, ASAP. Cloris and Doris invited me to their bunco club the other night. Oh, it was such fun! But, as I was leaving, I overheard some of the girls talking about going to New Orleans for a convention. Since they'd already welcomed me into their club, I knew they'd want me to go along. Oh, you should've seen the stunned looks on their faces when I assured them I'd love to go! Why, they were speechless!"

Stunned? Speechless? I could picture that.

"Although I can't afford it," she continued, "I whined to Dougie about missing out on all the fun until he agreed to pay for the whole trip." She fumbled in her purse and pulled out a slip of paper. "Here are the details. I need a room—no make that a suite—next week at the Sheraton. That's where the convention is being held."

"The Sheraton?" I'm certain I heard Stewart tell Ellie that Grace's convention was there, too. "What convention is it, Ruby?"

"Oh, I don't know. Some kind of picture-taking deal. Sounds boring, especially since I don't know diddley-squat about cameras. Haven't even learned to use the one on my phone, yet," she chuckled. "But it's time for me to get out of this ol' rut I'm in and spread some joy." She threw her arms wide open as if greeting an invisible, adoring crowd.

I marveled at her resiliency and self-worth. Even at

19

age sixty, I couldn't picture Ruby ever being in a rut. "But, what about your trip to Cancun? Wasn't being accused of murder enough excitement?"

"Oh, silly goose," Ruby chuckled. "When are you ever going to stop badgering me about that? I didn't murder that Lenny fella, and I was cleared, thanks to my lawyer-friend, Bert. Oh, and you, too, of course."

I wanted to bang my head on the desk. Instead, I took a deep breath and thanked my lucky stars Ruby and I no longer shared the same living space.

After our Cancun horror trip, she'd ditched her Florida block-built ranch and had occupied my bedroom for a month, while I slept on the fold-out couch. "I don't think I could stay alone in that house, especially at night," she'd sniffled. "Besides, Andi, honey, this can be so much fun! Just two available *girls* living together, going shopping, painting the town. Why, it'll be just like we're on vacation."

You mean, like your vacation in the Cancun jail and my vacation flying to Las Vegas, to catch the real culprit? Not to mention, almost getting killed in the process. That kind of vacation?

"Besides, think of the money we'll save!"

"You're going to pay rent?"

"Oh, of course not," she'd scoffed. "But, I have all kinds of money-saving ideas!"

I couldn't deny her gift for saving money—hers. No house payment, no rent, no utilities. Sure, she bought an occasional grocery item, but most expenditure revolved around her beauty regimen.

I would've never agreed to such an arrangement except for my promise to Dad to watch after his new wife if anything ever happened to him. *Lucky me. He had five years with her and now I'm going to be stuck with her for the rest of her life.* On the bright side, staying patient had paid off. It didn't take dear stepmom long to move on to her next target. *And, how's this for irony?* While trying to set me up with every single man in North Miami, despite my protests, Ruby was the one who'd latched onto a rich widower who loved to dance and party as much as she.

I'd had the pleasure of meeting her latest source of income and extravagant gifts, Douglas Windleman, III, the first time he picked Ruby up at my house. "Having this adoring red-headed jewel on my arm keeps me young and sexy," he'd schmoozed. The slicked-back, silver haired septuagenarian patted his date's derriere producing a spasm of giggles from his newest *arm candy.* Thank God, Ruby moved out before I was subjected to the spectacle of a *second* date pickup, or worse.

Yuck! I didn't need that visual stuck in my head for the rest of the day. I pulled up info on the Sheraton in New Orleans. The sooner I booked her reservation, the sooner I'd get her out of the agency. "What are the dates?"

"Oh, let me see. I believe they said Tuesday through Saturday. To tell you the truth, they were talking so low I had a hard time hearing them."

Why am I not surprised? I hesitated to ask but, "By any chance, is Grace Payne going to this same convention?"

"Why yes, she is. I believe there are fifteen going, plus me, of course."

Should I mention Grace is staying in the French Quarter instead of the convention site? *Naah.* Ruby asked for the Sheraton, so that's what she'd get. My fingers flew across the keyboard. Whew. *Six night availability. Non-stop flight from Miami to New Orleans.* Got it! I fought the urge to book a *one-way* plane reservation. "Let me print it out. How will you be paying?"

She rooted around in her purse, I assumed to pull out her wallet or a credit card. Instead, she peeled the wrapper off a piece of gum, popped it in her mouth and dismissed my question with a hand flip. "Oh, silly goose! Charge it to Dougie, of course. He said to put it on his account. Trust me. I'll make it worth his while." Her pencil-drawn eyebrows danced around like two bacon strips on a hot griddle.

Oh, dear Lord. I could get sued six ways to Sunday for this. But I did have his credit information. "Fine, Ruby, but have Doug call me. I want to hear it from the horse's mouth."

Ruby huffed, "Now, Andi Anna. When have I ever lied to you?"

"There aren't enough hours left in the day, Ruby. Just have him call."

I printed the itinerary and handed it to her, reluctantly. I'd be willing to bet the bunco club ladies were less than thrilled to have Ruby tag along; especially Grace Payne. They'd never been friends and ran in completely different social circles. Grace came from an "old money" family. Ruby came from a "no money" family. Oh, well. *Not my circus. Not my clowns.*

Chapter Four

I called Lucy the following Wednesday to let her know I'd finished booking her three-week Alaskan cruise and tour. "I was just ready to call, Andi! I was out of town until late last night. Did you try to reach me?"

"No, I just completed the details this morning. Come over, when it's convenient."

She burst through the agency door ten minutes after we hung up. "Oh, Andi, this is just perfect." She hugged the itinerary to her chest. "Three weeks of pure bliss, cruising the strait, photographing the glaciers, before they all melt." She clucked. "And, this eco tour, complete with adorable little cabins, is a dream! I can't wait!"

She was delighted with the extra days. I knew she would be. *That's just Lucy.* Always grateful, constantly happy, and looking on the bright side, even after a nasty divorce. Unlike some, she never caused problems. Her unlimited supply of travel money, thanks to her ex, so she said—easy to please demeanor, and phobia about personally booking online, made her the dream client. Traveling gave her such joy, along with a break from being ignored—almost scorned—by her daughter and grandchildren. I never understood why she continued to live next door to such an ungrateful family. Her confidence in the agency was undeniable, so I had no

23

wish to question her personal decisions. *It's her life.*

Lord knows I'd had my own share of family drama with Ruby. About the same age, Lucy and Ruby were polar opposites. Lucy was attractive in an old-timey Florida kind of way. Always pleasant, and willing to listen. If she were my mother, I'd never take her for granted.

Lucy cleared her throat and brought me back to business. "Sorry, I just spaced out for a moment." I assembled her travel packet, complete with flight and cruise information, excursion dates and times, and gave her everything she'd need for her three-week adventure. "Always a pleasure helping you, Lucy. Wish all my customers were as appreciative as you."

I considered spilling my recent frustrations with Mr. Payne since she knew both Grace and Stewart. Before Lucy and her ex-husband split, they'd gone on several trips with the couple. Had their friendship continued, or was Lucy now considered a "third" wheel?

Turned out, I didn't have to bring up the subject because she did it for me.

"I heard Grace Payne is taking a trip, too. A convention in New Orleans. I assume you made her reservations."

I was a little surprised by her knowledge of Grace's travel plans, but at least my question was answered. Lucy and the Paynes must still be in contact. "Ellie took care of her or rather, she dealt with Stewart. To say he's difficult is an understatement. But, Graves Travel is here to serve." I bit my tongue. Saying more would be a disservice to the agency.

"Well, don't you worry about unpleasant people,

24

Andi. Some spend their lives looking for problems."

I'd always been a "glass half-empty" kinda gal myself, and the past few years had given me no reason to change perspective, but still, I envied Lucy's optimistic view. Pessimism shrouded me like Batman's cape, especially when it came to certain difficult acquaintances, but I tried to put on a happy face for my customers. "I'll try to take your advice. Thanks for the pep talk and please take plenty of pictures!"

She gave me a hug at the door. "Oh, you bet I will. I'll be mostly out of touch while there, but I'll see you when I get back and we can plan my next adventure."

"Wait, Lucy." Not used to seeing her with flashy jewelry, I followed her to the sidewalk. "Where did you get that beautiful necklace?" On more than one occasion, she'd stated that wearing anything beyond a plain, gold chain and simple charm, was pretentious. Had she broadened her taste?

"This gaudy thing?" She held out a bright yellow sun burst pendant surrounded with turquoise and silver. Instead of showing pleasure with a new piece of jewelry, her lips tightened. "Darryl gave it to me a week before he walked out. Said it was 'one of a kind' like I'd believe anything he said. *Hmmph*. His leaving was the best thing that ever happened to me."

Her words said one thing, her body language, another. I was thrown by the cold, angry expression on her face. Why wear something that raised such negative emotions?

As quickly as her smile disappeared, it was back. "Well, gotta go! Those suitcases aren't going to pack themselves." She strolled to her car, displaying the same carefree demeanor she'd brought in.

Maybe I just imagined her momentary flash of anger. At least she was pleased with her cruise. Wonder why I can't please all my clients? For some reason, my brain misfired when I faced a screen filled with airline flights or resort itinerary options. Maybe a kind of dyslexia. Or maybe, my lack of confidence caused me to freeze when faced with impatient, demanding people like you-know-who.

****

Tuesday and Wednesday were surprisingly busy, but for some weird reason I'd yet to figure out, Thursdays were typically dead. Ellie had the afternoon off, and the phones were quiet, so I opened my tablet and scanned the latest news. "Pileup on I-95 injures six, Miami city council discusses flooding issues, North Miami Beach woman missing in New Orleans, movie filming causes gridlock in South Beach."

...Wait. What was that about a woman missing in New Orleans? I scanned the article.

Grace Payne, North Miami Beach, was reported missing when she failed to register at her hotel on Tuesday, friends told NOLA police. "She texted she was on her way from the New Orleans airport around 6:00 p.m. last night," said convention attendee, Doris Dobson. "I texted back, but never heard another word." According to a police spokesman, a search is being conducted throughout the city and outlying areas."

I grabbed the phone to call Ellie, but it rang, instead. "Hello! Uh, Graves Travel."

"You better have a darned good explanation for this!" An all too familiar voice threatened through the phone.

26

"Mr. Payne? I just heard. Is there any news on Grace?"

"No, and it's your fault. I warned you about putting her into some sleazy hotel and now she's missing! What kind of half-baked business are you running? First you fly me to Texas instead of Georgia, and now you've lost my wife!"

I shook so violently, my brain stuttered. *How could this happen?* I pulled up the reservation. "I'm looking at the hotel website, Mr. Payne, and it's very presentable. Dozens of 5-Star reviews and no complaints."

"I don't care what you or that website says! My wife's convention is being held at the Sheraton, miles away from the Quarter. Why did you ever make her reservation so far away? I'm worried sick. The police will be contacting you, Miss Jones, and you'd better have some answers for them!"

"But you approved the..." I stared at the silent receiver. The burning knot in my stomach moved its way up to my throat. Where was Grace Payne, and did her reservation get screwed up? I called Ellie and left a message. "Get over here, ASAP. We have a problem."

****

Ellie stared at the computer screen. "I don't see how he can blame us, Andi. Remember, when he was on the phone with her? According to him, she insisted on staying in the French Quarter; some 'fancy-schmancy' place, were his exact words!"

I recalled the same conversation. "Could you hear Grace on the other end of the phone while he talked to her?"

Ellie thought for a moment. "No, but I was

27

concentrating on finding a place that would satisfy Grace and get him out of here before he blew a gasket."

Something nagged at me. "You don't suppose he set up that call and pretended to have Grace on the line? Maybe so he could sue? Oh, that's silly. Why would he?" Sure, he still held a grudge about that mistaken airplane reservation, but would he go that far to make Graves Travel look bad? Book a different hotel reservation for Grace and claim she was missing?

Ellie didn't give my suspicions much validity. "Yeah, Jonesy, that's a stretch, even for your active imagination. He could get in serious trouble for filing a false missing person's report."

I walked to the front window, arms folded. Oh, Ellie was right, but *what is missing—besides our client?* I played the scenario back in my head. "Do we know the convention Grace was supposed to attend?"

"No, but I can probably narrow it down." Ellie googled, *Current New Orleans Events.* "Here we go. This week they're hosting, 'The Cajun Citchen: From Andouille to Mudbugs to Turducken'. Guess they thought spelling kitchen with a 'C' was clever."

"What? Oh, sorry. I'm still trying to process, 'turducken'."

"I had it once when we visited my St. Charles Parish relatives. Would you believe it's a turkey stuffed with duck stuffed with chicken?"

"Ah, similar to a recipe your spell-conjuring neighbor would cook up," I quipped.

"Oh, this sounds good." She continued reading, "Phantoms and Photos. Does your camera see dead people?' Ooh, Jonesy! That's right up my alley! Wish I'd seen this earlier. I would've taken my va-ca a little

28

early this year."

"Your 'va-ca' will have to wait until we locate Grace. Call Mr. Payne and find out the name of the convention. Maybe we can start there."

She huffed, "Sure, make me talk to him. Bad enough when his wife's *not* missing!"

"Please, just do it."

I'd walked into my office when a thought struck me. *Oh, no, Andi. Don't get her involved.* I scrolled through my contacts, took a deep breath, and tapped the little phone icon next to the name, Ruby Jones.

"Hell-*oooooo*."

"Uh-Ruby, this is Andi."

"Why Andi Anna. I can't remember the last time you called me. Usually, it's the other way around. To what do I owe this pleasure, honey?"

I could still hang up; pretend I pocket-dialed. "Sorry to interrupt your trip, but I'm calling about Grace Payne. Has anyone in your group seen or heard from her?"

"Why, no. According to the scuttlebutt at breakfast, she was supposed to meet up with a few of the girls last night, but she stood them up. We're all anxious to know where she is, but I think it's silly to worry. Like I told Cloris and Doris, she probably just met up with a handsome paramour and decided to skip this boring old convention. I mean, seriously? What is there to learn about ghosts? I'll stick to living, breathing humans, thank you very much."

"So, you and the girls are attending the photography convention?"

"That's the plan. At least it's their plan. Listen, honey, can I get back to you? I'm heading down to the pool bar. Rumor has it there's a sexy entertainer this afternoon, and I need to grab a good seat in the shade before they're all taken. It's crucial I protect my flawless porcelain complexion, you know."

"But, Ruby, remember the last time you got involved with a performer?"

Dead air. Could speaking to *dead air* be any less productive than speaking to a *dead head?* Probably not. I was confident an MRI of Ruby's brain would reveal a mass of marshmallow fluff. I fought the urge to call her back. Even if she answered, trying to get any useful information out of her would be hopeless with pools, booze, and men occupying her mind.

I struggled to remember every detail of Ellie's and my conversation with Stewart.

Why didn't I encourage him to take his business elsewhere? Why did I agree to take over this agency? Why was I born in Florida? I crossed my arms on the desk and planted my throbbing forehead. *Think something good, Andi. Margaritas, maybe. Manny, definitely.*

"Jonesy," Ellie yelled. "It just hit me! Grace signed up for that 'seeing dead people with your camera' convention. Do you believe it? Now, she's missing! Maybe her camera knows where she is. Ha!"

"Not funny!" It was, but this was no time to humor her sick jokes. At least Ruby's vague description about ghosts made more sense. "Try to find a phone number for the person in charge of the convention," I yelled from my office. *It's a start.*

Chapter Five

True to Stewart Payne's word, the North Miami police showed up that afternoon. Detective Maxwell Carter, the portly, balding man behind the badge was no Manuel Rodriquez; not even close.

We sat in the front office. He casually pulled a notepad and pen from his jacket pocket with the enthusiasm of a politician kissing slobbering babies. "I'll take your statement first, Ms. Jones," he droned, in a flat, nasal tone.

I was glad Ellie and I had discussed the chain of events earlier in the day. "From what I remember, detective, Grace signed up for a convention along with several friends. While the others stayed at the convention site, The Sheraton, according to her husband, Stewart, his wife requested a quaint hotel in the French Quarter. The plan was to meet Tuesday night. Grace sent a text saying she was on her way, but didn't show. No one's heard from her since." I wasn't about to mention my phone call to Ruby. Getting my stepmother involved, a suspect in a murder case several months back, would be a huge mistake, for many reasons. "I don't know what else we can say, Detective. I just heard this morning Grace is missing." I didn't elaborate on Stewart's threats, blaming us for her disappearance. I'm sure he gave the detective an ear-full.

31

"So, you're saying neither you nor your assistant has a clue why Mrs. Payne failed to check in at the Chateau Maison. Is that correct?"

Before I could answer, Ellie jumped from her chair in a state of frenzy. "Do I need a lawyer? Because if I do, I'm not answering any of your questions until you let me make my one phone call! "In fact, I'm leaving!" She grabbed her purse off the desk. "I don't have to take this abuse! Jonesy, I'll be back tomorrow, maybe."

I grabbed her arm before she could sprint to the door. "Sit back down," I hissed. "This is not helping."

"But, Andi," she whispered, "I might have a few unpaid parking tickets. Okay, about fifty, and if this turkey runs a background check, I'm going to jail!"

Ellie needed work on her whispering technique as well as her parking decisions. "This, uh, turkey is not here about your tickets, Miss Clanton," scoffed the police detective.

He stood and grabbed his notepad and pen. I was surprised to see someone still used such antiquated information-gathering tools. Why not just hit "record" on your phone?

"Here's my card, Ms. Jones. Please let me know if you remember anything pertinent." He walked to the door and glanced sideways toward Ellie. "While I'm not interested in your criminal past, you might want to be more careful about where you park. Pay the meter the next time, and get those tickets paid, too."

Ellie heaved a sigh when the door closed behind him. "Whew! I thought I was dead meat, Jonesy."

"You still might be!" I was livid. "What got into you? Are you trying to raise suspicion on us and on this agency?"

"Well, of course not," she shrugged, dismissing my fury. "Guess I just panicked. But, at least we know from the text Grace sent her friend that she *was* staying in the French Quarter. Her reservation was correct. I swear on my granddaddy's moonshine still, I booked her into the exact place Stewart Payne okay'd. You know how efficient I am about work."

I couldn't argue with that. My anger subsided until she added, "Now, if you'd made the reservation, I could see how—"

"Point taken, Ellie. Ridiculing my skills, or lack thereof, is not helping your cause. Detective Carter said Grace texted Doris when she first arrived, but no one's heard from her since. From what they said, her lack of communication was out-of-character. They're worried about her safety, and so am I."

I paced up and down the hallway hoping activity would force me to think clearly. The radio news report popped in my head about the four mysterious deaths around New Orleans. Should I mention that to Ellie? *Oh, sure.* Get her more paranoid than she already was! Not a good idea—at least, not yet.

Besides worrying about Grace's well-being, I was afraid Stewart would sue to the tune of more than this place is worth ten times over if this mix up turned deadly. *Oh, Andi, don't imagine the worst!* I hated what my instincts shouted, but was there another possibility? Maybe the Universe was telling me I need to change professions. I took a deep breath. "Find the next flight to New Orleans, Ellie, along with every discount travel voucher you can scare up."

Well, I said I wanted to travel more. Cancun, and now the Big Easy. One involved a murder and this, a

33

mysterious disappearance. Would I ever be able to travel for fun?

****

By the time Ellie found a flight, I had just enough time to run home, throw a couple of outfits and essentials in a bag and race to the airport. Fortunately, rush hour was over, and I made it to the gate exactly two minutes before it closed.

I called Ellie as soon as I boarded. "Sprinting through Miami International was fun. I'm expecting a call from the U.S. Olympic committee." Sarcasm hit its peak when I was stressed.

"You said, ASAP, Jonesy," Ellie grumbled. "No good deed goes unpunished, my Granny Dumont used to say."

Having heard more than enough sage advice from her granny to last a lifetime, I didn't argue. I was on edge about making this trip in the first place, but settled in my seat, and my tension eased. Added bonus; I had a whole row to myself. The eerily quiet cabin was about one-third full. Guess South Floridians had little reason to travel to New Orleans in the summer. Rumor had it you could leave a dry rag outside overnight and wring out a cup of water in the morning. Heat and humidity hadn't been an issue the two times I'd visited during Mardi Gras in February. In fact, I recalled it being downright chilly. That wouldn't be the case in August.

I checked my hotel reservation. Ellie found a room for four nights at the same place she'd booked Grace. *Wonder how she managed to pull off that miracle.* "The hotel had a last-minute cancellation," she explained. "Suppose that was Grace's unused reservation? Well, whatever, just remember you're the *Southeast Regional*

Hospitality Director and you're there to do a site inspection. That's the only way I could get the room free, well except for taxes."

"Am I there under an assumed name, or can I use my own?" I half joked.

"Use your own. I didn't have time to get fake I.D.'s."

"I was kidding! You mean you could do that? No, never mind." No way would I want any part of that shady business. I checked my watch. "Gotta go. We're about to take off. I'll keep you posted on my return. Oh, and *please* let me know if Stewart Payne shows up with a bulldozer."

I must've snoozed because the thump of the landing gear was my next semi-conscious sensation.

"Welcome to New Orleans, the home of jazz and jambalaya. Please stay seated until the captain has turned off…"

Yeah, yeah.

Two rows ahead, a toddler covered his ears and shrieked displeasure with the landing. I pulled my suitcase from the overhead bin, ready to exit the flying elevator, but plopped down, defiantly clutching my bag when the flight attendant glared. Seated close to the front, I wouldn't have to fight my way through passengers dawdling in the back; taking *years* to retrieve their carryon bags. The toddler now stood, quietly, on his mother's lap, thumb in mouth. He appeared to survey the sea of faces before him. I caught his eye and waved, presenting my best, "I love kids" smile. He collapsed onto his mother's lap and resumed crying. *Oh, well. I tried.*

"Ladies and gentlemen, please show courtesy to

35

other passengers as you exit to the front of..." Jumping to my feet, I rushed to the door, mumbling a hurried "thanks" to the pilot and flight attendants. Finally, freedom!

True to expectations, humidity hit me like a wet sponge as I trudged up the Jetway. *Déjà vu* slapped me in the face. *Cancun, Manny.* Oh, how I wished this plane had mistakenly flown straight to the Yucatan Peninsula. Visions of our night together in Miami sent shivers racing up spine. *Snap out of it, Andi, and focus on the task ahead.* Find Grace Payne. Halt the inevitable lawsuit that would surely bankrupt the agency and put Ellie out of a job.

Oh, who am I kidding? Ellie would be snatched up in a Miami Minute. Me? Not so much.

I followed signs to the exit. Ellie promised to arrange for a pickup so I wouldn't have to fight for a taxi. Sure enough, an older gentleman held up a small placard that read, "Jonesy".

I sighed, "Uh, I'm Andi Jones, Jonesy to my assistant."

"Pleasure to meet you, Miss Jones. I'm to take you to the Quarter, correct?"

I rooted in my purse for the address to the hotel and grabbed a note from Ellie, instead. "Look up my cousin, Clem and his wife, Clementine. If you need anything, here's their phone number." Chicken scratches—possibly numbers—followed the two implausible names. *Clem and Clementine Clanton.*

"Uh, Miss? The address?"

"Oh, sorry." I wadded up the note and dropped it back in my purse. "I can't seem to find it but it's the *Chateau* something, on Toulouse Street. Do you know

36

it?"

"Miss, there's nothing in this here city I don't know. Been 'round these parts for close to seventy years," he assured, in distinct Cajun dialect. "Name's Marcel, but you can call me Mudbug. That's what my kin calls me. The *grands* gave me that name 'cause I made it a ritual to give them their first taste of mudbugs, or crawfish as you probably know 'em, soon's they had enough teeth in their mouths to bite off the heads and suck out the juice."

I'm gonna barf, I just know it. I'd seen platters of the tiny, boiled crustaceans on my last trip, five years ago. Eating a cousin to the critters I used to spot crawling out from under rocks in the creek that trickled behind my grandmother's house in Indiana, was not on my menu.

"I'm sure you're proud of them." Bile stung my throat as I choked on the words.

He laughed. "Oh, I am. Now the young 'uns catch 'em and bring 'em to me. 'Course I still have to do the cookin'. They balk at throwing live critters into boiling water."

That did it. "Mr. Marcel, uh, Mudbug, how long until we get to the hotel?" Changing the subject was imperative if the chili dog I inhaled on the way to the Miami airport stayed in its proper place.

He peered through the rearview mirror. "I 'spec we'll be there in about twenty minutes, since traffic is light. So, are you here for business or pleasure?"

I resigned myself to continuing whatever conversation Mr. Mudbug preferred. "Business," I answered.

"What kind?" he persisted.

"Travel." Might as well practice my deception. "I'm Southeast Regional Director." I prayed he wouldn't ask, *for what*! *What the heck do I regionally direct?* Ellie forgot to spill that tidbit of information.

"Ah." He rubbed his grizzled salt and pepper beard with one hand, his other on the well-worn steering wheel.

I settled back in the seat, grateful he probed no further. The last half of the trip was spent in silence; well, except for the driver's soft rendition of Randy Newman's song, *Louisiana 1927*. Not the least bit cold, I shivered; suddenly in a strange, melancholy mood. "Someone's walking on your grave, Andi," Grammy Kate used to say when that happened. *I hope not, Grammy.*

I must've drifted off because my next semiconscious act was swiping at a trickle running down my chin.

Was that drool? Nice, Andi.

The back door opened. "Here you are, miss. Can I help you with your bag?" Marcel held out his hand.

"What? Oh, no, I just have this small one. I can manage." Emerging from a trance-like state, I sensed a steadying hand underneath my elbow.

"You okay? You look a might peaked," he remarked.

"I'm fine. I must've dozed off for a few minutes. Your singing put me to sleep."

His keen brown eyes twinkled. "Well, missy, you're not the first to say that. I do believe it's the first time I've thought of that song since I sang it, years ago, to my grands at bedtime." He shook his head. "Nowadays, they all think they're too old for such nonsense. Don't know what made me serenade you." He chuckled softly. "Anyways, you have a nice stay in our fair city, y'hear? Oh, and if you're in the mood for authentic Cajun cuisine, check out my old friend's place just west of the city. Gator Bill's. They have the sweetest alligator nuggets..."

"Yes, yes, I'll do that." *Like Hell, I will!* I scurried through the wrought iron gate before he had the chance to describe another Louisiana delicacy. I checked in at the front desk, got my room pass, and hurried across the courtyard. The room was the answer to my stress. Warmly decorated, comfortable bed, and all the amenities I'd need for a short stay.

Which didn't explain the chill that settled in the middle of my chest.

Chapter Six

I woke with a start to the sound of clomping hooves and horse whineys, stretched my arms and legs and opened one eye; only then remembering I was in New Orleans. What a night! I hadn't slept that soundly in months. Was it the pillow-top mattress that caressed my body? The heavy drapes that shut out the brightest sunlight? Or, maybe I missed my Miami upstairs neighbors, and their four kids, stomping around at six in the morning like a troupe of River Dancers.

Relieved the apprehension from last night had diminished, the other eye popped open recognizing a familiar aroma. Coffee! The one thing that got me moving in the morning, and glory be, I was in the coffee capital of the world! At least, in my world. French roast, chickory-brewed, espresso, café au lait…take your pick. My stomach growled with anticipation of a couple of powdered sugar-covered beignets to complement my morning beverage of choice.

I rolled out of bed and stretched, again, enjoying the relative quiet of the room, the hotel, and The Quarter. If rollicking partiers were out and about, they hadn't kept me awake last night. Compared to my living quarters overlooking Flamingo Drive, this place was an auditory paradise.

So much for paradise. My "Bad to the Bone"

ringtone disrupted the solace. Probably time to change, but I'd uploaded it when Dad died, almost two years ago, and hated giving up even one memory of him. He'd go around singing it until my sister, Georgia, and I would plead with him to stop. *I'd give anything to hear him sing it again.*

The agency calling. "Hullo, El."

"Mornin', Jonesy. How's the Big Easy-Peasy treatin' ya?"

"Pretty good, so far. Hope you're not planning to change that."

"'Fraid I am. Has the NOPD gotten in touch with you?"

"Noooo…" I braced for the explanation as to why I was being hunted by the police.

"Oh, man. I hate to be the bearer of bad news, Andi, but here goes."

Uh-oh. Ellie calling me Andi instead of Jonesy? This can't be good.

"They found Grace late yesterday. At least they're pretty sure it's her body from the description the Miami PD gave them this morning."

Her body? Oh, my God. I fell back on the bed. "What happened?"

"It's weird. Some crawdad fisherman found a woman in a lake about 20 miles from the city, tangled up in his traps, I think. No cause of death, yet, but it's doubtful she drove into the boonies, got caught in a critter cage, and drowned herself."

I reeled imagining Grace's body floating in some snake and alligator-infested bayou. "Was the woman, uh, Grace…dressed?"

"Oh, yeah, fully clothed. Stewart apparently

41

confirmed to the cops the, uh, corpse had on the same outfit Grace wore when he dropped her off at the airport."

"They've talked to Stewart? Is he here? In New Orleans?"

"No, the police contacted him in Miami. I imagine he's on this way, though."

While the thought of Grace being dead sickened me, for some odd reason knowing she wasn't found naked gave me a small amount of comfort. Maybe because she went to such great lengths to dress fastidiously when she was out in public. "So, am I supposed to get in touch with them, or are they going to call me?" I was stumped. What could I possibly offer their investigation except what I knew from the time "Mr. Obnoxious" walked into the agency until he stormed out? Didn't the North Miami police pass along my previous statement? I shivered at the thought of being in the same city as Stewart and his deceased wife. Wouldn't surprise me if that foul-tempered man had gotten rid of Grace, himself.

"I gave them your cell number. Okay?"

"I appreciate your asking, El, but your timing sucks. Sure, you had no other choice. Besides, I-we, have nothing to hide—other than your parking tickets."

"Not funny, Jonesy. Let me know what you find out, oh, and look up my cousin and his wife. They know more about the people and goings-on in those parts than the *National Enquirer*. You still have the number I gave you, right?"

I remembered stuffing it back in my purse, so I assumed it was still there. "Have it right here. I'll be sure to call them," I lied.

"Okey-doke. Tell Clem and Clementine I said 'hey'."

"Will do. Gotta go, El. I'll keep you posted."

****

Coffee, I need coffee. After throwing on yesterday's clothes and running a brush through my hair, I began a systematic search for caffeine. The charming travel-poster-worthy courtyard, with its fountain and lush ferns, would've been an inviting spot to enjoy a café au lait, were it not for the oppressive humidity and the horrifying information I'd just received. I couldn't bring back Grace, but I also couldn't fully absorb the news until I'd absorbed the proper amount of caffeine.

Sweat began the inevitable journey from my scalp to my eyebrows. "Glad I didn't waste time jumping in the shower." I could tell today would be a baseball cap kinda day. No sense washing *or* styling my hair. *Meanwhile, where is the coffee?*

I followed my nose along a stone path to a set of French doors and walked inside to the small cafe. A whiff of freshly-baked pastry almost knocked me over.

"Good morning, Miss. Do you prefer coffee or tea?"

I smiled at the petite older woman whose skin reminded me of, what else, smooth light mocha. She was living proof that humidity did wonders for the skin.

"Regular coffee, please, and one of whatever is attached to that sweet aroma."

"You must mean Mama Louisa's croissants. I'll bring you one, fresh from the oven."

I settled at a bistro table overlooking the courtyard. Even in the early morning heat, the black wrought iron chairs cooled my thighs and my mid-back. *The air conditioning bill in this place must be ginormous!* Why, oh why couldn't this be a pleasure trip? I could *so* get into spending a couple of weeks chilling in this slow-paced ambiance. I couldn't remember the last time I'd had a vacation that didn't involve work, inspections, or, lately, murders. *That's what excites you, Andi. Why not admit it? A passion for investigating, is now, and always had been, stronger than anything else in my life.* When I was a kid, I'd curled up in the easy chair with Dad and read Sherlock Holmes, or watched TV detectives, Colombo and Jessica Fletcher. The fascination, for solving mysteries, carried into adulthood.

My cell vibrated. *A local number so this might be the police.* "Andi Jones."

"Miss Jones, this is Sergeant Andre LeBlanc of the New Orleans Police Investigative Division. Is this a good time to talk?"

The hostess—name tag, Marie—brought a small pot of coffee to the table, along with a charming cup, saucer, and a plate with two golden croissants; butter dripping from the top. I smiled and nodded my appreciation. "Uh, sure Sergeant LeBlanc, just hold on for a moment." I added condiments to the black brew and took a mind-clearing sip. *Ah.* "Okay, sorry to keep you waiting."

"I understand, from your assistant, you're here because one of your clients disappeared and is now deceased." Although Ellie had given me the sparse details, the finality of the words still shocked my system. "Well, unofficially, that's right. She just called to let me know about Grace's body being found." I didn't reveal the initial motive for my trip, to avoid my livelihood being ripped away by my client's irate husband—now widower. The pettiness of that reason didn't escape me, given the current circumstances.

"I have a transcript of your statement to the North Miami police. Is there anything you've thought of since? Something you'd care to add?"

So, the police did have my previous statement yet still had more questions. I tried to recall everything Ellie and I had told Detective Carter, which wasn't hard because we'd told the truth. "I can't think of anything, Sergeant, but if I do, should I call this number?"

"Yes, this is my cell so you can reach me anytime; day or night. Thank you, Miss Jones. I'll be in touch, and enjoy your stay in our city."

Enjoy my stay checking out a client's murder? Yeah, that'll happen. Everyone must be schooled on Big Easy tourism.

I took a couple more sips of coffee and bit into the luscious pastry. The news about Grace had ruined my appetite, still, the flaky goodness melted in my mouth. The butter on top was overkill since the entire roll oozed creamy richness. I scarfed down the croissants, despite the knot in my stomach, and reluctantly refused when Marie offered a second plate.

"No, thanks." *I don't even want to guess how many calories I just consumed.* "I will take a refill on the coffee, though. To go, please."

I made sure to save Sergeant LeBlanc's number in my phone before returning to the room. Glancing at my reflection in the hotel window, even a futile attempt to make myself presentable for what the day might bring, would be better than nothing.

Chapter Seven

Giving up on the useless hotel dryer, I ran my fingers through my hair in a futile effort to straighten the ringlets that expanded with each degree-rise in humidity. A vigorous, but ineffective brushing followed. Why did I inherit my dad's kinky, blonde hair instead of my mother's sleek, black locks? Oh, yeah. My sister, Georgia got those.

I studied the pair of beige cotton, blend capris and white linen shirt I'd chosen to wear that day. *I'll be wrinkled as a full-grown shar pei by noon, but at least I'll be cool.* I quickly dressed, grabbed my phone. Before sticking it in my purse, I noticed a text had come in, probably during the tussle with my hair.

Hi Andi. Ellie filled us in on ur deceased client. Said she gave u r #. Might have info for u. Call. Clem Clanton

Ellie's cousin. She must've called him right after we hung up. I'd had no intention to contact any of her backwoods relatives, despite my promise. But, since she'd probably told him to expect my call, I owed her the courtesy to at least hear him out. Besides, his message intrigued me a little. It could be, at the very least, a much-needed lead. Besides, Ellie swore her cousin and his wife knew the goings-on in the area. Could be helpful. I put down my bag and punched in Clem's number.

46

"*Yel*-lo!"

"Uh, is this Clem Clanton?"

"Yep. Andi? Wasn't sure I'd hear from you. Ellie told us the reason for your visit. Wow, what nasty circumstances!"

"It sure is." Not in the mood for small talk, I pressed on. "Ellie speaks highly of you and Clementine, and...well, uh, you texted you might have some information I can use?"

"I might. I read online that Luther Bertrand is the one who found the body of your client. I've known him for at least ten years. We run into each other, on occasion, doin' our trapping gigs. I do more shrimping, but also dabble in crawfish, just to mix things up. Anyway, he's a good guy. Not the brightest star in the sky, but I'd bet my fishing boat he had nothing to do with killing anyone."

"So, that's your information? He's not a suspect?" *Did I waste time and a phone call on something I'd already presumed? Even if this Luther fellow wasn't very bright, why would anyone commit murder and then call it in to the police?*

"No, that's not all. You see, we bayou shrimpers and trappers are a pretty close-knit group. We hear things. Things the police aren't privy to."

Now it's getting interesting. "Such as?"

"We need to talk in person. Do you have a car? Can you meet me somewhere? We're only about twenty-five minutes out of town."

"I don't have a car, Clem. I'd have to call a ride."

"Tell you what. I'll come and pick you up. Be there in less than an hour. Gotta get Bertha gassed up. Oh, and wear old clothes and a sturdy pair of shoes. See ya."

"But…wait. You don't know where I'm staying."

"You don't think I'm smart enough to get the name of the hotel from the person who set up your trip?"

Ellie, of course. "But, how will I know you?" And, what was I thinking agreeing to meet a virtual stranger? On the other hand, he was Ellie's cousin, and she'd never suggest I connect with anyone who wasn't on the up and up. Would she?

"No worries. You'll hear me coming." He laughed and hung up.

I stared at the phone. *You'll hear me coming? What in the world is Bertha? A military jet?* I took a couple of deep breaths and tried to remember a meditation Georgia had taught me during the stressful months after Dad died. How she managed any quiet time, with four kids, blew my mind. I couldn't shut off my mind when I was alone, in a dark room! In a flash, I nixed the meditation exercise and called Ellie, instead. Maybe she could provide added reassurance about Clem. In any case, she'd have current information for the police when my dead body turned up in Lake Pontchartrain.

"Graves travel, Ellie speakin'."

"Hey, El. How's it going?"

"I've been busier 'n a cat coverin' crap on a marble floor. You picked a heck of a time to go out of town, Jonesy."

"I didn't pick the time," I reminded her, "Grace Payne's disappearance and death did. Speaking of which, I got a call from your cousin, Clem and—"

"You did?" Ellie shrieked. "Oh, he's just my favorite cousin on earth, and Clementine is a real peach, too. You don't wanna cross her, but oh, my, is she ever

48

smart. Are you meetin' up with 'em?"

"That's why I called, if you had just let me finish my sentence before piercing my eardrum. Clem's picking me up and wants to discuss the murder, for some reason. He hinted at information from sources in the bayou. Other fishermen, I guess."

Ellie paused.

"Everything good, El? Clem's okay, isn't he? I assume it's safe to go with him."

"Oh, uh-yeah. Clem's a solid guy. I'm just not sure about some of that crowd. Just be careful where you go and make sure he's with you at all times. Don't, I repeat...do *not* go anywhere without him or Clementine."

The statement and foreboding in Ellie's voice sent a chill up my spine. Before hanging up, I weighed whether to call Clem back, and tell him not to come, when the room began to vibrate. "They don't have earthquakes in Louisiana, do they?"

"Not that I know of, Jonesy. Why?"

"I'm not sure, but I suspect a convoy of semis just parked out front. Okay, the rumbling stopped. Better hang up and watch for your cousin."

"Let me know how it goes and give them both a big ol' hug for me." Ellie snickered, knowing I wasn't the huggy type.

"I'll give them your best."

"Okay-doke. Gotta go, three lines are flashin'."

We'd no sooner hung up than I heard light tapping on the door. "Miss Andi? It's Clem."

I opened the door and braced for an introduction to Ellie's cousin from the boondocks.

"Nice to meet...you...Clem?" To say his

appearance surprised me, was an understatement. Let's just say, Clem Clanton looked nothing like the image his name portrayed. About thirty, clean cut with wavy, light-brown hair stylishly trimmed; nothing in his appearance suggested the wild, grime-coated chaos I'd expect from a Louisiana shrimper.

He stuck out his hand—properly cleaned with manicured nails—and smiled. Yes, he had all his teeth. "Nice meeting you, Andi. Ready to go?"

"Sure, let me grab my things." Fortunately, I'd stuffed everything but the kitchen sink in my very ample denim bag. Cell, water bottle, phone charger, billfold, and debit card. Thinking back, wish I'd grabbed a brush.

We walked through the gate onto the street. Not one single mud-splattered pickup truck with 60 inch tires and gun rack in sight. No customized muscle cars, either. Only a very large, intimidating motorcycle that looked like one Batman might ride if he ditched the Batmobile.

Clem saw my mouth fly open. "Meet Bertha. Prettiest, most reliable gal in Louisiana. Well, except for my Clementine." He reached behind the seat and pulled out a helmet. "Here. This is Clemmie's. She also sent along this lightweight leather jacket for you."

I could understand the helmet, but, "It's hot and humid. Why would I need to wear leather?"

"You haven't done much cycle riding, have you?" He chuckled. "Trust me. Once we get going you're gonna be glad you have this on to keep the air from stinging your arms. It'll also protect you from rocks or debris flying up from the road."

I'd ridden on exactly one motorcycle in my life.

No, scratch that; a motor bike, and my mom had a fit when I'd come home with a burn on the inside of my knee from the exhaust. How she knew about motorcycle burns and where to look for them, was still one of life's great mysteries.

"Are you wearing those shoes?" He looked, disapprovingly, at my turquoise and taupe sandals."

A twinge of annoyance at his critique of my footwear didn't deter my common sense. Flimsy t-straps weren't the best choice to tromp around the bayou, or ride a motorcycle, for that matter. "I have a pair of sneakers. Let me run to the room and change."

After a five-minute delay, we finally wound our way out of town. Clem took the backroads in order to avoid the traffic on I-10. I zipped the jacket tight around my neck, with new appreciation for protective leather apparel, along with the basic necessity to hang on for dear life. Fortunately, instead of struggling to stay upright, the art of leaning into a curve came naturally to me. In fact, I downright enjoyed myself as Clem, Bertha, and I became one, traveling the backroads of Louisiana. *Take that, Mother!*

Chapter Eight

The narrower and rougher the roads, the faster my riding confidence vanished. To keep from sliding off the seat, I squeezed the life out of my companion, leaving little opportunity to scan the cypress swamps bordering both sides. Clem pointed to a couple of alligators eying a nutria relaxing on the bank. Thanks to nature TV shows, I learned the large otter-type mammals were exported, decades ago, from South America by fur ranchers. Sadly for the ranchers, but fortunately for the nutria, the fur market collapsed allowing the over-sized rodents to breed like rabbits and overrun the swamps. I turned away from the impending carnage, having seen my share of hungry gators in Florida. Witnessing the inevitable lunch-time "buffet" had no appeal.

To the relief of my aching arms and sore behind, the road opened to a clearing with a charming white frame home perched on stilts at the edge of the bayou backwater. A large dock and shrimp boat drifted to the right of a boat house. Clem stopped to let me off before backing Bertha into a small, custom garage. No doubt he loved his *Harley*. Yep, even *I* recognized the century-old insignia. I crawled off the back seat; none too gracefully, handed him the helmet, and attempted to smooth my hair. Why bother? *Clementine is probably decked out in Daisy Duke cut offs or a gingham house*

52

dress.

Clem closed the shed door and snapped the padlock. "Hey, Clemmie! We got company!"

Clemmie, the woman I had foolishly dismissed as backwoods and barefoot, strolled out the door onto the front porch. Surrounded by planters brimming with buttercups, blue bellflowers, and pink sweet peas, she presented a stunning contrast to the harshness of the bayou. Two natural wicker rockers, tucked between the planters, completed the unexpected setting. Identical to my introduction to Clem, his wife was the polar opposite from expectation.

A tall, slim woman tossed a head of sleek midnight black hair. Shocking, topaz eyes peered from behind stylish silver-framed glasses. She spoke in a soft, Cajun drawl. "I hope your ride out here wasn't too uncomfortable, Andi. I know how Clem loves to kick up the dust on Bertha."

Clem chuckled. "Naw, I took it easy." He turned to me. "You're a natural on a bike, Andi. I figured a Miami girl wouldn't have a clue how to sit on someone like Bertha."

"Oh, I've ridden before." I fought the urge to rub my sore backside, and purposely skipped the laughable details of my first ride on what could only be described as a glorified bicycle.

"Clem and I are heartsick about your client."

Clem chimed in. "We sure are. Cousin Ellie isn't one for sentimentality, but Miz Payne's death shook her to the core."

I nodded. "That's Ellie. Tough as nails exterior. Sentimental and caring inside."

Clementine slipped her arm around my back and

led me toward the house. "Here, let me take that jacket. You'll need it for the ride back, but not in this afternoon humidity."

My soaking armpits beat her to the weather report. I slipped off the jacket, took a subtle sniff while pretending to shake off the dust. Thanks goodness! The smell of leather, instead of perspiration, greeted my nostrils. "I appreciate your thoughtfulness. More than one rock flew at my arms during the ride out here." I rubbed the angry red welt on my ankle, wishing I'd had leg protection, too. I glanced at Clemmie's tall, slim frame. Wishing would never squeeze me into a pair of her leather pants, even if I were lowered from a crane, my legs plastered in butter. For darn sure, I'd never get them off; minus a sharp pair of box cutters.

She slung the jacket over her shoulder and led the way up the stone path to the front porch. "You two sit out here where it's cooler and I'll bring some sweet tea."

Sweet tea. I hate sweet tea. After eating road dust for the past hour, my mouth was so dry, my tongue stuck to my teeth. A glass-full of sugary brown liquid goop would not help. "Perfect," I lied.

I sat in the porch swing on a thick flowered cushion. "Clemmie made all these," Clem pointed proudly.

Seamstress, runway model looks; Bet she can't whistle through her teeth. Hmmph. Clem sat in one of the wicker rockers, decked with cushions matching the swing. How did these two fit in with beer-swigging, curse-like-a-sailor, snorts-when-she-laughs, Ellie?

Right on cue Clem asked, "My cousin says she's worked for you about three years, now."

Add "mind reader" to his many attributes. "As the beneficiary of a travel agency with no clue how to run it, I had just stuck a small, 'Now Hiring' sign in the window when she drove up."

"In that orange rattle-trap Camaro?"

"One and the same." I laughed. "Anyway, she got out, tugged at the back of her cutoff jeans, and burst through the door. Once inside, she snatched the sign out of the window and announced, 'Y'all won't be needin' this.'"

Clem laughed at my spot-on impersonation of Ellie's twang.

"And, she was right," I continued. "Most employers would be turned off by someone wearing a 'I Work for Money-If You Want Loyalty, Buy A Dog' t-shirt, but when she rattled off her qualifications, using booking and airline reservation terms I'd never even heard before, I hired her on the spot."

"That's our Ellie." Clementine came out the screen door with a tray. "Here we are. Three glasses of tea and a plateful of iced sugar cookies. Like my tea doesn't have enough sweetness," she snickered.

Mama Louisa's croissants had already expanded in my stomach. I swear, just looking at those scrumptious cookies made my mid-section grow two inches. That didn't stop me, though. "Hey, what's another pound or two of sugar?" If I had to drink that godawful Southern tea, those buttery cookies would be my reward.

Clem gulped half his tea and set down the glass. "Did Ellie ever tell you about our great-great-grandmother? She was quite the witch, so we're told."

Clemmie's eyes lit up. "Oh, yes, we have pictures of her somewhere around here. Even those old tintypes can't hide her 'crazy eyes'." She fidgeted in her chair and added, "I've never been comfortable with the voodoo stories that were passed down, though."

I felt a blast of cold air pass through me at the same moment Clemmie shivered. "That's odd. Normally, the only air movement this time of the year is stifling."

"Maybe a breeze moved across the water." I didn't think it was a big deal.

Clemmie hesitated. "We do get an occasional storm this time of the afternoon. Guess we'd better watch for one. You don't want to be riding Bertha in the rain."

I scanned the hazy sky for ominous clouds, but saw nothing to indicate an imminent storm.

Clem joined the conversation. "Marie Josephe was her name. Clemmie's right about the crazy look in her eyes. Her great-granddaughter, whose reputation is nearly as frightening as Marie's, still makes potions around here. Legend says Marie knew how to turn men into swine."

I laughed. "Considering some of the men I've met, that's not a stretch."

Clemmie smiled, but I could tell she wasn't too comfortable with the conversation. "Can we talk about something more pleasant than witchcraft, spells, and pig men?"

Clem obliged and said nothing more about his eccentric ancestor.

We sat, quietly, sipping tea and enjoying the serenity of the Louisiana bayou country. I breathed in the briny air and almost forgot the reason for my trip to the boonies. Hating to disrupt feelings of peace and contentment, I sighed. Fear and guilt, however, wouldn't allow me a moment's peace until the mystery of Grace's death was solved. "You said you might have information for me about the body found in the bayou? My client, Mrs. Payne?"

He leaned forward. "I can't say I have direct knowledge about that poor woman. There's been talk of a stranger asking very pointed questions about the area and the fishing industry; particularly the process and time of day the crawfish cages are checked. Wiley Boudreau said a young guy he'd never seen before spent a couple of nights at Gator Bill's. I guess he stuck out like a sore thumb because he spent more time quizzing a group of fishermen than he did drinking beer." He chuckled. "Oh, and Wiley said he had on a brand-spanking new *Saints* hat, I supposed to make himself fit in with the crowd. Anyone around here knows if your cap ain't tattered and sweat-stained, you're not a local. He couldn't have raised more suspicion if he'd strolled in that bar wearing a Dallas Cowboy jersey."

Well, that's a start. A suspicious man, wearing a brand-spanking new ball cap. Still, not much to go on. My detour into the bayou could've been nothing more than a wasted trip. At least the company was pleasant, but I needed something concrete to investigate. "Did anything else about this guy stand out? Surely it's not unusual for curious strangers to show up on occasion. Is it always that odd for one of the main industries around here being of interest to outsiders? Maybe he was looking for a job or a new career."

Clem gave me one of those looks you'd give an eight-year-old who'd just asked why she couldn't jump off the roof with her new *Wonder Woman* cape. "First of all, only those born and bred around here consider harvesting crawdads a *career*. Second, Wiley got the idea he worked in the city. His hands were soft and his fingernails clean as a fresh manicure. Besides, everyone around here can spot a phony fast as you can say, 'Pinch the tail and suck the head.' In case you don't know, that's the customary way to eat crawfish."

I threw up in my mouth a little. "Yeah, I've heard about that experience." Wait, was Gator Bill's the place Marcel, aka, Mudbug mentioned? Wish, now, I'd spent more time talking with him. Should I mention yesterday's conversation with my Cajun driver?

Clementine, who'd remained silent to that point, set her glass firmly on the wicker table. "Clem, did you drag Andi all the way out here to give her a hard time about crawdads? Tell her everything you know, or take her back to New Orleans so she can appreciate the city while she's here."

Clem smiled and hung his head. I suspected his wife was the only person in those parts who stood up to him. "Sorry, Andi. Guess I get a little protective of the people and lifestyle in this part of the country. I wouldn't have dragged you out here if I didn't think there might be a connection. Don't know if you're aware, but there have been a number of unsolved murders. What I heard this morning from one of the local deputies, your client's death was different."

That perked me up. "How so?"

"First, the other victims were all born and raised in these parts. Your Mrs. Payne was a tourist. You might know otherwise, but it's believed she wasn't born anywhere near here."

I nodded. "The fact her New Jersey accent was still

obvious, after thirty years living in South Florida, pretty much verifies that."

He continued, "Second, and no disrespect to the deceased, but she was also a lot older than the others. The next oldest just turned twenty-five."

"That is a stretch. Grace was in her early sixties. So, did the deputy you spoke to have anything else to say? Maybe any other clues as to how or why she died?"

"Forensics won't be completed for a few days to see if she had water in her lungs, but he said all signs pointed to the fact she didn't die in the swamp. I am sure 'natural causes' will be ruled out, too. Reckon it was just Luther's bad luck she got tangled in one of his cages."

"Clem!" Clemmie snapped.

Well," he added, "besides Grace Payne's bad luck to be there in the first place. Didn't mean to sound insensitive."

While the information shouldn't be discounted, frustration mounted, not at Ellie's cousin, but at me. *Why had I been so gung-ho about flying down here in the first place?* Oh, sure, I got Ruby out of jail in Cancun; a decision I'd lived to regret on a regular basis. But a travel agent, and not a good one at that, would never be confused for Jessica Fletcher. Still, something in my psyche drove me on. "Do you think I could talk to your friend, Luther? Maybe he can add some detail about the scene."

Clem glanced at his silver dive watch. "He's probably at Bill's by now, chugging down a Ragin' Cajun—that's the beer of choice in these parts—and complaining to anyone within earshot how he lost an entire days' wage because of a dead body."

Chapter Nine

Gator Bill's lived up to its wildlife description. I should've taken notice when Clementine stayed behind.

"I'd love to go, but, I just took a shower and washed my hair," she'd explained. "You understand."

Understood, Clemmie. I couldn't imagine her ever stepping into this place without a giant bottle of hand sanitizer and bubble-wrap parka.

A mounted gator head hanging on the wall opposite the entrance, stared, menacingly, at patrons who dared walk through the front door. The wooden floor crackled and crunched under layers of grime and peanut shells. I whispered a silent "thank you" to Clem for convincing me to change into a pair of sneakers before I left the hotel. The feel of peanut dust between my toes wouldn't have the same soothing sensation as beach sand. A quick glance around the small, stuffy eating area (No cigarette ban here!) reaffirmed Ellie's advice to stick close to her cousins at all times.

"Hey Clem," yelled a burly man behind the bar. "Who ya got there? Steppin' out on Clementine?"

With that boisterous question, heads turned. All talking and beer swilling stopped. I scrunched in a little closer to my escort.

Rather than take offense, Clem laughed. "Now, Bill, you know better than that. I value my life and all my body parts too much to risk setting off that Cajun

61

temper of hers."

A few cackles ricocheted through the bar. Soon, the drinking commenced. Whew! I'd never been comfortable in the spotlight, and here, in the middle of nowhere with a bunch of Louisiana fishermen, was no exception. *Aww, suck it in, Andi. They're just people who would gasp at some of the sights around Coconut Grove in Miami. Or, worse yet, tourists and locals parading around Hollywood Beach in thongs.*

Clem, sensing my discomfort, took my elbow and steered me to a back table where a couple sat downing longnecks, along with a basket of cheese fries and battered *somethings*. "Hey Luther. Marlene, how ya doin'?"

Marlene looked up and grinned. "Hey there, Clem. Where *is* Clemmie?"

Did everyone need an answer? Clem and Clementine must be joined at the hip.

Clem pulled out a chair. "Awe, she had something better to do," he laughed. "Mind if we join you? This is my cousin Ellie's boss from the travel agency in Florida. Andi, meet Luther and Marlene."

Luther stood and stuck out a work-calloused hand that belied his youthful face. "Pleased ta meet ya'll. Any friend of Clem's is welcome to set wit' us."

From the sound of his thick dialect, I wondered how I'd question him without an interpreter.

Marlene's sunny-blond hair and welcoming smile conflicted with penetrating hazel eyes and facial lines that suggested struggles beyond her years. "Hey Andi, have a seat."

Clem pulled out my chair and one for himself. "Andi's here on business. Some pretty nasty business, at that. Seems the woman you found the other day was a client of hers, Luther."

Luther pushed back a greasy lock of hair from his forehead. "I kin barely close my eyes 'thout seeing her hair twizzled ever' which-ways in my crawdad cage." He shook his head in disbelief. The pain on his face was evident, just mentioning the incident.

"I'm so sorry you had to go through that, Luther." Already a little queasy hearing his initial description of the scene, I swallowed hard, and pressed on. "Is there anything else you noticed about her, uh, appearance? Any wounds or unusual marks?"

His gray eyes widened; the whites rimmed in red. Obviously a man who'd had too little sleep, or too much booze. Maybe both. "Miz Andi, I don' stick 'round long 'nough to give no phyis'cal zam! I skeedaddle outta dere and call da po po."

I looked to Clem for translation. "Luther didn't touch the body, but instead he got out of the swamp as fast as he could and called the police."

Ah-ha. I thought "po pos" were sandwiches. No, wait, those are po-boys. Speaking of which, I'm hungry.

Right on cue a waitress, I'm guessing was about a hundred and three years-old, shuffled to the table. "Y'all gwanna et or just set hare jawin'?

Again, I looked to Clem. "Do you want something to eat, Andi?"

Now, that I understand. "May I see a menu?" The words were barely out of my mouth when raucous laughter rocked the small room. "What did I say? I just want to see the specials," I countered, a little too defensively.

Marlene chuckled and pointed to her plate. "You're

lookin' at 'em, honey. Cheesy fries and gator nuggets."

Gator nuggets? Ah! The *authentic cuisine* Marcel had suggested. The thought of consuming anything "gator" made crawfish sound yummy…almost. "Uh, how about an order of plain fries? Oh, and a beer." I wasn't going to make another tourist mistake by asking for a Corona.

"Mmmm." The ancient waitress mumbled and shuffled to the kitchen.

Clem leaned over and whispered, "That's Sylvie, Bill's grand-mère—grandmother. She and her husband, Horace, built this place back in the 1950s, and she's been here ever since. Bill's tried to get her to retire, but she won't have it; thinks the place will go under if she leaves. So, he goes along with her but always has another waitress keeping an eye on her if he can't."

Luther smirked. "'Member when ol' Bill caught 'er pourin' kerosene in da fryer 'stead a peanut oil?"

That, I also clearly understood, and immediately questioned my decision to order fries, or anything!

Clem sensed my unease, and chuckled. "Don't worry. He stopped her before she could cause any damage. Ever since, Bill has managed to keep her out of the kitchen by emphasizing how much she's needed out front to schmooze with the customers."

Marlene chimed in. "I heard her cooking was lousy even back when she and Horace owned the place. He didn't want her in the kitchen, either. My daddy said one time when Horace was laid up for three weeks with a broken leg, he had to stumble around in a cast to keep the place from going under. No one would go near the place with Sylvie cooking! He tried to get Sylvie's older sister to help, but Sylvie wouldn't let her in the place. Said she'd probably cook up some kind of witch's brew and poison everyone who ate there."

"Excuse me? Don't tell me Sylvie's older sister is still around." *I'd hate to meet her in a dark alley.*

"She's still with us and has a little business in the city. I guess the sisters had a falling out decades ago, so Bill doesn't bring up her name. He discourages anyone else from asking about his aunt, at least in front of his mama."

After Sylvie brought my fries to the table loaded with cheese, despite my "plain" request. I sniffed them, subtly. At least there was no fishy smell; fresh vegetable oil and salt, along with something I didn't immediately recognize. Again, Clem read my mind. "Bill puts Louisiana Hot Sauce in the oil, so don't even think about smothering them with ketchup. He might just throw you out."

Two items on the menu, plus one kind of beer, and a ban on ketchup. *What the hell is the fascination with this place?* That question was answered with one bite of the best cheesy fries I'd had in my thirty-six years.

I wiped grease off my mouth and fingers with paper napkins so thin, they stuck to my hands. "Clem, you mentioned a stranger hanging around here. Is there anyone who could identify him? Maybe that friend of yours, Wiley Boudreau?"

Marlene perked up. "Hey, I saw that fella, too. Me and Wiley were giving him the stink eye the other night. He tried to blend in with the locals and didn't do a very good job, mind you."

Clem leaned in and repeated the description he'd given back at the house. "Wiley said he was kinda tall and thin, had on a brand-spanking-new Saints hat didn't appear he'd spent much time in the bayou. Anything you can add, Marlene?"

She shook her head. "Naah. You described him pretty good, Clem. Although, his skin was on the dark side, it was smooth and citified. Not like around here where folks out in the sun all day get red and leathery. I'm guessing he made it a point to steer clear of the outdoors."

Hmmm. New cap—stays out of the sun. Not much, but something.

Clem waited until I'd scarfed down the last of my fries and finished my beer. "Ready to go, Andi? We should get on the road before it gets too dark."

Oh, crap. *Bertha*. I'd forgotten about having to get back to the city the same way I arrived.

"Ready as I'll ever be. If you think of anything else, Luther, or you, Marlene, you can get in touch with me through Clem." I turned to my escort for confirmation. "Is that okay with you?"

Clem nodded. "Sure thing. Clementine and I are here whenever you need us."

We said our goodbyes to Luther and Marlene. "Ah hope da po po find the nasty critter whut killed yer friend, Miss Andi," Luther offered. "Same here," Marlene echoed. "Clem, you bring her back with you, again. And, drag Clemmie along, too. It's been weeks since we've had a good gossip-fest."

Another ten minutes spent on "farewells" to every single patron at Gator Bill's, and we rumbled back to the city. I was grateful to Clem for driving at a slower pace. Sting from wind and flying rocks was kept at a minimum.

I clamored off Bertha at the curb in front of

Chateau Masson and thanked Clem for suggesting we meet. "Please let me know if you hear any more about the stranger at Bill's place. Oh, and thank Clementine for loaning the jacket, and for the hospitality. I'd begun to question why I was here, but talking with you two, along with Luther and Marlene, restored my goal to get justice for Grace. Thanks for being willing to help."

He took Clemmie's jacket and tucked it into a pouch under the back seat. "Not sure we were much help at all, I'm afraid. Luther added little about the crime scene, but I might not be in an observational frame of mind, either, finding a dead body instead of a cage full of crawfish. I'll check with him tomorrow to see if he remembers anything else. I'll also ask around about that stranger."

I walked through the gate, looked back, and waved as he roared away. The ground vibrated beneath my unsteady feet. I covered my ears and noted how pleasant the day had turned out, despite the rocky start. At the very least, I'd gained a couple of clues, along with a whole new perspective on Ellie and her family. An added bonus, experiencing a raw, but beautiful section of Cajun Country.

I peeled off my sweaty clothes and stood under the shower for a good ten minutes; grateful to wash off the dust from the road and the grime from Gator Bill's. *Maybe tomorrow something will click.* I slid between the cool sheets and fell asleep before anxiety over Grace's death, and her husband's foreseeable revenge, took over.

Chapter Ten

The next morning presented a hair nightmare rerun. Frizz, inefficient hairdryer, heat, and humidity. On the bright side, the breakfast special featured café au lait, along with two yummy beignets. To say I'd died and gone to Heaven wasn't much of a stretch. A sip of the creamy, sweet liquid and a bite of fried, powdered-sugar paradise threatened to send me into a coma. Again, I thanked the higher powers for my efficient metabolism. I consoled myself by reasoning, no matter how many pounds gained on this trip, they'd quickly melt away with just a little effort. Ha! That's one thing I have on my sister. Georgia fought her weight, constantly. I had to admit that four kids, in less than ten years, might have something to do with her struggle.

If not for the urgent task ahead, I might've stayed there eating and drinking myself into a stupor. In hindsight, I'm glad I enjoyed breakfast because what I saw, next, was an appetite-killer.

"Miss Jones. May I join you?"

A tall swarthy man in black pants, black shirt, and gray windbreaker hovered. "I'm Sergeant LeBlanc. We spoke yesterday on the phone." Unsmiling, he pulled out a badge.

My shoulders relaxed when he revealed his identity. Now, if I could just slow my heart rate. *Breathe, Andi. Breathe!*

He ran long, slim fingers through silver streaked black hair. "Hope I didn't interrupt your breakfast, but it's necessary we talk face-to-face."

"No problem. I just finished." My voice sounded tinny, but at least my heart had stopped pounding. I motioned toward an empty chair. "What can I do for you?"

He sat down and pulled a tablet out of a small satchel. "I'm afraid I have a rather troubling request. Grace Payne's next of kin, her husband Stewart, is flying in this evening, but in the meantime, we need someone to verify the victim in these photos. Rather than faxing them to Miami, Mr. Payne suggested I track you down."

Oh, did he, now? Thanks for that, Stew! "I, uh…is this necessary? When will her husband be in town? Surely this can wait until he gets here."

"I'm sorry, Ms. Jones. It can't. As you may know, we have our hands full investigating several other homicides in the area. The longer the delay, the more likely this, uh, incident will turn into a cold case."

He pulled out his cell phone. "Do you mind if I record your answers?" I barely had a chance to nod when he pulled up photos and placed his tablet on my "*Attractions* in the *Big Easy*" placemat. *I doubt looking at pictures of dead bodies is on this list.* I lowered my eyes. "Oh, my God!" The photo of Grace floating beside Luther's crawfish cage, and one of her body sprawled out on the bayou bank; eyes sightless, staring blankly into space, made me light-headed.

"Ms. Jones? Are you all right?"

I cleared the lump in my throat and murmured, "No, I'm not." What an asinine question! "Just give me

69

a minute." Although my brain had registered Grace's death, the photos slammed me with a dose of reality.

I took a deep breath and a second look. "Yes, that's Grace Payne. I recognize her."

Sergeant LeBlanc nodded. "Would you please verify her clothing, and general appearance? I need to know if you spot anything unusual or out of place."

I gulped and looked, again. I recognized her turquoise and navy suit. She'd worn it to a chamber of commerce dinner we'd both attended. Regrettably, a combination of mud and swamp water had turned the vivid colors to sludge brown. I imagined how upset she'd be to know pictures revealing a filthy wardrobe, were being viewed, especially as part of a police investigation. Not to mention that tangled mess of hair. *Bold Hold Hair Spray* and Grace were inseparable in life, but not, however, in death.

I couldn't reconcile the gap between those cold pictures and the lively, talkative Grace planning a trip, or attending one of many charity events. Before asking the sergeant to get the pictures out of my sight, however, I noticed something oddly familiar. "Could you enlarge this one for me? I want to see what's around her neck."

He spread his fingers across the screen and magnified Grace's chin and neckline. Where had I seen that pendant? I slumped back in the chair. Wasn't Lucy Minor wearing the same piece the last time I saw her? No mistaking that unusual sunburst. I'd even considered trying to find one, myself, until Lucy announced it was "one of a kind." How could that be, since I'd just laid eyes on a duplicate?

"Do you notice something, unusual, Ms. Jones?"

"This might be my imagination, but I'd swear I saw the same necklace a few days ago on another client. She told me her ex-husband had given it to her. He swore it was an original. In fact, both women knew each other, and while I can't confirm their friendship, they did run in the same social circle."

Sergeant LeBlanc's eyebrows furrowed. "Are you sure they're the same? Could they be designed by the same company or jeweler? Since both ladies knew each other, it's possible they shopped in similar places, right?"

Of course. "That must be it. They just look similar. Whenever Grace was out, she always wore at least one piece of hand-crafted metal jewelry." *Although...* "Just to be on the safe side, is there any way I could see the actual pendant? The picture enlargement is a bit grainy."

And I never want to see it again!

"I'll check with the 'chain of custody' property clerks to see how they want to handle it. This may take some time, but if I present you as a witness, there should be no problem." He stood and collected his tablet. "I'll be in touch, Ms. Jones." He handed me his card. "In the meantime, please call if anything else comes to mind."

I took the card and slid it in my pocket. "I'm anxious to get to the bottom of this. Grace was a client and a family friend. Although I didn't know her, socially, she'd introduced me and the agency to the Miami business community. So, please, Sergeant, keep me posted."

"I'll do just that, Ms. Jones." He nodded and left the restaurant. I sipped my coffee, coaxing my brain to visualize Lucy's pendant. "I swear Grace had on the same one!"

"Excuse me? Miss, did you say something?" Marie stood beside me with fresh beignets.

"Oh, no. Just talking to myself. Nothing else to eat, thanks, but I will take a regular coffee." *Might as well get hopped up on caffeine while I plan my next move.*

Marie placed a fresh cup on the placemat and poured steaming liquid. "You're not going to sit here all day, are you? There's a whole city out there just waitin' for you to explore. I'm more than happy to recommend a few of my favorite spots." She beamed.

"How could I ever turn down such a generous offer." I couldn't do much here anyway, except wonder, worry, and wait. "In that case, may I have my coffee to go?"

****

I stepped onto the sidewalk in front of the hotel, greeted with a blast of mind-numbing heat. *Why didn't I ask for iced coffee?* I pulled out the short list of Marie's favorite shops. Hmmm. Two book stores. *Wish I had more time to read.* Three antique shops. *Nope.* French art museum. *Huh-uh.* Polly's Pralines. *Now we're talkin'!*

I was on Chartres Street and Polly's was a block away on St. Ann's. I walked past Jackson Square on the right and St. Louis Cathedral on the left. Such history. Much of it troublesome, though. On second thought, "troublesome" underestimates the horror of public executions that took place in the 18th and early 19th centuries. On a happier note, visiting the premier jazz spots could bring me closer to my dad. He loved one of New Orleans' favorite sons, Louis Armstrong, and his legendary trumpet.

I turned left at St. Ann's and searched for the praline shop. How in the world could I even think of sweets after two beignets this morning? *I'll just take a few back to the room. Yeah, that's what I'll do.* I strolled past a couple of antique stores, another coffee shop, and one-stop food mart. Finally, the smell of caramel alerted my nasal passages. Polly's Pralines was one door up. Heaven! The moment I walked in I knew I'd never get out of there without sampling at least one...or three. Funny how, at that moment, one of my mother's favorite phrases jumped into my thoughts. "A moment on the lips. A lifetime on the hips." *Go away, Mother!*

I perused the cases stuffed with pralines from traditional, chocolate, café au lait, Bananas Foster (yuck!), to sugar and spice. Shelves of gourmet foods lined the opposite wall. I scrutinized a jar of Voo Doo Mango Hot sauce. *Suppose a couple of drops on Ruby would turn her into a toad?* I smirked at the thought.

But, back to the reason for my stop. *Pralines*! I debated, at the counter, how many to buy; or rather, how many I could afford. Those luscious pecan treats didn't come cheap!

"Have you made up your mind?" A cheery young lady in a pink and white candy-striped apron, with chef's hat to match, held an opened box ready to fill my order.

"I'll take six of your traditional pralines. Uh, make that seven. I'll have one here."

She chuckled. "I get that request a lot." She scooped one out with a gloved hand, laid it on a piece of waxed paper and handed it to me. I savored the sugary, melty goodness before taking the first bite. Nothing compared to a New Orleans praline, except maybe one from Charleston or Savannah. That's it! I'll become a praline taste-tester! *Remember, Andi...A moment on the lips...Yes, Mother.*

I moved to a small table at the front window and scanned the charming shops and diverse blend of tourists and locals going in and out. A middle-aged woman standing across the street in front of Claudia's Candles & Magic, the incense, candle, and herb shop, caught my eye. Her back was to me, but by the body language and hand gestures, she and a tall young man were engaged in a heated discussion. In fact, she got right in his face forcing him to back up. *Whoa! Wouldn't wanna cross her.* He shrugged and walked back in the store. She stood for a minute, possibly deciding whether to go back in and continue the *discussion* or leave. She did the latter, crossing the street a few stores down from my view through the candy store window. Pressing my head against the glass to get a better look, I did a double-take. Her posture, body type, gait, all reminded me of... *Could it be?* Not possible since she was on an Alaskan cruise. If I didn't know better, I'd swear Lucy Minor had a twin.

Chapter Eleven

I'd been in my room about five minutes when Sergeant LeBlanc called. "Miss Jones? I wanted to let you know you have clearance to view the pendant Grace Payne had on when she died. Could you come to the police station today?"

Already 4:00 p.m. and I'd planned to relax, maybe find a place to listen to some blues and sample a plate filled with authentic barbeque shrimp. *Hmmph. So much for plans.* "Where is the station located? Can I walk or do I need to catch a cab?"

"I wouldn't force you to do either. If you can come, now, I'll send a car for you. Is that all right? I promise not to take more than an hour of your time."

"Uh, sure. I'll wait outside the hotel."

"Detective Giles will pick you up in…can you be ready in fifteen minutes?"

Do I have a choice? "Sure. I'll watch for him."

"*She* will bring you back to the evidence room. See you soon, Miss Jones."

Swell. I did ask to see the pendant, but why did it have to be so soon? My mind and body were worn out—perhaps from those awful crime-scene photos, walking the entire perimeter of the French Quarter, or snacking my way into sugar shock? A big dose of each, if I had to guess.

The image of the couple arguing on the sidewalk

briefly crossed my mind, but I dismissed the notion it was Lucy. She was too excited about her Alaskan cruise to skip out on it. Besides, I'd be the first one to know if she'd changed travel plans. Wouldn't I?

I brushed through my hair, smiled into the mirror to check for bits of praline stuck between my teeth, and set out on what I hoped would be a useful fact-finding mission. Wonder if seeing Grace's pendant in person would confirm my memory of the one Lucy had on the day she stopped by the agency, or create more confusion?

A dark blue SUV waited at the curb. *That was fast!* A young woman dressed in crisp khakis, white shirt, and navy jacket slid out of the driver's seat. "Hello Miss Jones. I'm Carey Giles. Sergeant La Blanc sent me to give you a lift to the station."

"Nice to meet you, Miss, er…uh, Detective Giles. Thanks for picking me up."

She chuckled. "Andre…Sergeant LeBlanc is known for his spur-of-the-moment requests, so in the interest of expediency, we thought it best I drive you to the station while he completed the paperwork."

I hopped in the passenger seat. Lights and beeps, from electronic equipment, obscured the dash. I turned toward the driver, and bars separating the front from the back caught my eye. "Oh, sorry. May I sit up front?"

The detective laughed. "You're not going to pull a gun on me, are you Miss Jones?"

"Not me. Not a fan of firearms." I settled in my soft leather seat and buckled up for the short ride.

"Thanks for coming, Miss Jones. I sensed urgency when you requested viewing the pendant."

"Not a problem, Sergeant." I sat on one of two

stark wooden chairs that matched the charm of the scratched metal desk. I studied the dingy walls, yellowed fluorescent lights on the ceiling, and papers stacked on rusty file cabinets, it all made me wonder how this department could afford my luxurious transportation.

"You need me for anything else, Andre?"

The Sergeant shook his head. "No, Carey, that's all for now. I'll escort Miss Jones to the evidence room. Thanks for your help." With that, he stood and gestured toward the door. "I don't want to take any more of your time than necessary. Follow me."

All business, this one. We walked down an equally dingy corridor lined with offices and large windows; most of which were hidden behind grungy venetian blinds.

The sergeant stopped and opened the evidence room door. "Please, take a seat at the table. I'll get the piece in question." He walked to the back and returned with a large, white box, removed the lid, put on gloves, and began sorting.

Ugh! Watching him root through Grace's belongings made me ill. Why didn't he bring the pendant, and leave the rest in the back? I caught a glimpse of a soiled navy skirt and mud-stained blouse. *If he pulls out Grace's underwear, I swear I'm outta here!*

"Ah, this is it." He opened a plastic bag, containing several pieces of jewelry, and removed a pendant. "Have you ever seen Mrs. Payne wearing this?"

I scrutinized the bright yellow sunburst surrounded by silver and turquoise hammered metal. No, I hadn't seen Grace wearing it, but I swore I'd seen it on Lucy!

77

Should I spill my suspicions to the sergeant? Wait! What suspicions? *Andi, you're getting way ahead of yourself.* "I-uh, don't ever remember seeing this on Grace." *Good! I didn't have to lie!*

"Yes, I assumed that from our previous discussion, however, I also had the impression you'd seen it on another client. Is that the case, or not?"

Curses! He remembered. I studied the piece, again; struggling to recall the one Lucy had on the last time we spoke. Not wishing to send him on a wild goose chase, I admitted, "I just don't know. It looks similar to one I saw last week, but I can't be sure."

He leaned forward in his chair. "Where, and on whom did you see it?"

Whoa. Seriously pointed questions and good grammar. I'm cooked.

"On another client, Lucinda Minor. She'd stopped by the agency to pick up reservation material for a cruise, but as I said before, it looked *similar*. I can't be one-hundred percent positive it was identical. The two women live, well, uh, lived close to the same shops and may have bought the same, or similar piece of jewelry without knowing it."

Sergeant LeBlanc leaned back. "So, where does that leave us? You're the one who brought up the possibility of the two pendants being the same. The one found on the victim is very distinctive, wouldn't you agree?"

I nodded, regretting the minute I'd opened my big mouth about the second pendant.

"Is there any way to get in touch with this client in order to verify whether there is a connection?" The frustration in his voice, evident.

"She left on a cruise four days ago." I repeated my last conversation with her. "Said she'd be mostly out of touch for the entire three weeks. Lucy loves taking side trips off the beaten path, but maybe I can contact the ship and leave a message."

The sergeant stood, abruptly. "Why don't you do that, Miss Jones? Meanwhile, I'll speak to Mr. Payne and try to get more credible information."

Well, that was a little harsh! "I-uh, I'll let you know if, and when, I talk to Mrs. Minor."

He opened the evidence room door and nodded. "Thanks for coming in on such short notice." With that, he picked up the evidence box and disappeared into the other room.

"Guess our interview is over," I mumbled. *Hmmph.*

"'Scuse me?"

I jumped at the sound of Detective Giles' voice. "Oh, sorry. Just talking to myself."

She laughed. "Spending time with Sergeant Le Blanc tends to do that to the best of us." She stood at the door, indicating it was time for me to skedaddle.

I squeezed past her and waited as she locked the door. I supposed Andre either had his own key or left another way. Whatever, they sure didn't want anyone to saunter into that back room.

The dingy hallway looked no brighter on our way to the exit. *You'd think someone in this place could spring for a couple gallons of paint.*

Getting back into the police car, I sighed. That station had some seriously bad vibes going on! Or maybe despair was dragging me down. Why again did I think I could fly to New Orleans and solve a disappearance/murder? Helping Ruby out of hot water in Mexico and stumbling into Lenny La Mour's killer in Las Vegas was more dumb luck than anything else.

Grace's murder, however, is a whole other ball game.

Carey dropped me at the hotel. Still light enough to do some touristy stuff, I turned one direction, then the other. My mind wanted to explore. My body said, "For Godsake, sit down and rest!" I listened to my body and shuffled into the café for a light *Creole* meal before bed; a bowl of shrimp *étouffée* and grilled French bread. Spicy Cajun fare would have to wait.

Chapter Twelve

I'm blind! I gasped for breath. My lungs had turned into two squished Nerf balls begging for air. A shrill rendition of *Bad to the Bone* pierced my eardrums. I swatted the air in the direction of my phone.

"'Lo?"

"Well, hey there, sleepyhead. It's 'bout time you answered."

I squinted through matted eyelashes. Wiping drool from the corner of my mouth with the back of my hand, I searched with the other for the two-by-four crushing my lungs. I must've fallen asleep on my stomach—a *no-no* according to my chiropractor—and spent the night hugging my computer tablet. No wonder I couldn't breathe. Thank God I'd slipped on a T-Shirt last night or, my luck, I might've accidentally taken pictures of my boobs and posted them on Instagram! *Snicker.*

"Are you there?"

I rolled over and propped two soft pillows under my head. "Uh, yeah, I'm here, El...sorta. What's up?"

"Well..."

Uh-oh. When Ellie hesitates, something is definitely wrong.

"We just got notification from the Alaska Cruise Line that Lucy Minor is missing."

"Say again, El?"

81

"I repeat, Lucy Minor is missing! What's going on? First Grace, now Lucy? Something weird's up."

"Ya think?" One client dead and now another, missing? *Is the Bermuda Triangle up to its old tricks?* "You say the cruise line notified you? Did you speak to anyone, directly?"

"No, I just got a fax advising us and the client, no refund will be issued until we submit a valid request, and it goes through the approval process. Even then, she'll only get a partial refund. Guess I can see their point. After all, she—"

"Ellie! I don't give a rat's behind about their refund policy. Two people, directly booked by Graves Travel, are missing!"

"Well, technically, one's missing and the other one's dead."

I just heard that, but where? Oh, yeah. My brain. "Gee, thanks for the clarification." When did my assistant turn into a literal thinker? "Did they tell you anything else? Did someone call the tour company and cancel? Did they try to get in touch with her?"

"All they said was she never showed up for a side trip to the Mendenhall Glacier and whale watching. I swear, this is plain peculiar."

Peculiar, indeed. "I can't believe Lucy would miss whale watching. That particular excursion excited her as much as the whole cruise. Okay, let me make some calls. Guess I'll see if her daughter and son-in-law have heard from her. Fat chance since they don't much care whether she comes or goes, except when she's frittering away money they think should be saved for their inheritance. At least that's what Lucy tells me."

"Kids these days," Ellie sniffed. "I don't expect a

darn thing from my parents, not that they have anything to give. Still, you'd think her kids would have better things to do than whine about—"

"Gotta go, El. Let me know if you hear anything and I'll do the same."

I laid on the bed and stared at the ceiling. A gecko ran halfway across the tiles, cocked his head to get a good look at me, completed his trip, and disappeared behind the mahogany dresser. Any other time, I'd probably freak out, but not today. I had no unoccupied "worry space" for reptiles running rampant in my room. Not when my problems just doubled.

Well, this certainly changes things. If Lucy missed her excursion, maybe she was the woman I spotted across the street from the praline shop. Maybe I wasn't seeing things. But why would she skip out on the trip of a lifetime to argue with a man outside a candle and magic store in New Orleans? I couldn't quiet the voice in my head from connecting Grace's murder to Lucy's disappearance and possible re-appearance. If Lucy was in New Orleans, instead of Alaska, I would darn-sure find out why!

Andi, don't shout. I made short time of getting dressed and brushing my hair; primping just enough to be socially acceptable in the cafe. After all, coffee, and lots of it, was the only credible cure for a throbbing head.

****

The hotel café was practically deserted. A different waitress, Daphne, walked over carrying a carafe of coffee in each hand; regular and decaf. Obviously, she'd never waited on me. "Fully-leaded, please. Half and half and stevia. Oh, and please just leave the pot."

She returned with a trivet and set down the pot. "Will you be joining us for breakfast? The special this mawnin' is eggs N'awlins' style. Sunny-side-up on an English muffin topped with poached oysters."

I gave her a, "Have you lost your mind?" stare. If I'd had any inclination to eat, Daphne's menu description put an end to that internal debate. "Just coffee, for now." She opened her mouth for one last attempt to coerce me into ordering, but the "Leave me the hell alone or I might just kill you," look on my face sent her scrambling back to the kitchen.

I sipped the hot liquid; wishing, now, I'd ordered an iced brew so I could slug it down in one mind-clearing gulp. I blew on the top and sipped. Added a little more half and half and sipped again. Ah-that's better. Back to my dead and missing clients. *Nothing I can do for Grace, but where the heck is Lucy? Here in the Big Easy? If that question is affirmed, the next question is, why?*

I finished my coffee and filled a go-cup for the road. Well, technically, the sidewalk. Maybe I'd make a casual stop at Claudia's Candles and Magic to see if the man I saw arguing with Lucy's doppelganger was hanging around.

The stupid decision to wear sandals instead of sneakers made the walk twice as long. When will I ever learn? *Never, Andi. You're too vain about your tanned, Egyptian-shaped feet.* I might not have dark, exotic looks like my sister, Georgia, but I had one enviable asset and by golly, I was gonna flaunt it! No matter how much it hurt!

The store windows, at Claudia's, brimmed with oils, incense, tarot cards, and statues more frightening than magical. A grass voo-doo doll, complete with blood-red dress and gold-colored scarf, perched on a top shelf. Next to it, a piece simply called, "Death." My relief at spotting a *Saint Francis of Assisi* statue was short-lived. Three wolves—teeth bared—sat at his feet. "Even one of my favorite patron saints looks creepy!" I sucked in a deep breath and exhaled, hoping to dispel any evil spirits lurking about.

Expecting to enter a bat cave-like décor, vivid yellow walls and bright lighting shocked my senses. Cheery and inviting similar to many souvenir shops I'd frequented in the Bahamas. Well, except for the plaster skulls hanging from the ceiling and racks of zombie shirts decorated with ghoulish faces and half-eaten flesh. Ick! *I'll never figure out the "Undead" craze. Give me a sexy, fang-toothed vampire, any day.*

Among the blood and gore, a T-Shirt, emblazoned with a white ethereal-looking image, caught my eye. Not bad. My shade of purple, too. Next to the shirt hung a six-foot long satin banner, decorated with the seven chakra wheels. *Hmmm.* Perfect for the blank wall between my bed and dresser. My condo definitely needed some color and—added bonus—my chakras could use some balancing, too. Whoa! $129.00? Maybe I'd just get a colorful, free travel poster at the next convention.

Two large display cases, loaded with stones and crystals, set back-to-back. I picked out a smooth pink stone; rose quartz, for love. Maybe I'd buy a couple pounds and send to Manny. It had been several weeks since we'd talked. Those old demons, *Paranoia* and *Insecurity* crept into my subconscious. Had he moved on with someone else? Guess I should've listened to those who warned me time was the enemy of long-distance relationships. "How could I ever think it would work?"

"May I be of assistance?"

"Oh! Geeze-Louise! You scared the crap outta me!" I grabbed my chest, sure my heart was about to beat its last, and did a one-eighty towards a silver-haired woman with black painted eyebrows, and more tracks on her face than the Talladega Raceway.

"I'm the owner, Claudia. So sorry I frightened you," she smiled. Okay, *smiled* might be a stretch. Her red-spackled lips turned up, menacingly.

Every sane and rational thought disappeared from my brain. Why had I come into this place? Oh, yeah. I'd planned to ask questions; maybe find out if anyone had seen, or waited on, Lucy or her twin. A furtive glance around the shop revealed no clerks in sight. Quizzing this woman, who'd make occupants from Madame Tussauds Wax Museum look lively, could be the worst idea, ever. "Uh-thanks, but I'm just browsing. Tourist, you know." I chuckled, swallowed wrong, followed by a coughing, or rather choking, fit.

"I have some slippery elm bark tea in the back that will soothe you," *Wax Lady* offered.

I sneezed, twice—something that always seemed to accompany one of my choking sessions—and shook my head. "No, really, I'm fine," I wheezed. *Oh, way to keep a low profile!* How could I expect to investigate on the sly when I broadcasted my presence?

"Scuse me, dearie. Do you have this headscarf in violet?"

That voice. That unmistakable shrill voice.

86

"Why Andi Anna! Imagine the luck finding you here!"

"Yes, imagine the luck. Hello, Ruby."

Chapter Thirteen

"I just had a feeling we'd run into each other! It's fate. The girls are across the street smellin' those *praw-leeens*, and prob'ly stuffin' their faces. I'm so glad I have self-control when it comes to sweets. Who are we if we don't look after our girlish figures, right, Andi?" She gave me a critical, head-to-toe, perusal. "So what if yours is more *boy-like*, I'm sure you still have to watch those calories."

I should be used to Ruby's subtle insults by now, yet, I felt the inevitable face flush. I'd never been self-conscious about my body until she came along. I had to admit, though, for a woman who just turned sixty, she still rocked a bikini; even if those 38's of hers did come straight from a plastic surgeon's office.

She slipped her arm through my elbow and led me around the store. "So, what are we buying today? Healing crystals? Essential oils? Oh, I know! A love potion!"

"I don't need a love potion, Ruby. I'm content with my long-distance relationship."

"Oh, fiddlesticks! Content? That's how you describe your liaison with that handsome Cancun sheriff? Just how many times have you seen him since we got back? Once?"

She had me there. "That's not the point. We talk on the phone and Facetime, regularly." Well, at least we did until a few weeks ago.

"Facetime," she scoffed. "The only face time I appreciate is lip-to-lip."

"Did I hear someone needs a love potion?"

I jumped, again. *I swear Claudia's feet must not hit the floor when she walks!* Her stealthy movements didn't startle Ruby one bit. "Why darlin', this one needs somethin' quick! She's moving into that awful 'middle-age' and not a beau in sight."

Oh, dear Lord, take me now.

Claudia studied me for a moment, moved closer and rubbed her hands together. "May I touch you?"

Huh? I swallowed, hard. "I, uh-guess so."

She moved beside me and wrapped a bony hand around my wrist. Her head moved back and forth, her eyelids blinked, rapidly. I was wondering if the scenario could get any more bizarre when her eyes rolled back in her head. Was she having a stroke? If so, she was in the throes of a doozy.

A deep growl, I swore emanated from the bowels of the earth, seized the small woman's throat. "You follow death. Now, death follows you. Beware of those seeking to do harm."

Her eerie warning sent shivers all the way down to my shoes. Heat from her hand, seared my arm. I jerked away so sharply, my wrist popped in the process.

"A dangerous presence is closing in!" Her voice darkened, even more. Her eyes shut tight. A low moan rattled in her throat a split second before her lids flew open revealing pupils reminiscent of glazed white cupcake frosting.

"Leave! Leave! Leave!" She groaned, dropping my wrist like a hot potato.

Believe me, I wanted to leave, but with concrete blocks for feet, you're pretty much stuck in one spot. Ruby, unconcerned about *my* well-being, turned to run and plowed straight into a rack of tie-dyed T-Shirts. Meanwhile, Claudia stood, motionless, unblinking.

Fast as you could say, "Archangel Michael, get me the heck outta here," the older woman's eyes cleared. She asked, softly, "May I help you find something?"

"No-no," I stuttered. "I'm, uh, just looking around." Ruby's eyes were so big I feared her fake eyelashes would pop across the room.

Barely flinching, Claudia nodded and eased away. I did my darndest to peruse a table teeming with essential oils and charms, but my hands shook so badly, I was afraid to pick up the merchandise. I couldn't swear it was her gaze, but something evil pricked the back of my head. I dared not turn around for fear her eyes had turned black and looking directly at them would transform me into a muskrat or-or a shrunken head!

"Andi?" A whisper of hot breath tinged the back of my neck triggering a blood curdling scream. "Ahhh…!"

In the same instant, a young man dashed from behind a back-room curtain. His eyes, angry and unfriendly, bored holes through me like two lumps of coal. "What's going on out here? Are you trying to wake the dead?"

"So sorry. I-uh, thought I saw a, uh…spider." Shaken to the core, I backed away from his menacing gaze, straight into Ruby.

"Oww! You just stepped on my foot," she shrieked. "Oh, and you smudged my new Ferragamos! I just bought these for the trip. What's wrong with you?"

I spun around; eyes blazing. "Don't ever sneak up

on me, again. Understood?"

She raised her palms and, for once in her life, quietly backed off.

By the time I'd gathered my wits, the young man's head was bent in conversation with Claudia. "I found the box you needed, but it is almost empty. You'll have to order more from Gizelle."

Claudia scoffed. "Jules, you're new here, so let me explain something. I'd be safer pulling the tail of a female wildcat protecting her young than to *order* more supplies from Gizelle. She is adamant about making potions on her terms, only when the moon is right." Claudia shook her head and murmured, "That old witch will not change long as she draws a breath."

Old witch? I wondered if Claudia's description was literal?

Jules cleared his throat when he noticed Ruby and me staring; his dark brows furrowed. For the first time, I got a good look from head to toe. Although I'd been across the street during the confrontation with the Lucy-look-alike, the height, weight, along with gestures and mannerisms, fit the description of the male participant. I broke off the uncomfortable gaze between us, and pretended to scrutinize a rack crammed with multi-colored stones. *Sure could use a protective crystal about now.* I vowed, from that moment on, to carry at least one Labradorite with me at all times.

"I'm sorry I overreacted." Jules had slipped beside me. "Please let me show you our best stones and crystals." He cupped my elbow with chilled fingers and led me to a display case. "These were shipped from all over the world." He pointed to a startling turquoise stone. "Some are used to ward off evil"

Did his eyes narrow when he said, "evil"? *Oh, stop it Andi!* "They are all beautiful. Uh, any specific protection stone you can recommend?"

He smiled and I relaxed a bit. No horns popping out from the top of his head. Ha!

"This beautiful deep blue stone, lapis lazuli, is from Egypt. Topaz and peridot were also used in ancient times as jewelry and in amulets. However, you might consider this emerald." He turned me toward a mirror next to the display case and placed the brilliant green crystal just below my chin. I had to admit, it was gorgeous. He wasn't bad, either. My negative opinion, of the scowling young man I'd first encountered, slowly changed. In fact, I considered buying the stone and having a necklace made.

Before I could ask the price, Claudia called from the back room. "Jules? Please come here. We need to discuss the inventory. Now!"

A dark shadow crossed his face. "I'm so sorry for the interruption. Could you give me a few minutes?"

"Sure, take your time. I can wait a little while."

He stormed to the back.

Whoa. No mistaking the boss around here. I let out the breath I must've held for at least five minutes, and feigned interest in a display of tarot cards conveniently positioned near the muffled discussion behind the curtain. A powerful-looking angel on the front of one deck offered *extraordinary protection* and a *quick and easy guide for the beginner. Hmmm, that's another option, along with the stone. I could also use a covert listening device.* My hearing wasn't worth a hoot after teenage years full of rock concerts and blaring headphones.

Funny how I clearly heard Ruby *whisper* from across the room, for all to hear, "Andi, what are you doing?"

I silently "shushed" her and moved perilously close to the curtain, hoping to catch a bit of conversation. By that time, fading footsteps, followed by the opening and closing of an outside door, were the only sounds.

I scurried to the front window past a confused Ruby just in time to see a car exit the side ally and turn left toward The Quarter. My guess was *Scary Claudia* remained in the back of the store, and Jules had *left the building.*

"What in the *Sam Hill* is going on with you, Andi Anna? If you wanna stay and talk some more to that nutso in the back, it's your funeral. I'm leaving!"

For once, Ruby and I were on the same page. "Right behind you!" I placed the emerald on the display case and sighed. "Maybe I can come back for you."

"Who you talkin' to, Andi? Let's go!"

We exited the store and walked across the street. Well, I walked, and Ruby pretend-limped, all the while complaining about her smudged shoe and possible broken toe. *So much for acting casual with Claudia and Jules!* Between my coughing attack and Ruby's histrionics, that ship had sailed.

Now what? Andi, you're getting nowhere! Dead ends, nothing but dead ends. Pardon the pun. Plus, the addition of Ruby baggage.

Chapter Fourteen

Several women from the convention group greeted us when we walked into Polly's Pralines; friends of my mother and dad's, plus two others who'd also accompanied Ruby on her ill-fated cruise to Mexico.

"Oh, my goodness. Andi Anna? Ruby didn't mention you were in town," Cloris squealed.

Her "twin" sister, Doris shook her head, glumly. "You look terrible, Andi. Is this about Grace?"

Cloris's eyes widened. "Oh, please don't tell us you're involved in another murder! Remember, you almost got yourself killed, thanks to Ruby." She turned and smiled, sheepishly. "No offense, Ruby."

"Hmmph. None taken, I suppose." Ruby stomped off and plopped down at a table in the back with two other convention-goers.

Not much of a trade-off. Ruby for the twins, but my mood improved surrounded by familiar faces after the unsettling encounter with Claudia and her strange employee.

Cloris grabbed my arm and pulled me toward a bench at the front of the store. All 5 feet-185 pounds stood directly in front of me. I was sitting, she was standing, yet I couldn't help noticing my eyes were on the same level as the vertically challenged twin.

"Now, what's going on, Andi? We want to hear every gory detail!"

94

"Cloris!" Her sister scolded. "Leave Andi alone. Why do you insist on being such a gossip?" She folded her arms, giving her sister a withering look. "If Andi wants us to know something, she'll tell us. Right, Andi?"

I couldn't help marvel at the two. I supposed their mother thought it was cute to dress them alike when they were children. Sadly, they'd continued the tradition. Cloris, about a head shorter than Doris, also outweighed her tall, willowy twin by about thirty pounds. Yet, there they were, dressed in identical flared legged, beige pants, and pink flowered blouses. Ruby used to tell me how they'd brag about being able to shop at the same store. "You wouldn't believe it, Andi Anna. The sizes range from six tall to twenty-six petite! Why, I'd bet my new *Dolce and Gabanna* scarf that was the exact size range between them." Before seeing them side-by-side on the cruise ship in Cozumel, I assumed Ruby had exaggerated. For once, she was spot on. If not the oddest twins on the planet, they were certainly in the top five.

Between Cloris's pleading brown eyes, and the imploring expression in Doris's blue grays—too wide for her long, narrow face—I knew I was cooked. *No getting out of here without throwing them a bone.* "Yes, I came to New Orleans to get information on Grace's disappearance, but now that she's been found, uh-dead, there's nothing more I can do."

Cloris patted my shoulder. "Oh, it's just awful, isn't it? One of our own. We were all so fond of Grace, even if that husband of her is a pill!"

"Cloris, don't speak ill of Stewart. I'm sure he's grieving." Without missing a beat, she offered, "You're welcome to tag along with us, Andi since you no longer have to locate Grace."

Ruby had, somehow, quietly joined our conversation. "Oh, my yes, dearie, unless you need to get back to that little travel business of yours."

For once, I was grateful for the intrusion. *The perfect opportunity to make my exit.* "You're right, Ruby. Thanks, so much, for the invitation, girls. I'd love to stay but need to get back to Miami. According to Ellie, the phones are ringing off their hooks." I made a quick move to the door. "Have fun."

The twins looked crushed. "But…but, Andi," Cloris pleaded. "What about Grace?"

"How did she die? Did someone kill her? Oh, you can't leave us hanging," Doris begged.

"Sorry, ladies. Gotta go." I flew out of Polly's before they could pull me back into the inquisition, and before I could buy more pralines. Darn!

****

I limped straight back to my room and collapsed. Funny how I'd scoffed at Georgia's foot bath gift a couple Christmases ago. "How old do you think I am, Sis? A hundred and three?" But, after trudging back to the hotel in those godawful sandals, I would've given my right arm to stick my aching dogs in warm, pulsating water. I tenderly rubbed a blister that had formed on the bottom of my big toe, fell back on the lavender and blue patterned comforter, and closed my eyes.

I heard my mother's voice scold as I drifted off to dream land. *"Hotel bedspreads are germ magnets, Andi."*

"I know, mother…and I don't care."

A persistent buzz pierced the pitch-black room. My eyes flew open. How long had I been asleep? I rolled over and pulled my cell off the nightstand. Squinting to focus on the blurry text, four words popped out. *Andi-murder-meet-Lucy.*

That got my attention. I sat up and turned on the wall light beside the bed. The full text read, "Andi, have info on Grace's murder. Need 2 meet, Lucy."

Lucy? What the hell? I typed back, "Where are you?" A few seconds later she answered, "Pick u up in front of hotel. 15 min."

I struggled to process the unexpected request, or rather, *demand.* If the message was from Lucy, why is she in New Orleans, insisting to meet at...I checked my phone...*11:45?*

The notion of another midnight meeting had a particularly ominous feel, especially after my horrifying experience in Las Vegas at the bodies exhibit. Late night encounters could get you seriously killed! I debated whether to text back and cancel. Or maybe stand outside and make sure it was Lucy and that she was alone. I'd known her long enough to never, ever consider her a threat, any more than my own mother. Or at least, I did until she'd apparently skipped out on her trip for reasons unknown.

I channeled my best Ricky Ricardo. "Luuu-ceee. You got some 'splainin' to do."

Still dressed, but wrinkled from this afternoon, I threw my phone and room key card into my purse and shut the door behind me and mumbled to myself, "Wish I'd bought a pack of those Angel protection cards."

I considered whether to text Ellie to let her know the latest plan, when a small, gray four-door sedan pulled up to the curb. I stooped down when the passenger window rolled down. Lucy sat in the driver's seat. "Thank goodness you agreed to meet me Andi. Please, get in."

"Not until you tell me why you're here and not in Alaska."

"I will, dear, but not here on the street. Please get in, and I promise to answer all your questions, and more."

I glanced into the back seat—that, to my relief, was empty—and proceeded to flop into the passenger side. "Wow, why's the seat laid back so far?"

Lucy laughed. "I suppose the last person to rent this mid-size sedan must've set it that way. Adjust it and get comfortable, dear."

I made one vain attempt to fix the seat and quickly gave up. It wouldn't budge. "I might as well be sitting in a beach chair," I grumbled, "We're not going far, are we?"

She glanced at the side mirror and pulled away from the sidewalk. "Not too far."

A small chill prickled the base of my neck, but why? *This is Lucy, for gosh sake!* Still, I felt a strange vibe surrounding her. Maybe from her uncharacteristic outfit. Instead of crisp matronly white slacks and tropical shirt, straight out of a lavish Florida boutique, she wore wrinkled khakis and matching vest. Her typical, smoothly-coiffed hair resembled the asparagus fern on my patio; after I'd forgotten to water it for a month, or three. I could almost picture her piloting an airboat into one of Louisiana's thousand or so bayous. But it was more than just her look. Her demeanor showed an intensity I never knew existed in my favorite client.

We pulled onto Interstate 10. I squirmed as we drove west, past the Metairie exit. When we flew by three Kenner exits, I'd had enough of the mysterious road trip. "How far, Lucy? I need to get back to the hotel."

She gave me a cursory, sideways glance. "Just a few more miles, dear. I promise you'll be back in plenty of time to get your beauty rest."

Relax, Andi. It's Lucy! I pulled up and glanced out the window. The three-quarter moon cast haunting shadows on the tops of cypress trees thriving along the bayou. The clack, clack of the tires crossing the bridge expanse, reminded me of another of my mother's favorite Bee Gees songs. A trip across Biscayne Bay Bridge in Miami inspired the group to write one of their first number one hits. Neither Georgia, nor I, remembered Mom ever crossing that bridge without singing *Jive Talkin'*.

Anxiety revved into high gear when Lucy turned off the highway and headed down a narrow road, shrouded by eerie, overhanging cypress. Warm memories, of my mother's musical favorites, transformed into cold reality.

"You're not taking me to the swamp to kill me, are you?" I laughed, attempting to cover a nagging, creeping fear.

"Of course not, silly. You'll understand in a few minutes. Ah, here we are."

I pulled myself to a sitting position. *Here* set a tiny shack tucked in a horseshoe of scrub pine trees. Dried threads of Spanish moss covered the roof and the only window in the front. I silently scolded myself for ever agreeing to this, so-called meeting, and begged my guardian angels to please keep me safe.

Lucy unbuckled her seat belt and got out of the car. "Come, Andi. We can talk inside."

I hesitated. "Can't we just talk here?" I couldn't imagine the inside looking much better than the outside. *What in the world is Lucy's connection to this dump?* The Lucy I knew. Prim, proper, fastidiously dressed. Not this messy, back-woodsy character.

"Now, dear, you'll feel more comfortable if you come in. Trust me."

There it is. That familiar, motherly smile. Still the same Lucy. I had nothing to fear. Wonder what set off my sudden paranoia?

I slid out of the car and followed her across the rotting porch. Lucy held the door. I took a deep breath and stepped inside. *Whoa!* The shock must've registered on my face.

"I don't imagine you expected this, huh, Andi?"

A small alcove opened to a cozy room and décor; blue and yellow-flowered loveseat, a burnt orange armchair, and an antique, white rocker with cushions that matched the loveseat. A tiny kitchen and hallway on the left led to the back of the cottage.

"No, Lucy, I'm a little surprised." *Putting it mildly!* "Is this your place?"

She shook her head. "No, this lovely little cabin belongs to a friend of mine. It's been in his family for decades"

"I don't doubt that. Was it abandoned for a while?"

"I believe it was. His father built it many years ago. When he died, my friend moved away and only recently, moved back. He rented a room in town for a while until he gathered the funds to make the place livable. The outside is a disaster, but he's planning to work on it when time and money allow."

My suspicion eased...a bit. Should I ask about this male friend or leave well-enough-alone? I chose the latter. Anyone so determined to restore his family home was okay in my book. Still, I needed answers from Lucy.

Right on cue, she gestured. "Please sit. I'm sure you're anxious to know why we're here." I chose the padded rocker. The gentle back-and-forth motion had always relaxed me...especially in stressful situations. This qualified.

Lucy occupied the loveseat. "Andi, I know you're just as sick over what happened to Grace as I am. That's why I cut my trip short and decided to come to New Orleans to help."

"But, how did you know I was here, and how did you hear about Grace's murder?"

She leaned forward. "Well, you know Stewart and Grace were friends of my ex-husband and I, so when I read about her death on the internet, I called Stewart immediately from the ship. You do know there have been several deaths in the same area. News reports say this is the foul work of a serial killer." Her voice raised an octave. "It's a crime of national interest, Andi."

I nodded. "I heard a brief news report last week." Probably should've paid more attention before sending a client to her death! Before I could mention Sergeant LeBlanc's theory about the discrepancies between the first four victims and Grace, Lucy continued her explanation for our meeting.

"Anyway, Stewart wasn't there, but his son

answered the phone and said he'd gone to Louisiana so he could—uh-identify the body." She threw the back of her hand to her forehead, Scarlett O'Hara-style. "Oh, poor Grace!"

Hmmm, I hadn't realized they were such good friends. *You have to start paying attention, Andi! Life is passing you by and you're missing all the details.*

Lucy cleared her throat. "I hate to tell you this but, Jeffrey, Stewart's son, said his dad was determined to make you pay for what happened. He believes your agency mixed up Grace's reservation, somehow, which led to her murder. Frankly, I don't believe it. Neither you, nor Ellie, have ever made a mistake with my travel arrangements."

I thought back to my unease when Ellie first booked the trip, why I insisted she check and recheck the reservations. In hindsight, kicking Stewart Payne to the curb and encouraging him to book somewhere else, would've been a god-send. But that ship had sailed, and I was left bailing water from a sinking canoe.

"I'm well aware of his animosity toward the agency, Lucy." His anger over that little "wrong airport-wrong state" incident was epic, but nothing compared to the anguish of Grace's death. "I hate to admit it, but the thought of Stewart using Grace's disappearance to go after me, and the agency, is the main reason I flew here in the first place. Of course, I was worried sick about Grace and hoped she'd be found safe and sound. Never, in a million years, did I expect this ending! I'm just sick and don't know where else to turn." Tears stung my eyes.

Lucy slid off the loveseat and knelt beside me. She cradled my hands in hers. "I'm so sorry, dear, but your dead end, pardon the pun, may find some life."

I pulled my hands away. "What do you mean? For starters, why are you here, Lucy?"

She stood. "Please, just hear me out. I have reason to believe Grace's murder was set up several weeks before she got to New Orleans." She settled back on the loveseat and took a deep breath. "It's becoming all too likely her husband, Stewart, had his wife killed."

Chapter Fifteen

"Stewart? Stewart Payne? Oh, sure he's a jackass, but a murderer?" Questions raced through my mind. "But, why? What did he have to gain?" From my perspective, they didn't have the most loving marriage of all time, but I saw no indication it had deteriorated that completely. Other than the last testy phone conversation Ellie and I overheard at the agency, he'd never talked to, or about her, with anything but respect; a consideration he rarely gave to anyone else he encountered. Well, not to me or Ellie.

Lucy's icy gaze made me shiver. "I believe it was greed."

I settled back in the rocker, took a deep breath, and listened to Lucy's stunning accusations.

She paced back and forth with the focus of a female lion stalking her prey. "I understand you've had your run-ins with him at the agency, but you don't know the whole story. Grace, her husband, my ex, and I were frequent travel companions over the years. Our trips to New Orleans usually meant Grace and I would shop while Stewart and Darryl—*the snake*—would visit every bar in town."

Darryl, the *snake*? Her surly tone indicated their divorce was not only unpleasant, but downright hostile.

"Anyway," she continued, "While I never saw the Paynes fight, there was always this undercurrent

104

between them. Stewart made snide remarks about Grace and everything she did, seconds later pretending he was just kidding. He'd compliment her outfit one minute and the next suggest she needed to lose a few pounds. Passive-aggressive."

Hmmm. Passive-aggressive? I can see that being an issue, even though I'd never seen his passive side.

"He was also very jealous of her. You do know all their money came from her family, right?" Lucy sat back and crossed her arms with a look of smug satisfaction on her face.

"I had no idea." What a shocker. Grace was so unpretentious. I never would've guessed she came from money. Stewart, on the other hand…

"Grace's granddaddy bought acres of land along the Florida coast in the early 1900s. Unlike most investors, he had enough vision and cash to hang on through two hurricanes, a fruit fly invasion, the stock market collapse, and the Depression. After World War II, Miami Beach flourished, along with Grace's family. So, you see, Stewart depended on her for just about everything. House, clothes, and all those country club memberships. I think he has at least five."

"So, you're saying he got rid of her for money? Why not just continue to live with Grace, if he had everything he needed?"

Lucy leaned in. "Because of something he needed that his wife wouldn't condone—a woman on the side, if you know what I mean."

"He was having an affair?"

"Oh, not just an affair," she clucked. "He wanted to marry the floozy."

Why am I just hearing this? I need to get out more.

"I'm confused. Why go to the trouble to kill Grace here? Why not dump her body in the Everglades? Surely, he'd find equally remote spots in Florida."

"Because here, Andi, he had the perfect cover! Remember hearing about all those dead women turning up in the bayou? He figured Grace would be viewed as another addition to the serial killer victim list, removing suspicion from him."

Much as I wanted to disregard the story Lucy had spilled, I breathed a sigh of relief. I was no longer alone in wanting justice for Grace. If *Stewart the Pain* did kill his wife for her money, the police needed to know. Still, something else nagged at me. Let's see, the police, the police station, the sergeant, the evidence room—that's it! The pendant! *Andi, you lame brain! That's the reason you wanted to meet with her!* "Even if all this is true, there's something I need to ask you."

She walked over, leaned down and put her hands on my shoulders. "Of course, my dear. You can ask me anything."

Hmmm, that same sweet Lucy smile I'd seen so many times during the past three years. "I don't know what I'd do without you and your agency," she constantly affirmed. "I trust you to send me anywhere in the world!"

I wondered if that trust would extend to grilling her about possessing the same piece of jewelry that was found on a corpse. Although, if she had nothing to hide, she shouldn't take offense. "Do you remember when you came to the agency to pick up your Alaska travel information?"

"Oh, what a happy day." She clapped her hands, joy spread across her face. "So sad my trip had to be interrupted, but poor sweet Grace's death takes precedence over a cruise." The smile disappeared, replaced by concern. "Sorry, dear, please go on."

"Yesterday, I was shown a picture of Grace's body."

Lucy gasped, "Oh, my. Who would make you look at such a dreadful site? I'm so sorry, Andi. That must have been horrific."

I nodded. "Not something I would've chosen to see, but the police asked if I could identify her before Stewart got into town." No need to mention I was the one who brought up the possibility of identical pendants with Sergeant Le Blanc. "When I saw Grace's body, something stood out."

Lucy's brows furrowed. "What, dear?"

"Grace was wearing a pendant on her jacket similar, no, *identical* to the one you wore the last time I saw you. You know; the sunburst with the yellow and turquoise? Only yours was on a silver chain."

Lucy smiled, again, this time a bit more forced. Her mouth turned up, same as always, but there was no "smile" in her eyes. "Oh, that's such a silly story. Very easy to explain."

Her voice quavered.

"One night when the four of us were out to dinner, Grace showed off the pendant Stewart had given her for their thirty-fifth wedding anniversary. I gushed over it so much I guess Darryl thought I wanted one just like it. The next day, he found out Stewart bought it in one of those expensive boutiques at Bayside. Some hand-crafted jewelry place. Anyway, Darryl surprised me with it a couple months later." Her voice shifted from endearing to sarcastic. "The bastard moved out the following Monday. Miserable scumbag! Guess he thought it made an adequate going away gift," she scoffed.

I wondered if pride kept her from mentioning the pendant was a duplicate. Even though it was a gift from the ex she despised, I supposed she wanted admirers, including me, to believe it was one-of-a-kind. Still, I couldn't imagine wanting to wear something with such bad karma attached. "Since it came from Darryl, why do you still wear it? I'd think you'd want to sell it or bury it. Sorry, poor choice of words."

Her voice, softened. "Oh, I hoped, maybe, he did want me to have a lovely reminder of our marriage. It wasn't all bad, you know." She sat back on the loveseat. "I suppose that's silly, but," she grasped her hands, "you do what you must to survive disappointment."

I saw genuine hurt in her eyes. "I'm so sorry, Lucy. I didn't realize you were in such pain from your divorce."

"Well, how could you, dear. If I recall, we didn't meet until after that miserable piece of garbage left." All hint of melancholy gone, her clinched jaw and blotchy red cheeks left no doubt, Darryl was still on her hate list.

I would've gladly dropped the conversation, but one more question demanded an answer. "Tell me, Lucy, How did Stewart react to Darryl getting you the same piece? I can't imagine he was too happy."

"Oh, I don't think Stewart ever found out. I made sure not to wear it in their presence. She probably wouldn't have cared, but, you know, we all prefer to think we own something special, unique. Really, dear, you're making too much of a silly old piece of jewelry."

I'm making too much of it? Wasn't she on the brink of tears one minute and ready to bite the head off a rattlesnake the next? "Oh, I suppose you're right, but I should warn you, the NOPD know, too," I announced.

"But-but, why would they be interested?"

Was it my imagination, or did her voice sound thin, like every breath of air had dissipated from her lungs? "Oh, I'm sure it's no big deal," I assured her. "The similarity surprised me, so I casually mentioned seeing the same one...on, uh, you before you left on your trip."

If my revelation unnerved her, she recovered, quickly. "Well, I suppose the jewelry police are coming any minute to slap the cuffs on me," she joked. "Oh, my. I wonder what the sentence is for 'pendant plagiarism'."

I managed a wry smile. "Funny, Lucy, but have you forgotten a killer may be on the loose? If Stewart is guilty and catches wind of your suspicions, you could be the next victim...and I'll be right behind you!"

Lucy nodded. "Yes, you're right. This is serious. No jokes allowed until we plan our next move."

"Great. I'll call Sergeant LeBlanc and ask if he can meet us tonight."

A shadow crossed her face. I took a step back. "Uh, is there a problem? You can trust him, I swear."

"Of course, I can, dear." A slight smile returned, and she patted my arm. "You make your phone call."

Stop imagining the worst, Andi. I took out my cell to call the sergeant. "Hello? Yes, I'll hold." I glanced at Lucy and shrugged. "They didn't even give me a chance to say whether this is life or death." After a five minute wait, finally, "Is Sergeant LeBlanc available? This is Andi Jones and I need to speak to him, ASAP. What? Well, when will he be back? Is there no way to reach him?" *Click.* "Well, that was rude!" I turned back to Lucy. "Seems he's gone for the night and won't be back until tomorrow morning. You could still go in and give your statement to another officer."

"But, didn't you say your sergeant was the one running Grace's murder investigation? I'd rather wait and give him my statement, tomorrow."

"That makes sense. No sense repeating the whole story."

Lucy visibly relaxed. She took the keys from her purse and moved toward the door. "Tell you what. You set it up for first thing in the morning. I'd much rather talk to someone you trust. Besides, we must get Stewart off the streets!"

I followed her out the front door. "Don't you want to lock it?"

She dismissed my question with a wave. "No need. The owner will be back, soon."

Strange, we were in the middle of nowhere. Oh, well. Not my worry. I opened the passenger door and fell back into the car; once again sprawled out on the reclining seat. This night couldn't be over soon enough.

Chapter Sixteen

Lucy dropped me at the hotel around 2:00 a.m. I crawled out of the car. Before shutting the door, I confirmed, "So, it's all set? We'll meet first thing tomorrow morning, right? I'll call and make the arrangements."

She smiled and nodded. "I wouldn't miss it, dear. Don't worry. After a good night's sleep, we'll both be fresh as daisy bouquets."

I trudged to my room and plopped on the bed. How would I ever get to sleep? Stewart a killer? Could I trust Lucy? Never one to count sheep, I counted ceiling tiles. *Wonder how long they've been up there? And, how did they survive Katrina?* A better question would be *how do I get caught up in these dramas*? Lucy claimed she found out Grace had been killed through national news coverage. Decided to leave her cruise, fly to New Orleans in order to raise suspicions about Stewart Payne. The fact Lucy had a pendant exactly like Grace's was very easily explained. *Yeah, that about does it.*

While relieved I wasn't alone in wanting justice for Grace, Lucy's story made my head throb. *Ka-boom-kaboom-kaboom.*

Darn! I forgot to ask if she planned to pick me up the next morning. Exhaustion finally caught up with me. I fought the urge to crawl under the covers without

111

washing my face, brushing my teeth, or undressing. Yep, I was that tired. Recalling past hygiene lectures from my mother won the battle. I bypassed my comfy mattress and soft pillows and shuffled into the bathroom. After one quick swipe with a washcloth, and cursory teeth brushing, I turned off the lights, stumbled to the bed and fell fast as a spindly tulip tree in a windstorm; oblivious to any all-night parties in the Quarter.

****

I woke to the sound of my phone "dancing" on the nightstand. *Where the hell am I?* Oh, yeah. Little hotel, French Quarter, New Orleans, Louisiana. "Hullo?"

"Andi? Whoa, you sound terrible! What's up?"

Ellie. Why the hell was she calling this early? "You're asking, 'what's up'? You mean, besides the crack of dawn?"

My assistant let out one of her hearty guffaws. "Crack of dawn? Hey, I know it's an hour earlier there, but still. It's 11:00 a.m. here, so were you planning to sleep until noon?"

My bleary pupils squinted at the time display on the phone. Sure enough. It was after ten, but when you don't get to sleep before 3:00 a.m., ten was the crack of dawn. "I had a late night."

"Hmmm, cheatin' on the hunky sheriff, are we?"

Not a chance! "No, El, but you won't believe who I saw last night. Let me save you the trouble of guessing. Lucy Minor."

"Lucy? What in the name of King Louis IX is she doing in Louisiana? Didn't you say she was practically turning cartwheels over that cruise? What happened?"

Impressive. Ellie knows her Louisiana history! I

112

repeated every word from last night's conversation. "Coming straight from the horse's mouth, Lucy cancelled all her side trips and flew here when she heard about Grace. Guess they were better friends than I realized. Not only was she torn up about the murder, she had an interesting theory about the killer's identity." I bit my tongue soon as the words came out of my mouth. Stewart wasn't a legitimate suspect until Lucy's story could be confirmed—by the authorities.

Too late. "Spill! What theory? Does she know who offed Grace?"

"Who *offed* Grace? Could you put that any more crudely?"

"Stop stalling. Whadda ya know? My lips are sealed, now gimme the details."

What could I say? Telling Ellie would be equivalent to taking out a full-page ad in the Miami Herald. "She has her suspicions about the killer but didn't give me a name." I lied for my own protection against a lawsuit, and from Stewart's wrath if Lucy's conjecture was wrong. Although, for the life of me, I couldn't think of a reason she'd go to such lengths to lie.

Ellie huffed. "I'm not buying. You know something and don't want to tell me. Okay, if that's how you're gonna play it. Maybe I won't tell you what Grace Payne's son said."

I sighed. "You know as much as I do. When I find out more, you'll be my first phone call." *Another lie, but it's for my own good!* "So, keep her son's conversation to yourself, Ellie. At this point, I don't care what any of the Payne family members have to say about me or the agency."

"Well, Grace isn't doing much talking these days," she snorted.

"Did you just snort?"

"Sorry. Bad joke. Anyhoo, Ethan's comment had nothing to do with you, or the business, but if you don't care, well...

Wait for it. Wait for it.

"Oh, if you insist."

Do I know my assistant, or what?

"He called to book a plane reservation for his dad and mom. Well, you know; his mom's casket. His dad wanted him to call another agency, but, apparently, Ethan doesn't hold a grudge the way Stewart does. However, he does have a grudge against another one of our clients. Guess who?"

My patience had reached Vesuvius level. "I'm not going to guess! Either tell me or hang up. I don't care which!"

"Now, don't get your panties in a wad. After all, I'm the one stuck here taking care of business while you're down there in *The Big Easy* having a high ol' time."

"Ellie!"

"Okay, I may have let it slip that Lucy had disappeared from her Alaskan cruise. Now, before you chew me out, that was before I knew you'd met with her."

"I'd be foolish to think you could keep your mouth shut about anything."

"Ya got me there," she happily agreed. "Well, anyway, when I told Ethan I hoped Lucy was okay, he snarled, 'I hope she's not.' I'm tellin' ya, his voice sounded as cold as a Bud Lite straight outta my daddy's

Freezerator."

Hmmm. Why would Ethan resent Lucy? I thought the two couples were friends. This whole situation was complicated enough, without more controversy from Stewart's son. "Sounds odd, but there could be many reasons he doesn't like Lucy that have nothing to do with his mother, or her death."

"That's what I thought, at first, but I'm tellin' ya, his voice sent chills up my spine. There's something going on in that boy's head. You know me and my intuition, Jonesy. I have that Dr. Spock-Vulcan thing going on."

Huh? "You mean, Mr. Spock? Mind-meld?"

"Yeah, yeah, that's it! I can read people's minds, I swear."

"Can you read mine right now, El?"

"Uh-I should hang up?"

"Thanks for the info on your phone call with Grace's son. I'll try to pump Lucy for information. See if her reaction to Ethan is as cold as his feelings toward her. Talk to you soon."

"Okay-doke."

Thankful to get her off the phone without spilling everything, I flopped back onto the pillows. If I could just stay there for the next day *or fifty* and not have to face Lucy, Stewart, or Grace's corpse, I'd be so grateful!

My cell chimed. A text from Lucy. *No rest for the wicked, Andi,* I reminded myself.

"Had emergency. Back in a few days." She closed with a smiley face.

That did it. I pulled the covers over my head, longing for access to a worm hole or time machine to take me back *five minutes* before Ellie booked Grace's trip. Hell! Might as well go all the way back before I took over the darned travel agency! It had caused me nothing but trouble. *Where's a fairy godmother when you need one?*

Just after 11:00 a.m. My stomach growled. I threw off the covers. *Wonder if the café is still open for breakfast?* I dragged my aching body out of bed, greeted by the full-length mirror on the outside of the bathroom door. Drawstring pajama pants splattered with white daisies added a certain *joie de vivre* to the faded turquoise football jersey. Bed-hair and mascara streaks that would thrill *The Bride of Frankenstein* completed the cheery picture. "Why didn't I just stay in bed?" Oh, yeah. Coffee! Food!

I replaced the daisy jammies with white cotton capris, dragged a brush through my hair and grabbed a pair of sunglasses. Surely, I could slip in and out of the restaurant without too much attention. Considering my foul mood and lack of sleep, I didn't care who saw me. If anyone gave me a hard time, I'd just remove my shades and give them the scare of their lives. *Too bad it's not close to Halloween. Ha!* Wonder if I should brush my teeth, first? *Naah.* That first cup of coffee tasted better, sans toothpaste.

I peeked in the French doors of the café, and sighed. Just my luck, the lunch crowd had packed the place. My luck changed, however, when Marie, my waitress from the first morning, spotted me and stuck her head out the door. "You come in, Missy. I find a place for you."

"Uh, tell you what. If I wait out here, could you get me a huge coffee to go?"

"One cream and one stevia?"

"I'm hoping the cup is so big I'll need three of both."

She wrinkled her nose and giggled. "One huuuge coffee coming right up."

"Thanks!" Ah, that solved one problem. I could sit here in the courtyard without feeling conspicuous. I'd pulled the cell phone out of my pocket to check for additional texts when a significant shadow hovered overhead, blocking out the late-morning sun.

"We meet again," came the cheery greeting.

Shielding my eyes, I squinted into the smiling face of Mudbug, aka, Marcel. "Good morning, Mr. Marcel, or should I say, good afternoon?"

He chuckled. "Still morning, Miss, but only by a frog's hair. Don't look like your day started any too soon, if you don't mind me sayin'."

If anyone else had been that pointed about my lack of grooming, I might've taken exception, but, for some reason, Marcel's presence soothed me more than anyone since Dad died. "No, I don't mind. I didn't have a very good night and a worse morning, but things are looking up." Marie came outside lugging the biggest cup of coffee I'd ever seen along with, what had to be, the largest croissant in the city. "I swear, Marie, I'm already growing out of my clothes!" I grinned, just in case she didn't get my joke. *God forbid she'd take the pastry back to the kitchen!*

No reason for concern. My comment flew right over her head. "I know you didn't ask for a menu, but you look a bit peaked, and could use some nourishment, Missy. Let me know if you want a refill on that coffee." Marie turned her attention to my visitor. "Well, Marcel,

I swear, where'd you come from? I ain't seen you in weeks."

"Hey, Marie. How you been?"

Jez fine, Marcel. Can I get something for you? Coffee? How about some Monkey Bread? A fresh pan just popped outta the oven."

He grabbed his chest. "You're killin' me, Marie. Sounds scrumptious, but I can't stay. Be sure to say 'hey' to Sonny and the young 'uns for me."

"I surely will." She smiled and headed back to the kitchen leaving Marcel shifting back and forth beside the small table.

Andi wondered where her manners had gone. Her mother would be mortified. "Please, Mr. Marcel. Won't you sit?" I motioned to the chair across from me.

He shook his head. "I need to get back to work, Miz Jones. No rest for the wicked, as they say."

He was preaching to the choir, as far as she was concerned.

His easy demeanor turned deadly serious. "Since I'm the one who first delivered you to my city, I feel obligated to tell you to watch your step. Word on the street is somebody thinks you're getting too close to the truth about the crime around here."

Even the hot coffee and muggy weather didn't keep the goosebumps away. *Is Stewart after me now? Does he know I've talked to Lucy?*

"I'm not an investigator, Mr. Marcel. The victim was a client of mine at the travel agency, and I'm trying to get some answers about her murder and discover whether we could've done something to prevent it."

So, I stretched the truth, a bit, but Grace was my main concern. Saving my butt and the agency, a close second. "Where did you hear I about me being watched?"

"Let's just say they's folks keepin' an eye out for you, and I thought you should know."

Folks keeping an eye out for me? What could that possibly mean? And who were *they*? Before I could ask, my "informant" if he was one of those watching me, Marcel slipped through the hotel gate and disappeared.

Chapter Seventeen

I slugged down half the coffee and hurried back to the room to catch my breath. For the first time since arriving, I scouted the courtyard to be sure no one was following or spying on me. Paranoia—not my usual m.o.—but I couldn't shake Mud Bug's warning. Maybe a shower would help ease the anxiety. I locked the door and secured the privacy latch.

Like someone wanting to break in couldn't get around that flimsy piece of metal.

Lifting my face toward the warm, gently flowing water trickling from the rainfall shower head, my breathing slowed. The quaint hotel had all the amenities I could've asked for. While it appeared old, and could use some fresh paint, management hadn't skimped on little touches that made traveling easy and convenient. Scented lavender soaps, a pullout mirror that made applying makeup a whole bunch easier than trying to bend over a sink staring into a large, usually foggy, mirror topped with fluorescent lights. Now, if they'd just fix those godawful hairdryers!

Speaking of hairdryers; might as well wash my hair while I was in the mood. Maybe the fancy keratin shampoo and conditioner would wash the fear out of my brain along with the road dust and sweat collected in my frizzy locks over the past few days.

Hey, I could hope!

120

I would've been perfectly happy spending three or four days in that shower, if not for the prospect of getting pruney as my great-aunt, Eloise. Nightmares haunted my early years about the kisses she'd plant all over my face. Imagine a three-year-old seeing a wrinkled, purplish face with bright red lipstick coming at her. "Give me some sugar, Andi Anna. Give Auntie some sugar."

Still gives me the shivers.

I settled for a relaxing half-hour, dried off and slipped on the white, fluffy robe the hotel provided. Were it not for my principles, I would've looked for room in my suitcase to smuggle it back home. Ah, but my darned conscience, or my fear of being thrown in jail and branded a "hotel amenities thief" for the rest of my life, held me back.

Won't bore you with the grooming details; hair drying, makeup primping, two swipes of deodorant, yadda, yadda, yadda. For once, I'd hoped my *after* picture looked better than the *before* shot. *Sadly, no.* Still the same freckled-faced, non-descript Florida gal I'd always been and forever would be.

Initial panic at Marcel's dire warning diminished. Convinced I could take care of any and all scumbags trying to do me harm, I grabbed by purse and cell and left the hotel property. Maybe I'd take another walk to Polly's Pralines. Nope. I could barely zip my capris. Besides, I might run into Creepy Claudia. She had the same effect on *adult Andi* that Aunt Eloise had on *young Andi*. On the other hand, I do believe I could take either one in a wrestling match. Ha!

Maybe I'd check out some of the jazz bars. Get out of the heat, listen to the soothing wail of a sax or clarinet, and down an ice-cold brew. What more could there be? Besides, I'd be honoring my dad. After his last trip to New Orleans, all he talked about was the musical history of Preservation Hall. Maybe it was open! I should, at least, take a peek inside. "Depends on how quickly I find it, Dad." *And, how long I last in this heat.*

Lesson learned from my previous painful walking adventure, I ditched the fashionable sandals in favor of comfy sneakers. While my feet were content, nothing relieved the stifling humidity. Generous layers of "pit perfume" struggled with the heat. I thought South Florida was bad. *How do people stand it here in the summer?*

The plan to cut through a couple of alleys, I'd spotted the day before, significantly shortened the walk time. I suppose that meant I could discard my tourist badge. The main drag was just ahead. I stopped to catch my breath and quench my parched throat. Thank heaven I'd remembered to pack a small bottle of water. A plain ol' iced tea would've sure tasted good about now, but I couldn't be choosy. I screwed off the cap and emptied half the bottle in one swig.

Dropping the water back in my bag, I felt a tug on my arm. My entire life flashed before my eyes. "Stew...Stewart!" I scanned up and down the alley, frantically searching for anyone who might hear me scream. No one in sight? The middle of the afternoon in the French Quarter? Where were the crowds?

"I didn't mean to startle you, Ms. Jones. I just want to talk."

His voice carried no animosity or sarcasm. *Who are you, and what have you done with Stewart?* The calm before the storm, perhaps? "Why should I believe you?" I came *this close* to blurting out, "Did you kill Grace? Are you going to kill me?"

But, restraint prevailed, especially since imminent danger stood between me and the relative safety of the public sidewalk—a good half-block away. If I could get him to let down his guard, just for a moment, I could sprint to freedom.

Chill, Andi. Don't make your move too soon or it could be your last.

My voice steadied. "So, now that you have a captive audience, what is it you want to say?"

He slowly shook his head. "I don't blame you for being angry and suspicious. I've been a real jerk, especially toward you and your agency. Oh, sure, you can be incompetent and annoying at times…"

"Wait. Is this your idea of an apology?" The "old" Stewart was back, and I was fired up.

"No, no, I'm sorry. As you well know, I'm not a very patient man, nor am I good at diplomacy."

Duh. Tell me something I don't know.

"This horrible thing with Grace has, well it's made me rethink my attitude and my life. We had a terrible fight before she left, and now I have no chance to make it right."

His admission and smidgeon of self-reflection caused me to let down my guard, a bit. I'd certainly never seen this side of him. Sizing up a person's character, on the spot, was a special gift of mine; sometimes a blessing, sometimes a curse. No telling how many promising relationships I'd tossed in the dumpster due to snap judgements.

I studied his eyes. They appeared sincere, filled

with enormous pain, and the eyes never lie. At least not without extreme effort or good acting and he was no actor, to my knowledge. *Give him a chance, Andi.*

He shuffled back and forth and glanced toward the street. Maybe now I could make my getaway. But, before I could move, he said, "Why don't we get out of this alley? I noticed some benches on the sidewalk and if we're lucky, we might even find one in the shade. I swear this heat is a thousand times worse than anything I've experienced in South Florida. Even in August."

Well, that took me completely off guard. *No need to run for my life. No reason to feel threatened. He wants to be seen in public.* "Uh-sure. I have a few minutes to spare."

We spotted an empty wrought-iron bench in front of Polly's Pralines. My shoulders relaxed; a good thing because I sensed a case of "chicken neck" coming on; a "medical term used by my great-uncle, an Indiana farmer, about chickens whose necks fell forward due to nerve damage. I didn't know anything about chickens, but the condition had tormented me on more than one occasion. Maybe the whiff of sugary caramel would loosen my tight muscles and put me in a receptive mood. In any case, I prepared to hear what Stewart had to say.

He sported khakis, white shirt, with some kind of golf club insignia on the upper left, and blue deck shoes-no socks. In other words, Mr. Preppy had no place to hide a weapon. I settled comfortably on the bench.

He wasted no time. "She did drive me nuts, you know."

I glanced to my right, unsure whether I was

supposed to comment. He stared straight ahead. I remained quiet.

"Oh, please don't get me wrong. I never, ever would've wished for this. Our 40th Anniversary is, or rather *was*, coming up in September. I'd planned to surprise Grace with a European cruise down the Rhine. Her family's from that area and she'd always wanted to visit and research her ancestors."

Wonder who would've booked that trip? *Oh, stop it, Andi! Not the time for business thoughts.*

As if reading my mind, he added, "I probably would've asked *Graves Travel* to make the reservations. No matter how much I gripe, that assistant of yours knows her stuff."

"Can't argue with you, there." At least Ellie had his professional respect.

He slumped forward, hands clasped. I couldn't help noticing prominent male pattern baldness at the crown of his head. No wonder he wore golf caps or a wide-brimmed Aussie hat when he was in the sun.

Should I suggest 60+ sunscreen?

"Identifying her body was, by far, the worse moment of my life." His hands trembled. "Mercifully, I viewed morgue pictures instead of the ones taken at the crime scene, or worse, close ups of her actual body. I couldn't have taken that. It's bad enough having that blue, lifeless photo image in my brain."

Yeah, good for you. LeBlanc shoved those pictures right in my face right after breakfast!

He paused, so I took the opportunity to mention my visit to the station at Sergeant's LeBlanc's request. "At the time, I was the only one in town who could identify Grace, so they asked if I'd do it. I'm sure they would've waited for you had they known you'd be here just a few hours later. At least I assume you flew in not long after I got here." I stopped short of mentioning the pendant or that Lucy was in town. Feeling more at ease with him didn't include spilling suspicions or unsubstantiated links to Grace's murder. Especially when those matching pendants were still considered mere coincidence.

Seeing the sincere grief he expressed over Grace's death, how could I take Lucy's theory seriously? Just a few days ago, I was sure he wanted to throw me in jail for a variety of reasons—inaccurate travel itineraries and misplacing his wife, to name two. Ellie and I had agreed he was the most obnoxious client, maybe even *person*, on the face of the earth. Now, I felt sorry for him.

I wondered if he even knew Lucy was in town. Should I mention her to gauge his reaction? Conflicted, I erred on the side of caution. Best to stay quiet about her being in New Orleans and, especially, the fact she pointed the finger at him. That could lead to disaster, with me stuck in the middle.

If not Lucy, should I mention the Cajun fisherman who had the bad fortune to find Grace caught in his crawfish cages? *What would it accomplish*? Probably nothing, but I figured he had the right to know.

I gulped. "I met the man who found Grace's, uh-body if you want any more details. I don't mean the grisly details, just how and when he found her."

Stewart put his head in his hands. "I don't know if I can take any more right now. Maybe later." He sat up, looked me straight in the eye. "Do the police have anything to go on? I mean, Grace had no enemies. I did,

126

but not Grace. She was kind to everyone she met; maybe to a fault."

That last statement caught my attention. "To a fault? Was there someone who might've taken advantage of her?"

He turned away. "Oh, no, not really. I'm probably just grasping at straws."

I recalled the conversation between Ellie and Stewart's son. Should I get his take on Ethan's apparent disdain for Lucy and whether it had anything to do with Grace?

Before I had the chance to ask, he stood, abruptly, ending any chance for further questions. "I have to get going. It was surprisingly nice talking to you, Andi. I hope we can start over." He stuck out his hand. "Maybe we can't be friends, but can we stop being enemies?"

I smiled. "*Frenemies*, maybe?"

"Frenemies it is." He stuck out a card with his phone number. "I'm at the Hilton on Poydras. If you need to get in touch, call or text. And, please let me know ASAP if you find out something from the police."

I assured him I would. He turned the corner and walked out of sight. Standing for a moment, I mulled over the previous conversation until crowds of tourists pushed by interrupting my concentration. Lucy's main suspect—mine, too, before talking with him—didn't act like a suspect at all. But, if he wasn't the perpetrator of Grace's demise, who was?

Chapter Eighteen

Continuing my aimless wandering, I successfully fought the urge to pop into Polly's for a sugar fix. Nothing, whatsoever, to do with the fact the waistband on my khakis had obviously shrunk in all the humidity. *Crappy New Orleans weather! Ha!* You can't take a good, long run to burn off calories. Not unless you had a death wish. Me? I longed for the relative coolness of my hotel room and a shower.

Crossing the street toward the candy shop, I saw movement out of the corner of my eye. Using every speck of peripheral vision, I spotted a figure standing boldly at the window making no attempt to hide. Was Claudia spying on my meeting with Stewart? Before I made a left turn toward the hotel, I decided to confront her. Too late. Except for displays, the window was empty. Either she'd disappeared, or my paranoia was working overtime. "Another day, Claudia."

A cool-ish breeze swirled around making me shiver. *Ah! Relief from the crazy heat.* I took a deep breath, enjoying the clean, fresh air filling my nostrils and lungs. *Where in the world did that come from?* Low humidity in New Orleans, in August? Crazy! I checked the sky for ominous clouds, or perhaps a locust invasion signaling the end of the world, but only white, puffy clouds floated overhead. I swear one had the shape of a trumpet!

"The trumpet," I whispered. "Dad's favorite instrument. Must be an omen." He'd played in school bands from age ten-up. His words repeated, "Best music on the face of the earth, Andi, is in New Orleans. Do me a favor. If your travels ever take you to The Big Easy, stop in Preservation Hall or one of the old jazz clubs. Order a Hurricane or, better yet, a Sazerac, sit back and think of me."

How could I leave the French Quarter without honoring Dad's wishes? *Simple. I can't.*

A tourist map located Preservation Hall on St. Peter Street, a couple blocks over, if my memory served. With newfound energy, thanks to the unexplained weather change, I practically skipped down the sidewalk. From booking tours, or rather watching Ellie book tours, I remembered the famous hall set next to Pat O'Brien's; known for Hurricanes—the drink, not the weather disasters. I checked my phone. Hmmm, 3:00 p.m. A little too early for a drink, but, I reasoned, it's 4:00 in Miami. "Close enough."

Locating the jazz hall was easy as pie. Fifty, or so, tourists lined the sidewalk waiting to enter a dilapidated old building that hadn't seen a paint brush in a half-century. I checked the sign above the wrought-iron door and, sure enough, it said *Preservation Hall.* While I debated whether Dad would approve my standing in line for, who knows how long, the wail of a saxophone caught my ear. Across the street a young woman, eyes closed, sat on a black wrought iron bench playing the same mournful tune Marcel sang on my ride from the airport. I stood, mesmerized by the bond between musician and instrument. At that moment and time, they were one.

She ended with one final haunting run, laid the sax across her lap, and slowly opened her eyes returning, reluctantly—it appeared—to reality. A moment later she spotted me and grinned. I smiled back and walked across the street.

"I hope you enjoyed the performance."

"*Enjoyed* doesn't half describe it," I marveled. "Funny, but I heard that song earlier in the week, and both times, it gave me chills." I didn't mention that Marcel's rendition put me to sleep.

"It's a haunting tune," she agreed. "Know the name of it?"

I thought back to my dad's love of music—especially southern ballads. "I'm not sure of the name but wasn't it about a huge flood that hit New Orleans in the 1920's?"

She nodded, "*Louisiana 1927*. You got closer than most folks that ain't from around here."

Guess I still had the tourist look.

"Louisiana wasn't the only state hit," she continued. "Mississippi and Arkansas also got their fair share of rain. But this here city got 15 inches in 18 hours. Lots of folks lost everything."

"From what my dad said, the government response was somewhat less than desirable," I added.

"Yeah, you could say that, but that's all water under the bridge, or maybe water over the bridge." She laughed, softly at her joke. Changing the subject she asked, "So, what brings you here? Music, food, drink?"

Oh, if only. Guess there was no sense lying about my pretend business trip or even going into the real reason; my client's murder. "Yep, you hit all the highlights. I'm hanging around to hear some Dixieland or Cajun music at Preservation Hall, but from the looks of that line, they're already packed."

"Yeah, you have to get in line pretty early." She tilted her head toward the open door on her right. "This place will be jumpin' in a few minutes, if you wanna wait. Matter o' fact, I'll be playin' along with Smokey Sam on the bass and Bobby Joe Two Sticks on the drums. My name's Bonita, but 'round here I'm Bonnie Blues."

She moved over so I could sit on the bench beside her. "Nice to meet you, Bonita. You sure play a mean sax."

Hands at the back of her neck, she gathered long, woven strands of black hair, interspersed with purple, and added a green and yellow scrunchie. Purple, green, yellow. She definitely rocked Mardi Gras colors. "I picked music up from my daddy. This is his horn. He died when I was barely four years old, but I still have the sound of his sweet music rolling around in my head. Most daddies read bedtime stories. Mine played 'em, his daddy did the same, along with his daddy 'fore him. My great-great granddaddy, Gerardo, brought the tradition from the islands." She looked up and smiled. "You get my drift."

I chuckled. "That you come from a long line of musicians? I got that. Speaking of family tradition, I promised my dad to drink a Sazerac in his honor. Can I get one inside?"

Bonnie pointed at the sign above—*Sazerac's*—and smirked. "You sure can. And I'll join ya."

"Let me get this text and I'll be right in." I'd heard a message come in from Clem that read, "May have a lead. When can we meet?"

It sounded urgent, so I called him back and got a voice mail. "Leave a message for Clem, if that's who you're callin'. Otherwise, have a nice day." That's Clem, all right. Polite and no nonsense. "Hey, Clem. I got your text. Call me back. Oh, this is Andi." I stuck my phone back in my purse and stepped inside the bar.

The scuffed hardwood floor creaked with age, water damage, and more than a few spilled drinks. I'm guessing the large planks were originally white oak, but hard to tell under all the stains. Bonnie saw me reading a plaque about four feet off the floor.

The Ol' Mississippi paid us a visit when the levees failed. Katrina, August 29, 2005

"Nasty business, that. Locals didn't know if Sazerac's would open up again, but the music people around here are a close-knit bunch. They all pitched in to get 'er up and running before moving on to the next club. Guess we all had a stake in it, being we needed places to work and perform." She motioned to a table near the bar. "Hey, Lonnie. How about a couple of specials for me and my new friend?"

Lonnie, appearing less than thrilled at being interrupted during his bar setup, mumbled a string of words that were, thankfully, out of earshot.

Bonnie snorted, "Aw, don't mind him. Crabby comes naturally." She strolled to the bar, made a couple of remarks—again out of earshot—and returned with our drinks.

"Considering his rotten personality, he still makes one of the best Sazeracs in town. Besides, he manages the bar, so I have to be civil to him. Cheers." She clinked her glass against mine. "Here's to finding whatever it is you're looking for, Miz Jones."

I took a sip, having no idea what to expect. Being immediately transported back to my childhood days, eating licorice for the first time, was not on the list. Guess my shock must've shown. "It's an acquired taste," Bonnie laughed. "Take a few more sips and I guarantee it'll become your favorite drink."

"I seriously doubt that, but…" I lifted my glass and looked skyward, or ceiling-ward, in that case. "Here's to you Dad. Why you loved this awful concoction is a mystery to me." I took another swallow that burned all the way down but tasted better. Before I knew it, my glass was empty, and my taste buds savored the absinthe, bitters, rye, and lemon peel combo.

Warmth moved up my body, yet my skin stayed cool. Thanks to a couple of powerful ceiling fans, my only priority for the next hour, or so, was to relax and indulge.

Bonnie sat back with a smug look. "Told ya. Ready for another, Andi?"

"But I haven't paid for the first one." I dug for my wallet, but Bonnie insisted, "Your money's no good in here."

What? Surely Sazerac's couldn't afford to give away liquor. If this place was that successful, they should've used some of the profit to buy chairs and tables that didn't wobble every time you breathed heavy. Something else nagged at me while casually watching Lonnie make two more drinks. How did Bonnie know my name? I didn't recall introducing myself outside, or after we sat down inside. *Hmmm. Maybe I just forgot.*

Bonnie returned with the drinks. "Bottom's up."

We clinked, again, and this time I chugged the

sweet, sour, burning liquid, sensing a new appreciation for the drink that was, arguably, the oldest cocktail recipe in the country.

Through a mildly buzzed state, I noticed activity on the small stage. A young man, long brown hair tied with a blue bandana, positioned the drums. An older, distinguished-looking gentleman, with close-cropped white beard, pulled a huge base fiddle out of its case. Bonnie tilted her head and gulped her drink. "Gotta get to work. You're gonna stay for a set, aren't you?"

"Wouldn't miss it." I had nowhere to go and nothing to do. Although I wasn't getting any closer to solving Grace's murder, sitting in a bar the entire afternoon, I needed to regroup and recharge. One last check of my phone revealed nothing new from Clem, LeBlanc, or Stewart, although it was a little early to hear back from the latter. I tucked my only connection to the outside world back in my bag, determined to listen, uninterrupted, to good ol' Zydeco, jazz, bluegrass, or whatever Bonnie and her band chose to play.

Music, filtering out to the sidewalk, drew patrons two and three at the time. Soon, the place filled with noisy, raucous laughter and every kind of dance step imaginable. My knee bounced and my fingers tapped to the beat. Finally, finally, I could experience *The Big Easy* the way it deserved.

Bonnie, Smokey Sam, and Bobby Joe played their hearts out while I savored the combination of instruments, voices, and Cajun spirit. I cherished the connection with my dad. That is, until my eyes stopped focusing. Bourbon, licorice, and breakfast gurgled in my stomach, threatening a return visit. I must've looked as queasy as I felt. In between musical interludes, Bonnie mouthed, "What's wrong?" When I grabbed my stomach and indicated I was nauseated, she pointed to the back door exit. "Get some air," she mouthed, again.

I stumbled into the alley, searching for a place to sit down, or puke my guts out. The last sound I remembered was Bonnie announcing a short band break. I'd barely managed a couple of deep breaths when both arms were pinned behind me and a hood was draped over my head. I got out one muffled scream before the blow. A massive burst of white stars followed me to the ground. Through semi-consciousness, I heard someone yell moments before two sets of arms threw me into the trunk of a car and sped off.

Chapter Nineteen

"Are you sure about this?"

"I don't have a choice, and neither do you if you want your payoff."

Anxious undertones mixed with pain in the back of my head. Even in the throes of brain fog, I felt the chill of concrete. I lay on my side in a fetal position; arms tied behind my back. My eyes wouldn't, or couldn't, open, but even if they did, the suffocating hood covered my head. A gag, covering my mouth, ensured I couldn't scream if I wanted. Despite the chill of the floor sapping heat from my body, sweat trickled down the side of my face. In hindsight, a state of semi-consciousness probably saved me because I had no strength or will to panic.

"So, let's get this over before she comes to."

Get *what* over? That voice sounded familiar, but the hood muffled the conversation. The higher pitched voice was definitely female. That, I could tell. I just wished they'd speak louder and lose the annoying echo. Chances were good the echo resulted from the lump on my head.

The second voice hissed. "Can't we just leave her? She's in no shape to identify us. In fact, she never saw us!"

Definitely male. *That's right. Just leave me. I'll be good and lie here as long as you want!*

136

The woman's voice snapped, "You know we can't. She's getting much too close. It's only a matter of time before she's on to us"

On to them? Grace's killers? Who was this woman and her male accomplice? I wanted to scream, "You're not getting away with this, you scumbags!" *Oooh.* Just thinking loud made my head throb. Not only that, I felt sick, again. *Crap.* I'd had the misfortune a couple of times to throw up in an airsickness bag, but not with my whole head stuck in it! Damn those Sazeracs, and damn those breakfast beignets!

"I still don't see why we have to kill her. She seems like a good person," the male voice muttered. "At least to me."

Now I'm more confused. Had I met him? Where? Maybe I'd recognize his voice if he'd talk in a normal tone. If only I could get out from under this miserable hood! I knew better than to move, however. They couldn't know I was conscious—make that, semi-conscious—or I'd be dead meat, for sure.

"Look." The woman snarled, "I wish this could end some other way. I had a soft spot for her, too, but the sooner we do it, the better. I'm linked to evidence already, and trust me, she's not through snooping. So, get with the program if you want that money, you so desperately need."

He mumbled something out of hearing range.

"You're sure no one will find her here?" the woman questioned.

"Can't be positive, but most of these statues and props are used for replacement parts. I still say we should've followed the first plan."

"For the last time! I had to change directions," she

huffed. "From the police, that nosy husband and wife team, and practically every fisherman in the area, Nancy Drew here had too many eyes patrolling the bayous."

The male had mentioned a first plan. Referring to Grace? *Oh, Andi. Why didn't you just stay in Miami and mind your own business? I swear, if I get out of this, I'll give up playing detective.*

I almost wished they'd just get it over with. My joints ached. Every muscle in my body threatened to spasm. Not only was my well-documented claustrophobia thoroughly tested by that damnable hood, my breathing sped up, and the bile in my stomach built to a boiling point.

"C'mon. Let's get this done. We only have a few hours left before sunup," the woman ordered.

I braced for approaching footsteps. "You grab her feet," the male said. "I'll grab her under the arms and on the count of three, we'll lift."

What the hell? I'm not some 400 lb. Sumo wrestler! Oh, sure, I've gained a couple of pounds while I've been here, but…? I debated whether to continue playing dead or come up swinging. Even if I couldn't see and my hands were tied, I could still kick something. The internal debate ended the moment I was grabbed. Panic took over. I kicked and flailed with all my might, wishing I'd worn steel-toed work boots—even though I'd never owned a pair in my life—instead of my soft, comfy sneakers. "Let me go, you mother…!"

Bam! Stars, again. Black nothingness other than the vague sensation of my body being lifted off the floor. Either my two captors had picked me up or I was flying with the angels to my final reward. *At least I was going*

138

up! At that point, however, it didn't make much difference.

****

I woke to muffled scraping sounds. Raised voices argued in the distance, probably plotting my disposal. *Such warm, comforting thoughts.* Lying face-down on the cold floor, I fought the urge to flail and scream, again, since the last time worked out so well. Ha. Keeping still wasn't much challenge with my hands and feet tied and that damnable hood.

I listened for movement. Dead silence. Maybe my captors had decided to leave me. A nearby sigh dashed any thoughts of escape. A pair of hands rolled me firmly, but carefully, across the concrete.

"Sorry about this Miss Jones," whispered the distinctly male voice; the voice I'd recently heard. But, where and when?

Seconds later I was placed into a container.

The woman snapped, "Put this in, too. I've destroyed anything that could identify her."

An object plopped beside me, followed by the sickening sound of a door closing and latching. "Grab that wench," the female ordered.

The man complained, "I can't get her all the way up by myself."

"You're useless," his partner grumbled. "C'mon, this thing's made out of plastic, and she can't be that heavy. Groaning, followed by random curses accompanied my herky-jerky rise off the ground. I rolled, helplessly, from side to side. *What the heck is this? Where am I?* Face up, hands bound, a latch pressed firmly against my back. Unless I could get my hands free, I was trapped. Even that depended on how

139

high I dangled in the air.

Still in the grip of semi-consciousness, my self-preservation instincts faded fast. Every muscle in my body had gone limp. I pictured the gym equipment in my condo building, and swore, *Get out of this, Andi, and you are so going to work on your muscle tone!*

I tested the ropes around my wrists. *Someone had earned their knot-tying scout badge.*

The sound of fading voices and footsteps brought both relief and full-on panic. I was alone and trapped.

C'mon, Andi. How do you get your butt outta here? The first order of business was to remove that damnable hood so I could breathe! I twisted my head back and forth until I felt a slight tug on the material. A small shard of plastic must've snagged the burlap. Maybe it'll stay put while I move. Squirming with the enthusiasm of a newly hatched caterpillar, I freed myself from the hood. Great! Fresh air. Now, if I could just get the gag off.

Euphoria came to a screeching halt the moment I realized my situation. Complete blackness, except for light beams filtered from two rows of…what are those? Teeth?

I wasted no time squirming toward the faint glow.

Chapter Twenty

I struggled to my knees and stretched to look through one eyehole. Faint beams from the early morning sun broke through a small skylight. A room full of large floats, with heads of exotic human and animal characters, was revealed. Also obvious was how high my prison cell hung from the floor. If being kidnapped wasn't enough to make me light-headed, the fear of closed spaces and extreme fear of heights sent my heart pounding. I sat down, gingerly, panicked that an ill-timed movement could send me plunging to my death.

The hours passed slowly and silently. I longed for sleep, but if I dared close my eyes, would I wake up? Still, my body and mind suffered from physical and heat exhaustion. Maybe just a quick cat nap.

****

My eyelids flew open, saving me from a nightmare sending me and my cage plunging a hundred floors in a high-rise elevator. While my predicament wasn't that dire, a thirty-foot fall could do some serious damage. Voices chattered in the distance. I listened more intently but heard nothing but silence. Must've been a holdover from my dream. Nope, there they were again!

"Ain't this place cool, Dylan?"

My ears perked.

"Yeah, so. A bunch of old, dusty floats." Dylan

sounded unimpressed. "Besides, we ain't supposed to be in here. If my momma finds out…"

"You told her you were going to my house, didn't you?"

"Well, yeah, but she gave me the ol' stink-eye when I left at the crack of dawn since I don't usually roll outta bed until lunch time."

"An early start means we have a couple hours to snoop around before some guard shows up. 'Sides, no one comes here unless they need parts for the Mardi Gras parade. That's months away. Most folks won't step foot in this place 'cause they say it's haunted by voodoo spirits. Why, I'll bet a 'shaved ice' we're the only two kids with enough guts to walk around here 'fore sunup. Besides, if we do run into anybody, just look at all the places to hide."

"Crawl into some dirty ol' zombie head if you want, Chase, but don't expect me to follow."

Are they close enough to hear me? Only one way to find out. "Help! Help!" The gag muffled my plea. "I'm up here!"

"You hear something, Chase?"

"I dunno. Do you?"

"Thought I did, but I prob'ly just heard some poor critter outside bein' snatched by a gator."

No, no. I'm a human being! They're so close. Why can't they hear me? I tried banging my feet inside the shell. *What kind of container is this? Heavy and soundproof, for one. Think, Andi.* I was definitely in some huge plastic head. A blinding headache wasn't helping my thought process. While grateful for the stingy amount of air floating through the mouth and eye holes, I couldn't last much longer in the stifling heat.

I squinted through the gaps in the teeth. Far below, two boys scanned the area, pointing in different directions. They must be arguing about which way to go. Another muffled scream was useless. They didn't flinch. Didn't even stop talking. Getting their attention was hopeless.

When I scooted sideways to ease the strain on my back, my "prison" swayed. I moved more forcefully, and the swaying increased! I'd either get their attention or fall to my death. With all the strength I could muster, I rocked back and forth. *Back and forth.*

"D…Dylan? Look up! Is that skull moving?"

Dylan yelled, "Yeah, and it's moaning! Let's get outta here. This place *is* haunted!"

"No, no," I cried. "Don't leave!" The boys' frightened voices faded. I was doomed.

I peered, perhaps for the last time, at my limited view of the warehouse. Tears stung my eyes and soaked both sides of my face. Rays of sun poured into the surprisingly efficient skylight warming my "tomb" to a moderate level of discomfort. By afternoon, I'd be sautéed, baked, barbequed. Take your pick.

Sometime during the vain attempt to yell for help, the ropes around my wrists miraculously loosened. I strained to free my arms, but the more I pulled, the tighter my bonds became. Too tired, weak, and discouraged to struggle, I closed my eyes.

****

Diffused light snaked through the holes of my confines. I blinked. How many hours had passed? Must be high noon, or thereabouts. Clothing stuck to me with the gusto of a sweat-soaked rag. Random wisps of air had turned from restorative, to stifling. Resignation set in. I couldn't last much longer.

I whispered goodbye to my sister, Georgia, my nieces and nephews, and two of the three most important people in my life; Ellie and my caffeine guru, Bruce. Life would've been so much more difficult without them. Last, but not least. N*umero uno*. In a short space of time, Manny, my sheriff, had rejuvenated my spirit and restored my faith in the power of relationships. Why hadn't I let him know I was in New Orleans? The flight from Cancun was less than two hours. He could've easily met me here and talked me out of playing detective. *This is your fault, Manny! Why didn't you save me?*

Early afternoon sunlight filtered into my oversized, dimly lit plastic coffin, permitting the first clear view of my final resting place. I lifted my head high as possible. Seems I was encased in a human-shaped form, probably some fiberglass advertisement prop. Before they ran off, one of the boys yelled something about a skull. Was I in a voo-doo storage barn? In New Orleans? Made sense.

I pulled at the restraints, again. Damnable heat, exhaustion, and incredible fear had sapped my whole body. Worse yet, I felt a chill run up my spine. Was I going into shock? *That's it. The nail in the coffin.*

I closed my eyes and accepted the inevitable. The quiet sound of death. No noise except the blare of a far off siren. Shame they're not headed this way. *Wait! They are headed this way!* I listened for them to pass; leaving me to die.

The siren blared louder and louder and then stopped. Voices outside the building! Urgent voices drew closer and closer. A door scraped open.

"Is that it, boys?"

I strained to hear an answer, but none came. Kids! I could only hope one of them nodded.

"Okay, let's investigate your possessed skull."

A familiar voice barked orders from just below my perch. Carey Giles, from the NOPD!

"Carey." My muted cry was barely audible, even to me.

"Is someone in there?"

Adrenaline kicked in. I shouted through the gag. "Yes, hurry."

"Hang on. We're going to get you out. Someone call 911! Get an ambulance here, stat! Let's lower this thing and crack it open."

It took mere seconds to attached the wench and lower me to the ground. The trap door opened. Air whooshed in.

Detective Giles and two other policemen pulled me out and laid me gently on the floor. Carey supported my head and removed the gag. I took my first deep, refreshing breath in hours and whispered, "How did you find me?"

"Don't talk, Ms. Jones. We need to get you to the hospital."

"Get some water," she ordered.

I tilted my head toward the two boys I'd seen earlier, and two somber women standing behind them.

"The sight of this swinging skull scared the boys to death," Detective Giles confirmed, "especially since they'd illegally trespassed into a private storage facility. Both were traumatized when they got home from fear of what their parents would say, and fear of being haunted the rest of their lives. Fortunately, their families suspected something and called us the moment the boys were convinced to confess."

I turned my head and gave a weak smile to my pint-sized saviors. I must've passed out in the process, since I barely remembered the ambulance ride to the hospital.

Chapter Twenty-One

"Ms. Jones? Can you wake up? I need to take your blood pressure and listen to your heart and lungs."

Who was trespassing in my home to take my blood pressure? "Not today," I mumbled. "And, please let yourself out." I tucked the pillow under my neck and snuggled into a fetal position.

A hand pushed roughly against my left shoulder. "Sorry, Sleeping Beauty. I can't wait for your prince to come wake you up with a kiss, and I can't leave until I've taken your vitals."

Well, this is rude!

I rolled on my back and squinted at a very large bald man in blue scrubs with a stethoscope around this neck. "I'm Nurse Winston. Are you able to sit up?"

Not about to argue, I nodded.

"Good." He rested his hand on my back and easily pushed me to an upright position. "Take a couple of deep breaths. Good. Now, take one deep breath and hold it."

I obeyed. Deja vu. Another trip. Another stay in a hospital. You'd think I would've learned my lesson in Vegas.

"Your heart sounds strong and your lungs are clear."

The fog cleared and the horror of the last twenty-four hours rushed back.

147

"You're very lucky."

Oh, believe me I know. I wondered how long it would take me to realize just how lucky. Barely above a whisper, I asked, "Do you know when I can leave?"

He repositioned the stethoscope over his shoulders, fluffed the pillows and helped me lie back down. "Besides two very large lumps on your skull, you were in shock and given fluids all night. Don't rush it, Sunshine. Dr. Crawford will be in to see you, soon. Meanwhile, you have a couple of visitors. Should I send them in?"

I nodded. Moments after Nurse Winston walked to the door and motioned, Clem and Clementine rushed to my bedside.

"Thank God you're okay, Andi," Clem looked as washed out as I felt. "Ellie hasn't given us a moment's peace since we told her what happened."

Clemmie rolled her eyes. "I begged Clem not to call her after we knew you were going to be all right." She glanced sideways at her husband. "He wouldn't listen. As a result, I spent every hour, on the hour, giving her updates over the phone."

"I didn't know she cared." I grinned, somewhat surprised at my assistant's level of concern.

Clem moved, tentatively, to my side. "How are you feeling? I know the doctor said you'd make a full recovery, but...but you...you look awful."

I managed a thin laugh. "You sure know how to sweet talk a girl, don't you? Is he always this charming, Clementine?"

She smiled and pulled a chair beside my bed. "Men! They can be real jackasses, can't they?"

I remembered the heated discussions Manny and I

had when we first met. I thought he was an egomaniac, and he considered me stubborn and defensive. Thankfully, overwhelming attraction crumbled that wall of snap judgements in the nick of time. Still, I admitted a certain amount of envy for the Clanton's relationship. A couple made for each other. *Soul mates*. Living under the same roof. Not hundreds of miles apart like Manny and me.

"*Jackass* works," I grinned. "I appreciate your concern, but I'm okay. Now, would somebody help me up?"

"Not so fast, Andi. Your body bordered on shock when the police found you. Better let the doctors give you the okay."

In protest, I unleashed a loud exhale. Getting out of this place was my first priority. I'd show them!

An attempt to swing my legs over the side of the bed accomplished nothing. My upper body crumbled back on the pillows. "On second thought, guess my only choice is to agree with you and the doctors," I grumbled. "Oh, and Nurse Shaquille O'Neal."

"He is quite intimidating," Clemmie chuckled. "Do you feel up to answering questions about your ordeal? The police asked us to let them know when you're up to an interview."

All I wanted was sleep, but someone tried to kill me. The sooner the police were involved, the better.

"Anytime works for me. In fact, make that sooner before my voice gives out, entirely." I took a sip of water to ease my throat.

"Take it easy with that. You don't want to get sick." Clem cautioned. "You were dehydrated, so they pumped fluids into you as soon as you got here."

A chill passed over me at the thought of my narrow escape from death. "Guess I owe my life to those two boys. If they hadn't broken the law…"

"Yeah, we owe them a lot, but someone else notified the police you were missing. Detective Giles got a call from Bonnie, at Sazerac's. She said you'd disappeared from behind the bar yesterday evening right after you left for some air. By the time she got outside to check on you, a car sped away."

"Is she a friend?" Clemmie asked.

"She works and plays the sax at the bar," I explained."

Clem nodded, then added, "Yeah, we were there last year for Clemmie's birthday; full bar and fantastic entertainment."

"I've heard they go through musicians the way Clem goes through motorcycles," Clemmie added.

"Hey, Bertha's been with me for years, now. Although I have to admit, I had to test a few before I found my perfect road mate." He turned to me and winked. "Can you tell Clemmie's jealous of my love for good ol' Bertie?"

She rolled her eyes. "He wishes."

Their easy banter created a welcome distraction. "Yeah, I'd like to go back sometime without the kidnapping. Anyway, I met Bonnie outside. I was across the street, debating whether to join the long line to get into Preservation Hall or kiss it off, when I heard her sax wailing away. I walked over, and we started talking. Next thing I know, we're in the bar, and I'm getting loaded on Sazerac's signature drink."

"Is that why you left the bar?" Clem asked.

"Yeah, I guess so. I remember Bonnie pointing to

the back exit. I don't remember much after getting hit on the head and thrown into the car trunk." My breathing sped up remembering the tight quarters. Damned claustrophobia triggered panic attacks at the most inopportune moments.

"Clem, stop questioning her. She needs to rest," Clemmie ordered. "Take deep breaths, Andi. Let your mind go blank. Have you ever tried meditation?"

Are you my sister in disguise? I nodded. "Haven't had…much luck," I gasped, "but I'll give it another try." I closed my eyes and pictured Georgia's "go-to" place. Clem and Clemmie stood over me until my breathing slowed. "Whew! That came on fast. Guess my body is trying to tell me something."

"We're going to let you rest, Andi," Clem whispered. "I won't notify the police you're ready to talk until you're stronger."

I gave a half-hearted wave, shut my eyes, and imagined settling back under a beautiful shade tree, surrounded by a field of colorful wildflowers. A clear stream gurgled by. My mind calmed and my breathing slowed to normal.

Maybe Georgia was on to something.

My peaceful state didn't last. Clattering and clanging in the hall signaled dinner was on the way. If you call dinner, low-sodium cream of mushroom soup, a dinner roll that could easily substitute for a hockey puck, and fruit salad, straight out of the can. Seriously, if the hospital needed my bed, why didn't they just release me instead of starving me to death?

"Ms. Jones? Is this a good time?"

I'd braced myself for a visit from the surly Sergeant Le Blanc but was pleasantly surprised to see

Detective Giles outside the door. I pushed aside my *dinner* tray. "Sure. Please come in."

She smiled. "You certainly look better than the last time I saw you."

"I hope so. You don't know how happy I was to hear your voice in that warehouse." I expected my anxiety level to rise at the thought of reliving those awful hours. Instead, peace and tranquility surrounded me. Reluctant to acknowledge Georgia's meditation regime, I credited Carey Giles' calming voice and manner. Besides Clemmie and my driver, Marcel, I looked forward to her company more than anyone. Too bad her presence involved police work, crime, and my narrow escape from death.

The detective stood at the foot of my bed. "You can thank Bonnie at Sazerac's for my showing up. She reported the incident last night"

"Thank goodness she did. Although, I guess you found my location because of the boys."

"We had patrols out looking for you all night. When the call came in today, I had no reason to connect the mysterious happenings at a float warehouse with your disappearance. Sometimes, however, crazy leads pay off." She took out a notepad and flipped to an empty page.

"What? No high-tech recording device?"

She laughed. "Not on this trip, Ms. Jones. We save that for official statements. When you're released, and feeling stronger, we'll schedule a time. Meanwhile, can you provide a brief account of your kidnapping."

I filled her in on being abducted from behind Sazerac's. Tied up. Hood covering my head. Regaining consciousness in the warehouse.

"Do you think they drove straight there? Or were there any other stops? According to my estimate, the drive from the bar should've taken about fifteen minutes."

"Seemed like hours to me, but if I had to guess, that's about right. No stops along the way."

I described being semi-conscious when they dumped me on the concrete. "After a good bit of arguing back and forth, they must've settled on the skull. A man and a woman shoved me inside. The woman then threw my purse in beside me after she bragged about getting rid of all the identification. I don't know what happened to it. Maybe it's still there."

"We have it in evidence. You'll have it back tomorrow."

"Was anything left? My driver's license, credit cards, money?"

"Strangely enough, they left the money. Sixty-five dollars, I believe. But you're right. Everything containing your personal information was missing. I assume they hoped your body wouldn't be found for months, with no possibility of identification."

I sniffed. "Guess they weren't smart enough to think about DNA evidence. Some of those genealogy sites keep detailed records. Anyway, that's all I can tell you. Think I owe those boys an apology for scaring them to death? If I hadn't been able to swing that prop back and forth, I doubt we'd be having this conversation."

Carey laughed. "You scared the bejeeszus out of them. I seriously doubt they'll ever, again, step foot on posted property." She moved to the door. "Hope they spring you tomorrow. Thanks for the info. We'll collect more when you're feeling better." Before walking out the door, she reassured me. "You'll be the first to know if we get any leads. Take care."

After Carey left, I made a second attempt to get out of bed. Legs still shaky, I managed the short distance to the window. Lake Ponchetrain sprawled in the distance. Hard to believe I'd only been in New Orleans four days. I made a mental list of my accomplishments, met Ellie's cousins, took my first *real* motorcycle ride, then talked with the man who found Grace's body, had a surprisingly civil conversation with Stewart Payne, and after Lucy revealed he may have killed his wife, I finally became suspicious of Lucy. Oh, yes, and the crème de la crème—I got kidnapped.

Wonder what the next four days will bring.

Chapter Twenty-Two

I was discharged the next morning. The Clantons picked me up at the curb in Clemmie's comfy truck. I chuckled, imagining speeding through the hospital parking lot on Bertha. Probably best I was safely tucked in the back seat of large vehicle.

"You can recuperate at our house, Andi," Clem insisted before pulling away from the curb. "Neither we, nor the police, want you going back to your room until we find a guard. Someone tried to kill you. We can't risk a repeat performance."

"We'll swing by the hotel and pick up clean clothes and your personal items," Clemmie offered.

"You won't get an argument from me." Their small home in the bayou practically burst with good energy. Energy I needed replenished.

****

I spent a good twenty minutes in the shower at the Clanton home. The water, surprisingly soft, felt heavenly after all those hours imprisoned in that sweltering plastic head. A cursory sponge bath at the hospital barely scratched the surface. At some point, Clementine cracked the door and asked how I was, and if I needed anything. She hung a pink terry cloth robe on the door hook. "When you're through, a cup of hot tea will be waiting."

That settled it. I'd died and gone to heaven. For the

155

moment, fear dissipated. I placed thoughts of Grace, and her killer, in a small "worry box" and shut the lid. Heck, I didn't care when or if I ever got back to Miami. Life, however, had a way of kicking you forward—ready or not. I knew Clem and Clemmie would be anxious to hear the whole story and find out whether I had any idea who attacked me. I hated to disappoint them, but other than familiar voices, I had nothing to go on.

Grudgingly I shut off the shower, dried with a fluffy towel, and slipped into Clemmie's robe. The subtle lavender aroma infused in the terry cloth transported me back to my mother's bedroom. She had used essential oils back before they were trending. Whenever I complained of a sore throat, I'd get a dab of lavender, lemon, or peppermint. Sometimes, a slippery elm lozenge for good measure.

I ran my fingers through strands of damp tangled hair. Still a curly mess, but at least it was squeaky clean; free of any leftover kidnapping grunge.

Clem and Clemmie greeted me at the small kitchen table with broad smiles that contradicted the concern in their eyes. "Did you have everything you needed?" Clemmie asked.

My grateful nod and huge grin answered her question. I couldn't have been any happier if I'd just showered at the Ritz Carlton.

Clem stood and pulled out a chair. "Try some lavender and chamomile tea. Clemmie picks the flowers and dry the leaves."

Not surprised. Is there anything she can't do? I sat down to a steaming mug.

"I have raw sugar or stevia," she suggested.

"A little stevia is perfect," I answered. "That's my go-to sweetener since I broke the artificial junk habit. Plus, I'd rather use my sugar rations on chocolate fudge or *Polly's Pralines*."

We made small talk for ten minutes, or so, before getting down to the nitty gritty. The time and conversation eased the tension in the room and in my soul.

Clem sat quietly, hands folded, while I indulged in several satisfying sips of tea. Clearing his throat, he said, "I imagine you're still pretty shaken up, but we're anxious to hear the details, if you feel up to it."

Clemmie put her hand over mine. "Take your time. We have all day."

"I appreciate your concern, but I'm not sure what happened, or why. I already told you everything I remember. Talking to Bonnie outside Sazeracs, having several drinks, getting hit over the head, and shoved in the trunk of a car. Next, I remember lying on concrete with a hood over my head, hands tied behind my back, two people standing over me arguing over the plan for my demise."

"Do you have any idea who they were?" Clem's voice was patient, but all business. "Had you ever heard their voices before last night?"

"I-I can't be sure, but when the woman spoke, I swear I'd heard her voice before. Same with the man, although I am less certain about his."

I described trying to fight off my two captors before getting another serious conk on the noggin. "I barely remember being dumped into that awful plastic monstrosity."

Clem leaned forward. "Could they be employees of

157

your hotel?"

I shook my head. "The hood muffled their words. Besides that, the man whispered, most of the time. I did hear him express regret about what they were doing. He suggested leaving me there, tied up, but the woman overruled him. Said I was getting 'too close to clues' for that to happen." I took a couple more sips of tea and a bite from one of the blueberry muffins Clemmie set on the table. "The worst part was not being able to breathe. The air was stifling, as you can imagine. Clemmie choked back tears. "I feel just awful, Andi. Ellie went to the trouble to give you our phone number in case you needed us, and we let this happen to you."

"When I think how close you came to the same fate as the client you came here to find, I…" Clem hung his head.

"Wait a minute. You two can't blame yourselves. How could you know I'd get kidnapped from the Quarter? It happened so fast. One minute I'm listening to the band and sipping on a Sazerac or two, or three. The next, I'm in the alley getting some air, and you know the rest.

"What I can't figure," Clem debated, "is how they knew you'd be in the alley. Maybe they followed you there hoping to lure you out."

"I played right into their hands." I huffed. The last time I got stink-faced drunk on margaritas was in Cancun. Manny was there to keep me safe. I shivered imagining his strong hands removing my clothes and lifting me into bed. I had to rely on his account that he left soon after, since I was too smashed to remember much about that night. Sigh.

Clem's laughter brought me back from La-La-

Land. "Earth to Andi. We need to get answers without putting you, or anyone else, in danger." He scooted away from the table and moved to the kitchen window. I imagined him spending hours staring at the wall of cypress trees trimmed with Spanish moss, making life-changing decisions. I had no interest in disturbing his process. He turned back to Clemmie and me. "I suggest we take you back to the city. I know we said you'd be safer here, but our home is isolated, plus, I need to get back on the boat. Those fish won't catch themselves. While you were showering, we talked it over with Sergeant LeBlanc and agreed that Clemmie is experienced enough to keep you safe, especially with all the staff surrounding you at the hotel. Meanwhile, I'll make some time to snoop around Sazerac's to see if one of the other employees noticed anything."

Knowing I'd have Clementine's company and support gave me much-needed peace of mind. Not only did I sense a certain kinship between us, I suspected she could hold her own with just about anyone. "Fine by me, if you're okay with it, Clemmie."

She set her teacup in the sink and headed to the bedroom. "I've been wanting to spend some time in the city. Let me pack a few things."

"I have friends in the Quarter, Andi, so getting information shouldn't be a problem," Clem assured me. "You'll have someone with you at all times until those kidnappers are caught."

Clemmie returned to the kitchen with a small bag. To my surprise, she removed a pistol, loaded a cartridge, and announced, "Let's get you safely back to the hotel."

I poured a second cup of tea and retreated to the

guest room. I'd grabbed the bare essentials last night at the hotel, so packing was a breeze. Slipping on a pair of shorts and plain T-Shirt, I gave a final, wistful look around the small sanctuary, wishing I could hide out in the closet. I opened the bedroom door, took a deep breath, and announced, "Ready when you are."

Clemmie and I pulled down the driveway in the same F-150 truck that brought me from the hospital. Clem and Bertha, engine roaring, led the parade.

Chapter Twenty-Three

Afternoon tourist buzz, mixed with competing street performers, created stark contrast to the peaceful setting I'd left behind at the Clanton home in the bayou. The noise and bustle did provide a certain sense of comfort and safety. I had screamed my lungs out in that warehouse without being heard. In the middle of the French Quarter, any number of people would rush to my aid, if my screams could be heard above the commotion that is. Maybe "comfort and safety" was up to me, with help from Clemmie.

The Clantons and I sat in the hotel café sipping iced tea. As usual, heat and humidity made enjoying the courtyard impossible. Besides, sitting with my back against an inside wall gave me full view of the only door to the outside. No one could grab me out of my chair without a fight!

Clem stayed long enough to insure we were settled for the afternoon. He leaned over to kiss Clemmie and must've read her mind. "Don't worry about me. I've done enough sleuthing in my time. I'll be safe."

Clemmie's hand cupped her husband's cheek. "His unofficial title in our parish is 'Backwoods P.I.'. Not much gets by him." Hard to tell if the statement was meant for my reassurance or hers.

After Clem left, I couldn't help contrasting Clementine with Ellie. My assistant used toenail

161

clippers on her fingernails for keyboard efficiency (I don't wish to speculate what she used to cut her toenails). I seriously doubted polish ever occurred to her. To compare *anyone* to Clemmie and her beautifully manicured, topaz painted nails, however, was blatantly unfair. Fighting the urge to chew on my own jagged nails gave me no right to judge Ellie.

I did, however, recognize one similarity between Ellie and Clem. While Ellie gave off unpredictable, light-hearted vibes, she stayed infinitely aware of every movement around her. Nothing got past her laser-focused powers of observation. I suspected the cousins came from a family that wouldn't or couldn't afford to get pushed around. My recent brush with death, and spending time with Clem and Clementine, made me realize how sheltered my life had been. Since childhood, I was used to being protected. *That, my dear pampered Andi, has changed.*

I jumped as a flash of red rushed past the café. *Someone's in a hurry.* My grip tightened on my tea glass. Clemmie sensed my unease. "It's okay. We're safe in here."

Not safe enough. The door burst open. "Why, there you are! I've been looking high and low. Oh, Andi Anna, how are you? My precious stepdaughter! You had me worried!"

Why couldn't it be a kidnapper? Ruby's arms encircled my head, smashing my left ear into her underwired bosom.

Before I could pull away, she let go and crossed her arms. "Well, aren't you going to introduce me to your friend?"

Before I could answer, she announced, "Pleased to

meet ya, I'm Ruby Jones, Andi Anna's stepmother."

"*Ex*-stepmother," I muttered.

Ruby stuck out her hand. "And, you are?"

Clemmie responded politely and shook Ruby's hand. "I'm Clementine, a friend of Andi's."

Ruby snickered and broke out in song. "Oh, my darlin', oh my darlin', oh my darlin' Clementine…"

Fortunately, the restaurant lunch crowd had left. The tables were mostly empty. One young couple on the other side smirked at Ruby's booming rendition. I considered sliding off my chair and disappearing under the table.

Clemmie—the epitome of pure class—kept her composure, adding a playful dose of satire that flew straight over Ruby's head. "How lovely. That's the first time I've ever been serenaded with that song."

I'll just bet. "Why are you looking for me, Ruby? Did Doris and Cloris and the rest of the gang abandon you?"

She flipped her wrist in my direction and snorted. "Oh, Lordy, no. I just left them at that oyster place down the street."

"That oyster place down the street? Well, that narrows it down." I couldn't help it. Sarcasm oozed from me with Ruby around. *How many years are left on this damnable contract, Dad?*

Ruby flopped into the empty chair. "Mind if I sit? My dogs are killin' me! Wonder why they can't make six-inch heels that are comfortable?"

"It's a wonder, all right." Why did I continue to waste top-notch wit on Ruby? "And, please do make yourself comfortable." I knew when to surrender. She rooted in her bag for a file and commenced scattering nail dust all over the table. "When you finish your manicure, could you please explain why you're looking for me?" At no time was I under the delusion her concern centered on my well-being.

She dismissed my request with one of her own. "I'd love some sweet tea. I'm simply parched from this godawful weather. The only saving grace, oh how vulgar of me to say that poor dead woman's name in vain." She closed her eyes and bowed as if saying a prayer for the dearly departed. Seconds later, she was back to normal. "Anyway, this high humidity is refreshing for a lady's skin." She glanced at me and clucked. "Why even your dull, dry complexion should benefit."

Clemmie sent a sympathetic shrug my way. *If she only knew the half of it.* I flagged down a wait person and ordered a sweet tea.

"With a lime," Ruby interjected.

"Now, spill it," I commanded. After my recent experience in captivity, I would not be captured by mindless blather.

"Well, you see me, and the girls were coming outta this weird shop on Choppy Tulip Street and…"

Choppy Tulip? "You mean Tchoupitoulas?"

Her face scrunched like a toddler sucking on a lemon. "Yes, that's what I said!"

Clemmie turned her head and pretended to cough.

"For heaven's sake, Andi, do you want to hear what I have to say or just criticize my *pronouncements*?"

"You mean…oh, never mind. Please go on, Ruby."

The waitress delivered her sweet tea to which Ruby promptly added two pink packages of sweetener, plopped a lime slice in the glass, and took a long slurp. "Ahhh. That hits the spot. Well, I know you've been in a tizzy over this Grace-murder deal, but did you know Lucy Minor is here, too? She's also a client of yours, right?"

I nodded, not wanting to get into my meeting with Lucy or the fuss over the matching pendants. Why confuse Ruby's brain even more? Or supply gossip material?

"Well, as I already mentioned, we were coming out of that shop when I saw Lucy across the street having a very heated exchange with a young man. She was shaking her finger something fierce. Why, I was afraid it would fly clean off her hand!"

Lucy arguing with someone else? I thought she'd left town. I dismissed the visual of 'flying fingers' and prodded, "When was this? Could you hear what they were saying?"

Ruby huffed, "Well, I coulda if it hadn't been for the earsplitting music coming out of that bar behind them. I can't remember the name of the place but it's like the drink."

"Like *what* drink? *Hurricane? Bloody Mary?* Surely not *Manhattan*," I quipped.

Ruby tapped her cheek with a long, point, fuchsia-painted fingernail. "Oh, I know! Like the tea, ya know, Sassafras!"

I thought I'd heard the names of most of the bars in The Quarter, but I couldn't imagine one specializing in tea. Then it hit me. "Uh-would you happen to mean, *Sazerac's*?

"Lordy! That's it," she squealed.

A cold chill slithered down my spine. Clemmie

reached over and tapped my wrist. "Could that be the same man who—"

I shook my head, hoping Clemmie would take the hint to keep quiet around Ruby. "This man arguing with Lucy; do you remember anything about his appearance?"

Ruby rolled her heavily black-lined eyes and huffed, "To tell you the truth; I was too shocked at Lucy's awful outfit to notice much else. Imagine, a woman her age wearing dirty old khakis and a big ol' vest. Not to mention that olive-colored shirt. Trust me. Olive is not her color!"

Oh, please, Lord. Help me. "Anything, Ruby. The color of his hair? How tall was he?"

"Let me think. I believe his hair was dark; almost black. His skin was medium brown. Oh, and he was kinda tall and thin." She sat back and crossed her arms; obviously pleased with what she considered an F.B.I.-worthy description.

Her meager account did convince me however, Lucy had been arguing with the same man as before. The fact she could've had another fight with Claudia's employee, Jules, the day after my disappearance from the alley behind Sazerac's, was no coincidence. But why?

I scooted my chair back. "I just remembered I'm supposed to call Ellie, and I left my phone in the room. Gotta run, Ruby. Don't be a stranger."

I headed for the door and called over my shoulder. "Clementine, are you coming?"

She jumped from her chair, startled by my hasty exit. "Uh-yeah. Nice meeting you, Ruby. Hope to see you again, sometime."

"But-I, uh, Andi Anna?" Ruby's neck stretched like a startled ostrich. "Should I wait for you?"

"No, Ruby. We'll talk later," I yelled, as the door closed behind Clemmie.

Chapter Twenty-Four

I collapsed on the bed; thankful I'd escaped Ruby before totally losing my composure. Reliving a blow-by-blow account of my awful night to a rational person would've been torture. I had no tolerance for her histrionics. I took a couple of deep breaths before realizing Clemmie had slipped quietly into the room, busying herself with a *Big Easy Sights & Sounds*, magazine.

I sat up and managed a sickly smile. "You must think I'm a real whacko!"

She closed the magazine and sat back in the armchair. "Compared to Ruby? You're as sane as they come." She laughed. "Did your lightening departure from the café have something do with the altercation Ruby described outside Sazerac's, or were you simply making your escape? Either way, care to talk about it?"

"I'm still trying to process, but maybe if we put our heads together, we can make some sense of it." I explained my meeting with Lucy; the matching pendants, and the NOPD. "Sergeant LeBlanc wasn't too impressed and passed that investigation back to me."

"How professional of him. And did you investigate?"

"Well, sort of. Lucy explained she'd admired Grace's pendant so much her ex, Darryl, located the same shop and bought a duplicate. But that's not the

168

story she told when she came to the agency to pick up her tour packet. Something isn't adding up. Although I didn't know him well, I never had the impression Darryl was the type to rush out and buy gifts, especially since they divorced a short time later."

"Maybe it was a 'see ya later' gift," Clemmie suggested.

I nodded. "That's sort of what Lucy implied, but her anxiety level soared the last time we talked about the pendant. Now we have her arguing, again, with the same man from Claudia's Candles and Magic."

"Could they be your kidnappers?"

That sickening thought had occurred to me, too. I wasn't ready to go there. Not Lucy! "I only met Jules, briefly, but I can't imagine Lucy being involved. Still, what's their connection? I can't continue to ignore facts."

I flipped on the TV and scrolled through the channels. Game shows, Soaps, endless news commentary, DIY, *Friends* reruns, and a couple of movie stations. "Wish this place had satellite," I grumbled. Clemmie nodded. We both needed a diversion.

I'd finally settled on a Hallmark Channel cozy murder mystery when my phone rang.

"If you don't recognize the caller, don't answer," Clemmie warned.

"It's the police station," I whispered. "This is Andi Jones. You're on speaker."

"Hello Ms. Jones. This is Carey Giles. How are you feeling today? Better, I hope."

"Much better, Detective, thanks. In fact, I'm back at my hotel, along with my 'bodyguard', Clementine

Clanton."

"Good to know, Ms. Jones. Would you be up to making a formal statement this afternoon? The more information you can provide, the faster we'll catch the pair of 'would-be' killers."

Yikes! I still had qualms admitting the danger I'd faced, but facts were facts. I'd come way too close to death. "Sure. I'm available any time. Can you pick me up, or do you want me to catch a ride?"

"I will pick you up," the detective stated, firmly. "I'd rather you stayed close to your hotel, unless you're with one of us. I know that's inconvenient, but we'd rather not have to search for you, again. Next time, we may not be so lucky, and neither will you."

"Message received. When should I be ready?"

"I can be there in a half-hour. Oh, and there's no problem if Ms. Clanton wants to accompany you."

Clemmie shook her head.

"I'll wait in the courtyard."

****

I gathered my phone, a small water bottle, and a hairbrush, stuck them in a faded denim bag I'd tossed into my suitcase at the last minute. I held it by the frayed strap. "Cute, huh? I normally carry this to the beach, not in public."

"I've seen worse," Clemmie assured me. "Besides, you'll probably get your purse back today."

We walked into the courtyard to wait for my ride. "Sure you don't want to come with me? Carey said I could bring a friend."

"You mean your bodyguard," she chuckled. "No, I'd better stay here and wait for Clem to call. He should check in, soon. There's your ride."

Detective Giles got out of the police car, waved, and opened the passenger-side door.

"You'll do great," Clemmie predicted.

****

The station buzzed with policemen, phones ringing off their hooks, and a few handcuffed suspects. "Wow," I observed. "This place was dead the other night."

"Yeah, Fridays are usually hectic. Here in NOLA, the weekend starts on Thursday night and ends Tuesday morning."

I laughed. "Doesn't leave much time for work."

"That's why our nickname is The Big Easy," Carey conceded. "We'll do our interview in the second room on the left."

To my dismay, Sergeant Le Blanc greeted us. "Thank you, Ms. Jones, for coming to the station. I trust you've recovered." Without waiting for my answer, he continued. "I understand you gave a preliminary report last night, but this interrogation, er-interview, is being recorded, and will be officially on the record."

He's still a ray of sunshine. "I understand." I sat at the end of a large wooden table; the two detectives seated on either side. He set a phone recorder in front of me. My knees bounced up and down. What reason did I have to be nervous? I had nothing to hide...or did I? I hadn't exactly been forth coming about my contact with Lucy, but that was before her actions raised my suspicions. I had to tell the police everything I knew up to that point.

The sergeant pressed the record button. "We'll start with your kidnapping, first. If you wish to add anything further from your previous statement, you may do so at the end."

I re-lived, without interruption, the circumstances of my capture, confinement, and timely rescue. When asked for descriptions of my assailants, I wasn't much help. "Their voices sounded familiar, but I wish they'd been clearer."

"That squares with your preliminary report, Carey. Anything else you can think of, Ms. Jones?" Sergeant Le Blanc sat back and closed his eyes, appearing he might fall asleep.

I stammered. Did I have enough evidence to suggest questioning Lucy and Jules? "Not about the kidnapping, but, I-uh, may have relevant information about Grace Payne's murder."

That perked him up. "Is this about the matching pendants? Did you talk to your other client?"

I began with facts I could verify. "Yes, I asked her about it. She said her ex-husband got it for her because she'd admired Grace's, the one you have in evidence. Shortly after, Lucy's, uh-her full name is Lucinda Minor…" I watched him write it down. "Anyway, Lucy's husband left her not long after she received the pendant. She assumed the gift was a way to ease his conscience."

"And you believed her?" Carey asked.

"I did, but now? Not so much."

Le Blanc leaned forward. "Please explain."

I took a deep breath and voiced my surprise at seeing my client, Lucy Minor, who was supposed to be on an Alaskan cruise, arguing with a young man outside Claudia's Candles & Magic. "During the unsettling conversation she and I had, she pointed the finger at Stewart Payne. 'He did it for her money,' Lucy claimed."

"I'd had my own issues with him, but I never imagined him murdering anyone, especially his own wife."

Le Blanc stood. "Did she give you any concrete proof? Or is this just speculation on her part?"

I racked my brain to remember every word. "No, but she had a strange reaction when I said you knew about the possibility of matching pendants. For a moment, I saw fear and then hostility in her eyes. Reactions I'd never experienced from Lucy."

"Have you spoken to her, since?" Carey chimed in.

I shook my head. "That's another problem. She had agreed to come here with me the next day to explain any confusion about her pendant, but I got a text that morning saying she had to leave town and wouldn't be back for a few days. She didn't leave, though. My ex-stepmother, Ruby, who came here for the same convention as Grace, saw her arguing with a man the next day. They were in front of the same bar my abduction took place—Sazerac's."

Carey leaned forward. "Do you know who the man was? Is there a chance your client is, somehow, involved in your kidnapping?"

"I can't believe she would be, but, from Ruby's description, the man could very well be the same person who argued with Lucy." I shivered, remembering when the male kidnapper suggested letting me go, and the female's response. *"You know we can't. She's getting much too close."* Could those words have come from a client I considered a friend?

Carey put her hand over mine. "Are you all right?"

I could barely speak. "I...I...think someone just...walked across my grave."

Chapter Twenty-Five

Did I hear Lucy's voice? Or was my imagination running amok? The room spun. Someone caught me before I fell off the chair.

"Get her some water. Andi, stay with me."

Can't breathe! I was back in the warehouse trapped in that fiberglass skull.

"Carey, hold her head. Can you sip some water?"

Water? Oh, good. Maybe I'm not going to die in here. I took a small sip, then another. Hands grasped my shoulders.

"Take a deep breath. Another. That's good."

The spinning stopped. I opened my eyes. Two concerned faces stared back. "She's coming to," Carey confirmed. "Andi, are you okay? Maybe you should've stayed in the hospital another day."

"What happened? I heard a female voice before everything went black."

"You passed out," Andre explained. "Are you feeling better, or should we call an ambulance?"

Feeling confused and a little silly, I shook my head. "No, I'm just a little dizzy." I turned to Carey. "You asked, before, if I thought Lucy was involved in my kidnapping. Much as it sickens me, I believe she could be. Her accomplice may be the man she argued with in front of Claudia's and, again, at Sazerac's. Could money be the reason for their second, uh, *discussion?* I

174

doubt Lucy was eager to pay since the target—yours truly—is still alive."

"Any idea what her motive could be?" Andre pushed the recorder closer. "Surely it can't be those pendants. How would they figure in a murder?"

"I don't know whether this is relevant, but Grace and Stewart's son told my assistant, Ellie, that Lucy had a dark side, one I'd never seen. While Lucy implied Grace and she were best friends, Ethan Payne said his mother couldn't stand her."

"Do you think his father, Stewart, could corroborate that?" Andre asked. "He isn't leaving until tomorrow. Maybe we can get him down here."

"I, uh, guess I forgot to mention I talked to him the other day, too."

My admission was met with an icy state from Le Blanc. "For what purpose?"

"I wish I knew," I admitted. "I believe he just wanted someone to talk with who knew Grace. He also apologized." Their blank stares required an explanation. "Stewart and I have had our share of travel mishaps in the past. His anger came to a head when Grace was first reported missing. He blamed my agency for screwing up her reservation, threatened to sue me for everything I was worth." I snorted. "Ha! Pocket change to someone with his access to money. Well, anyway, that's why he apologized…for overreacting."

"Is that all? Are you sure there's nothing else you've 'forgotten' to tell us?"

I grinned, sheepishly. "Nope. That's about it."

The sergeant pulled a business card out of his shirt pocket. "Payne's in town until tomorrow and, so far, has been cooperative. Maybe he can shed some light on this proposed vendetta of Lucy Minor's."

"Do you want me to stay?" *I sincerely hope not.* A three or four hour nap sounded so much better than waiting around for Stewart.

Carey must've read the exhaustion on my face. "If it's okay with you, Sergeant Le Blanc, I believe Ms. Jones needs to rest."

"Oh, sure, sure," he agreed. "You're a lucky young woman, Ms. Jones. If an employee at Sazerac's hadn't called in a possible abduction, and those two boys hadn't trespassed, we might be investigating *your* death." With a wave of his hand, he added, "We'll let you know if we need further conversations."

Guess I was dismissed without even receiving a "Thank you for dragging your dehydrated, banged-up body in here, Andi." His personality rivaled that of my high school algebra teacher, Miss Askew. *Miss Jones. You got 100% on your test today. Did you guess at the answers, or cheat?* She sure knew how to cut you down to size. So did he.

Carey made up for her boss's lack of bedside manner. "Thanks, so much, for your statement. I'll drive you back."

I'd gotten past whatever caused me to faint, but her steadying hand calmed me as we left the station. "Don't be too hard on Andre," she urged, during the short drive back to my hotel. "He's a bit socially challenged. I've been here ten years, and nothing's changed."

I chuckled. "I got that the first time. Trust me. I've dealt with clients in Miami that would make Sergeant Le Blanc rival Chuckles the Clown. Will you let me know if you get any worthwhile information from Stewart? I'd like to think I'm not the only one with doubts about Lucy."

"I'll be in touch." She gave a wry smile and waved.

Hmmph. Wonder what that means. I crossed the courtyard to my room. It was empty. Guess Clemmie left to meet Clem. *Fine by me.* I collapsed on the bed, too tired to think.

****

Amazing how eight, uninterrupted hours of sleep could rejuvenate a body and soul. I might've slept another eight if not for the strong, nutty aroma filling my nostrils.

"Hey, sleepyhead. 'Bout time you woke up." Clemmie lounged on the small sofa, sipping a go-cup of coffee. "I believe yours is still hot." She pointed to a matching cup on the bedside table.

I pulled up and tucked a couple of pillows behind me. "You're an angel, Clemmie." I removed the lid and breathed in the aroma before taking a cautious sip. "Ouch! It is still hot." I set the coffee back on the nightstand to cool. "So, when did you get here?"

She chuckled. "I've been here all night. Clem picked me up after you left for the station. When I got back around 10:30, you were already zonked. I took a shower, pulled out the sofa bed, grabbed pillows out of the closet. You never moved. If you hadn't been lying on your back, snoring away, I would've checked your pulse."

"Hey, I don't snore. Well, maybe a little but it's this godawful weather." To prove my point, I grabbed a tissue and gave a hearty blow. "See?"

She rolled her eyes. "To be fair, when I finally moved you on your side, you didn't make a sound the rest of the night. Now, if we're through analyzing your sinuses, want to switch to murder and kidnapping?"

I took another sip of coffee, sat back, and nodded. "Ready when you are."

"After you left for the police station, Clem and I stopped by Sazerac's to talk to Bonnie. As luck would have it, she had the night off. Think it would be safe for you and me to go back there? She's supposed to be in this afternoon." She stood and peeked through the drapes. "Or do the police want you to stay here?"

"After giving my statement, they never ordered me to stay inside. I doubt that surly sergeant would much care, one way or the other, but Detective Giles was another matter. If she'd had any concerns, I'm sure I'd know about them."

"Did you learn anything new from the police?"

"Not much. They heard a few fresh facts from me, though; facts they wished I'd spilled, sooner," I conceded.

"About?" Clemmie prodded.

"Mind if I splash some water on my face?" I shuffled to the bathroom, shut the door, flipped on the light, and stared into the mirror. For someone who'd been shoved in the trunk of a car and nearly suffocated in a festival skull, I looked pretty good. That sleep must've done wonders. I covered my face with a cool washcloth and rubbed the junk out of the corners of my eyes. A quick brush (hair) and flush (duh), and I was ready to answer all Clemmie's questions, especially since she was clever enough to bring coffee!

I opened the bathroom door and jumped, kid-style, on the bed. "Okay, I'm ready to face the world!"

She laughed. "I must admit; for someone who's been through your ordeal, you're pretty darn spirited.

So, what's new?"

I explained the contradictions in Lucy's stories. How she'd accused Stewart of killing his wife, her strange reaction over the matching pendants, saying she had to leave town, being spotted, the next day, by Ruby. "Not only that, according to the Payne's son, Ethan, Lucy and Grace weren't 'besties' the way she implied. When you add it up, Lucy Minor is a 'person of interest' at the very least."

Clemmie tapped her fingers on the table. "In Grace's murder, your kidnapping, or both?"

"A voice in my head says, both."

"A voice in your head? Oh, this is good."

"Before my statement to the police, I would've been skeptical of the theory." I explained the disturbing comment I heard from the female kidnapper; how the voice sounded familiar. "Too familiar. There was no question in her mind about the necessity of my demise. At first, I thought my imagination was working overtime, but those words came through at the police station, loud and clear, in the voice of Lucy Minor. I passed out, as a result."

"You passed out?"

"Don't worry. After a few sips of water, I felt normal."

Clemmie stood. "That settles it. We're going out. I'm a Black Belt…"

Of course, you are.

"…and there isn't one self-defense course I haven't aced. I'll call Clem and let him know our plans. He may be able to meet us there."

Chapter Twenty-Six

I had to admit, even the damp New Orleans air felt refreshing. We crossed the street and grabbed a couple of café au laits and set out for Sazerac's.

The fifteen-minute walk gave us time to small talk. She met Clem at L.S.U. when he was a senior and she, a junior. "We were both interested in teaching, but life got in the way. I made the decision to quit school when my dad got sick. Mom was gone—she left when I was two—which left no one to care for him in his later years. He's gone now, too." She stopped to swipe at a single, stubborn tear. "With no money coming in for tuition, I had no choice but to leave school."

"But you got your degree, right?"

"Thanks to patience and persistence, I took night classes, whenever possible. Clem made sure I had enough money to cover classes and books. Believe me, there were weeks when the only food we had was harvested from the ground or fished out of the bayou. My granddaddy helped, too, whenever he could. Now, we return the favor when he lets us. His pride gets in the way, though."

My admiration for the Clantons, especially Clemmie, skyrocketed. *You just never know*. The gorgeous, poised, intelligent woman had life experiences that would keep most people down. She not only survived, she thrived. Losing my mom, in my

180

early twenties was tough enough, but until a couple of years ago, I had my dad. "Wow, Clemmie. You've overcome a lot."

The Sazerac's sign came into view, along with about a dozen, or so customers milling about. Not surprising. They were already open for business. Let the party begin.

Clemmie walked right in, but I hesitated outside. Bad vibes swept over me. How could I step inside and risk reviving those awful memories?

"You, okay?" She stuck her head out the door. "If you're not ready for this, we can take a walk and browse at some of the other stores. The Quarter isn't all voo-doo paraphernalia, and bars."

I nodded. "I need to build up courage before I go back in there."

"Tell you what. The display windows, in shop across the street, look intriguing. I'll check inside to see if Bonnie's here and meet you over there in a few minutes."

I agreed. "Sazerac's looks pretty full, already, so you should be able to mill around without drawing attention." *Who am I kidding?* Clementine could draw attention away from Miss World Pageant contestants or Supreme Court candidates. Take your pick.

She stepped inside the bar. I crossed the street and entered a store like no other I'd seen in my thirty-six years.

"May I help you?"

I spun in the direction of the pleasant voice. "I, uh, sure." Checking out the front window would've been a swell idea *before* I'd walked into a...*what the hell is this place?*

"Hi, I'm Daphne, the owner. Pretty unusual, huh?"

Daphne's purple and black streaked hair, too many lip studs and piercings to count, gestured, *Vanna White* style, toward shelves packed with taxidermy foxes, boar heads, a full-size black bear, and other indescribable wildlife. The skeleton of a huge alligator, hanging above my head, did nothing to ease my discomfort.

Daphne looked up and laughed. "Oh, don't mind Cecil. He's friendly."

My attempt to laugh mimicked the wheeze of a three-pack-a-day cigarette fiend. "Remarkable store."

"Well, since this is, obviously, your first time here, let me show you around."

I glanced through the grimy window toward Sazerac's and saw no sign of Clemmie. It had been less than five minutes. Might as well kill time—poor choice of words—in this *shop of the dead.*

"Here's one of my favorites." She guided me to a glass case. "This is Pricilla, a domestic cat skeleton. Some say burying one of these under your front porch leads to good luck. Others swear they keep bad spirits away."

My horrified look must've pressed her to add, "Don't worry. We only use skeletons of animals that have died, naturally; usually of old age. Never would we dishonor nature by killing one of her beautiful creatures."

"Still kinda freaks me out," I gulped. I pictured my mother's cherished calico, Chrissy who died of old age not long after Mom passed. The thought of having her beloved pet shoved under the porch to ward off evil spirits, made my skin crawl.

I'd guess the owner was used to similar reactions.

She smiled, patiently. "Feel free to browse, or not. I'll be here if you have any questions."

I debated whether to leave and take my chances in the bar or to just stay put in the creepiest shop imaginable. Daphne's smile and friendly manner, however, contradicted the sinister displays. I decided to stick it out. How long could Clemmie be?

I stepped, cautiously, around the room and fought my inner disgust. A case containing vials and instruments was labeled: Antique Embalming Kit. *Ick*! After what I'd witnessed during my stay in New Orleans, I had no interest in the art of embalming. I moved to the jewelry counter.

Finally, something I can relate to.

Or not. The sign describing a one-of-a-kind necklace, revealed it was "Made entirely of human bones." I grabbed the counter to keep my knees from buckling.

Either this jewelry is as gross as it looks, or I need to adjust my thinking.

"We have earrings that complement the necklace, if you're interested," Daphne pointed out.

"Uh, maybe I'll just look around for a while and come back to it." *Yeah, right. And I'll also take that cat skeleton back to Miami and stick it under my bed!* I shivered just imagining the horror.

"You waiting for someone across the street?"

"Yeah, a friend went into Sazerac's. I decided to wait here, if that's okay?"

"Sure. You're the first customer I've had all day. Although, it doesn't appear you're a customer."

I flushed. "Who knows? I may find the perfect, uh, bone accessory."

I continued strolling around the shop, keeping my distance from the most disturbing exhibits. I'd just about resigned myself to buying a pair of dangly skeleton earrings when Daphne asked, "Is that your friend coming across the street?"

Whew! *Thank you, Clemmie!* I was saved from spending money I didn't have on creepy jewelry I didn't want. Although, Christmas was just around the corner, and Ruby would love those earrings. *Sorry, Ruby. Hope another spa gift certificate will satisfy you.*

Clemmie burst through the door, glanced overhead at Cecil, and stopped in her tracks. "I, uh...what the hell is that?"

"That's Cecil." I calmly explained the hanging alligator skeleton, eliminating the fact I'd had the bejeeszus scared out of me when I walked in. "He's harmless. At least *now* he is. So, did you find Bonnie?"

"Once again, no luck. She won't be in until later tonight, and the bartender is pissed."

"Yeah, Bonnie said Lonnie stays pissed most of the time. Since he struts around like the last person on earth that would cover for anyone but himself, we can assume he's telling the truth. Guess I'll have to wait to find out exactly what Bonnie told the police." *Why didn't I ask Sergeant Le Blanc or Detective Giles last night?* Oh, yeah. I was busy passing out.

Clemmie clasped forearm. "Why not take a walk to Claudia's Magic shop? Maybe the guy Lucy argued with is there."

"Even if he is, I don't believe he's the talkative type," I scoffed. "Claudia must keep him busy in the back or he'd scare off her customers. Although, I did have a somewhat personable chat with him about crystals and such." Did I truly believe a conversation with Jules would be useless, or was my body rebelling at the strain of a long walk? *Suck it up, Andi.* "Sure, why not? We have nothing else to do, right?"

I dismissed taking shortcuts through back alleys. While my previous encounter with Stewart was remarkably pleasant, no sense tempting fate. We took it slow. Clemmie stopped several times, pretending to scan shop windows. I suspected her sudden interest in French antiques and imported cigars was for my benefit, for which I was grateful. One more corner brought Claudia's and Polly's Pralines in sight. Maybe my body needed a dose of sugar. Before walking straight into the magic shop, I glanced, longingly, across the street. My companion ignored my obvious plea. *Maybe on the way back.*

Once inside, Clemmie's eyes widened in wonder. "I haven't been here in years. Nothing's changed, except it might look a little less frightening." She chuckled. "Less frightening than it was to a ten-year-old."

"You haven't been here since you were a kid?"

"Natives stay away from the Quarter. If we want pralines," she tilted her head toward Polly's, "voo doo masks, or crawfish etouffe, we make them, ourselves."

"Now, don't you be runnin' down my store, Clementine." A scowling Claudia stood a few feet away, arms folded.

Clemmie and I were speechless until Claudia slapped her side and cackled. "I swear you haven't changed since your *grand-père* brought you in during his weekly herbal visits."

Clemmie smiled. "I remember. If I'm not mistaken,

185

he swore by your rheumatism treatment. But how did you recognize me after all this time?"

Claudia took Clemmie's hand. "I never forget an aura, child." She glanced at me in a less spiritual way. "What brings you back?"

Not in the mood to be intimidated by the old biddy, I got right to the point. "Your stock person, or whatever he is. Jules? I need to ask him some questions."

Claudia sighed. "I haven't seen him in three days. If you find him, he needs to answer to me, first." She turned to the essential oil display and absentmindedly picked through the inventory. "Not only that...he stole a strong sleeping potion I had locked in a trunk." She shook her head. "It's one of Gizelle's bests. Safe, but very effective. Well, you know how particular she is, Clementine."

Clemmie nodded, knowingly, and asked, "Do you have any idea why he stole it?"

"Oh, he's probably selling it on the street. He was always asking for money, even though I paid him twice the minimum wage." She continued fiddling with bottles of peppermint, lavender, bergamot, lemon grass, and some oils I'd never heard of. At one point, she knocked over a whole row, dominoes-style, cursed in Cajun, I assumed, and started the process over again.

I'd never seen this side of her; shaky, reserved. I wondered if her mood involved her missing employee, the missing potion, or both.

Clemmie noticed her behavior, too, and walked to her side. "Anything we can do to help?"

Claudia turned, flashing a bright smile that contradicted the worry in her eyes. "Oh, no, dear. I'm fine. Now, if you'll excuse me, I have inventory to sort.

Oh, and if I see Jules, I'll let him know you want to talk to him." She hurried through the black curtain.

"That was a little strange. I realize you haven't seen Claudia for years, but I was here a couple of days ago. Complete personality change."

Clemmie agreed. "She seemed very uneasy, especially when talking about this Jules person."

I started to ask how she knew Giselle when my cell rang. "Hang on. It's Detective Giles. Hello, Carey. No, I haven't talked to him since we met a couple of days ago. Did you try the hotel?"

I covered the receiver and whispered to Clemmie, "They can't locate Stewart Payne."

I removed my hand and continued listening. Carey said they'd called the hotel and discovered he checked out, but the airlines had no record of his departure.

"That's strange, Carey. We weren't on the best of terms, but I was sure he'd let me know if his plans changed. We're not too far from his hotel. We'll check it out. We? Oh, Clementine Clanton is here with me."

Carey wasn't convinced we should investigate on our own and tried to talk me into going back to my room. "Trust me," I assured her. "We'll be safe. My sidekick is a Black Belt, ya know."

I gave Clemmie the thumbs up signal. She pulled the handgun out of her bag, returned the thumbs up and added a wink.

Still shocked by the sight of her packing heat, I didn't hear the rest of Carey's conversation other than, "Be careful and keep in touch."

Clemmie tucked the gun back in her bag. "Hope this doesn't make you too uncomfortable. I have a license to carry and a Golden Bullet award for gun training and safety from the NOPD. I was top in my class."

Of course, you were.

No choice but to bury—pun intended—my disdain of firearms for the time being.

Chapter Twenty-Seven

The short drive to the Hilton in Clemmie's truck took less than ten minutes. Contrasting the tourist-crammed French Quarter, the streets and sidewalks on the other end of town were, for the most part, empty. I strongly considered telling Clemmie to drive back to my hotel. Sure, I enjoyed a good detective mystery, but was it fair to drag her along?

However, *stubborn* was my middle name, a fact my dad verified after a decades-old peanut butter and jelly sandwich incident. He'd made the inexcusable error of putting the jelly on top of the peanut butter. Imagine! Everyone knows they go on different slices of bread! *Then* you smash them together. I smiled remembering that battle of wills. Eight-year-old me—arms crossed, pouting—insisting I would not eat that *sullied sandwich*. Yes, I did say, *sullied* even though I was clueless about the meaning.

Stubborn won. We'd already pulled into the Hilton parking lot, so might as well follow through with the plan. Besides, Clemmie was a gun-toting, Black Belt. Me? I was the first in my age group to do a perfect back flip off the springboard during county-wide middle-school competition. Ha!

"This place is huge." I leaned back, imagining the view from the penthouse. "Chances of anyone remembering a single guest, are slim and none. I don't

189

even know where to start."

Clemmie pushed through one of the revolving doors. "I'd say the front desk."

Patrons, checking in and checking out, or simply passing through, crowded the lobby. My attention shifted from Stewart, Grace, clues, and murder, to a heavenly aroma drifting from the bar area. My stomach rumbled as I watched a woman stuff her face with...*what is that? Charbroiled oysters? Barbequed shrimp?* I licked drool from the corner of my mouth; regretting the decision to skip breakfast.

"Hey, Clemmie, should we grab a bite to eat while we're here? Clemmie?" *Rats! She's fully engaged with a clerk at the front desk. Hmmph. No wonder she stays so fit.*

"Yes, his name is Stewart Payne," Clemmie stated. "He was a guest for the past several days, but apparently checked out this morning."

The clerk, name tag, Michael Burdette, tapped the keyboard. "Yes, he checked out early this morning. Notes show the police already have this information. Is there anything else I can do for you?"

The bored look on his face indicated the offer was purely symbolic. My charming, investigative partner, however, was determined to win him over. "Oh, we were so sure you'd be able to help us locate our uncle. He's going through such a difficult time, his wife dying and all. Is there anyone else who might help locate him?"

The expression on the clerk's face changed from "Who do you think you're kidding?" to, "Let me pawn you off on someone else."

"Check with the concierge, Miss Felix. She might

know if your"—He paused for an air quotes gesture— "'*uncle*' made reservations for a side trip." He pointed to the right, around the corner, and turned back to his computer.

"Friendly, huh?" I scoffed. "Air quotes? What is he, ten?"

"He sure wouldn't qualify for a seat on the Chamber of Commerce welcoming committee," Clemmie quipped.

Miss Felix, the desk clerk's polar opposite, greeted us, warmly. "Hello lovely ladies! How may I assist you?"

Adalyn Felix smiled with every inch of her five-foot frame. Eyes the color of pure dark chocolate, shoulder-length white hair that shocked against bronze skin. A sing-song Jamaican accent completed the picture.

"I certainly hope you can, Miss Felix." I gulped at the sight of this gorgeous older lady. "We're trying to find out." Oh, why lie to her? "We're trying to locate a client of mine who booked your hotel for three nights. He, supposedly, checked out this morning."

She tapped her computer. "Name, please?"

"Stewart Payne." Clemmie and I answered in unison.

Miss Felix laughed. "You two must be soul sisters. One of mind, one of heart."

Her instant observation surprised me. I'd never been one to collect girlfriends. In fact, I tended to shy away from conversations about kids and family, since I had neither. My early life centered on my dad and sports which made me more comfortable discussing the Dolphin's lack of defense in a particular year, or the

Heat's need of another point guard. Meeting Clemmie, however, gave me a whole new perspective. Our connection, of just a few short days, had the familiarity of a lifelong friendship. Nice to know others recognized our connection.

Soul Sisters? I like that.

"Now, back to your Mister Stewart." She scanned her computer and paged through brochures of local tours. Another flick of the keyboard sent her scurrying into a back room. She returned showing a printout of Stewart's driver's license, being careful to cover everything but the picture. "Are you looking for this man?"

I nodded. "That's him."

Her smile disappeared. "I believe I saw him this morning leaving with two individuals. I can't be sure because I only caught a glimpse of his face. He looked stressed. I thought, at the time, he was inebriated because the man and woman who accompanied him were on either side, holding him upright." She pointed to the exit on her left. "They rushed him through the side door of the lobby. He stumbled a couple times and his escorts laughed, but I don't believe he was in on the joke."

Flashbacks to my kidnapping sent my stomach into cartwheels. Was Stewart taken by the same couple? "Can you describe the pair?"

The clerk shook her head. "I wasn't sure, at the time, but now I believe their clothes were disguises. They wore black raincoats and hats pulled down low, probably to keep their identities hidden from security cameras. Their attire appeared especially odd, since the sky was clear all morning."

"Any idea where they were headed?" Clemmie asked.

"No," she answered. "I wish I had paid more attention, but mornings are very busy. If I think of anything else…"

My shoulders slumped. "Thanks. Here's my card in case you do. How long will you be here?"

"I get off at 5:00 pm," she answered. "If you need further help, here's my phone number."

"Guess we're back to square one," I grumbled. We left the hotel through the same door Stewart and his companions exited hours earlier.

"Hot as Florida asphalt" heat and humidity slammed us the minute we walked out the side door. Ribbons of steam evaporated off the sidewalk. *Two people in raincoats and hats? I don't think so.* I pulled the cell from my bag. "Hello, Carey? This is Andi Jones. I'm doing okay, thanks. Listen, we're at the Hilton…yes, I know, but we're safe. We do have a lead. The concierge on duty may have seen Stewart Payne being escorted from the lobby this morning. She ID'd him from a driver's license picture. No, she isn't positive but did get a glimpse of his face. The others? Are you ready for this? They were in disguise. Black raincoats and hats. I know! Not a cloud in the sky. Okay, her name is Adalyn Felix. She's leaving around 5:00 this afternoon, but I have her phone number if you need it. Oh, and you'll spot her long white hair a mile away."

Clemmie was on the phone when I hung up with Carey. I couldn't hear the conversation, but she mouthed, "Clem" when she saw me looking. Speaking to her husband should've been a comfort, but her sober look suggested trouble. She hung up and walked toward me.

"Everything okay?" I held my breath. This week had been one nasty surprise after another. I prepared for the worst.

"Yeah, I guess so. Clem's stuck on the boat. Engine conked out and he's waiting for a tow. He's not happy Stewart has disappeared. Less happy we're trying to find him on our own." She stuck her phone in the back pocket of her white jeans. "Did you reach the police?"

"They're coming as soon as possible to interview the concierge." Hearing that Stewart appeared drunk that early in the morning, I recalled our conversation with Claudia. "Clemmie! Didn't Claudia suspect Jules stole a powerful sleeping potion? Could that be why Stewart had to be helped out of the hotel lobby? He was drugged?"

Her mouth flew open. "That has to be it. Jules and, and...Lucy?"

I searched for Stewart's business card. "I'll call his mobile number and hope he answers." The number connected and rang in my ear. A second later I heard another ring. Close by. I spun around and waited for a second ring. "It's coming from that stone planter!"

Clemmie searched among the coleus and purple pansies. "Here it is! I guess Stewart's escorts had no time to bury it or shut it off."

I identified Stewart as the owner of the functioning cell phone. "Well, so much for calling him or using GPS." I swiped the screen. "Let's see if we can find a clue. Maybe he arranged to be picked up." I scrolled through his messages, and shuddered when I spotted four, days-old texts to Grace, all undelivered. Three were sent to his son. One each, to the hotel and rental car company. "You might know he deletes old messages, unlike me. I still have some from three years ago." I scanned to the end of the short list and noticed an unsent message with no recipient. Just one word in the body. *Cabin.*

"What do you think this means?" I held the screen for Clemmie. "He types one word and stops. Strange, even for Stewart." I tucked the cell in my bag with every intention of dropping it off at the police station. Maybe they could extract something useful. If Carey was available, I'd also mention my conversation with Claudia about the stolen sleep potion.

Chapter Twenty-Eight

I tried calling Carey on our way to the police station. She was out. Wonder if she was on her way to interview Miss Felix? Or, more likely, conducting another of many ongoing investigations. Just because my priority centered on one particular murder mystery, didn't mean crime stopped in the Big Easy.

Behind the wheel, Clemmie asked, "Do you still want to swing by the station, or wait to talk to Detective Giles?"

Hmmm. Should I attempt to explain the latest information to Sergeant Le Blanc and hope he follows up? I cringed at the thought of describing Claudia's ravings about a stolen potion. He'd think we were both looney. Until the police got an official statement from the concierge on Stewart's condition this morning, and until Ms. Felix confirms Stewart was led from the hotel, I didn't have much concrete evidence. I should turn in his cell, ASAP. That one-word, unsent message, *cabin*, nagged at me.

"We're here," Clemmie announced. "Want me to wait?"

"Huh?" Deep in thought, I had no idea we'd stopped.

"The police station? Do you want to hand over the phone while we're here?"

A handful of questions crossed my mind. Why

didn't we leave the phone in the planter and wait for the police to get it? By taking Stewart's phone, could I become an accessory in his disappearance? Could Clemmie? Why did I consider myself the next Veronica Mars? Maybe I should stop believing in my ability to solve murders and just write stories about them. That's it! I'll be the next James Patterson...or Sue Grafton!

"Andi! What do you want to do?"

Cabin...cabin... "This lovely little cabin belongs to a friend of mine." That's it! Lucy! "I have a better idea. Get on I-10, West! I'll explain on the way."

Between filling Clemmie in on the cabin in the boonies where Lucy and I first talked, I made every effort to channel the GPS in my brain. Why didn't I pay more attention to the directions the first time? Possibly since I made the trip in a prone position? Better yet, why wasn't I *born* with a sense of direction? I knew we were getting close when the exit sign to LaPlace appeared. "Get off here. I think it's just a mile, or two from the interstate."

The tops of trees, growing alongside the two-lane road, looked the same. Frustration mounted along with fear that I'd never find the cabin. Fear we'd take a wrong turn and get lost in the bayou. *How many recent murders? Four, five counting Grace?* "Maybe we should turn around, Clemmie. It was dark when I drove out here with Lucy. Not sure why I thought I could find the...wait! That large oak tree just ahead! I remember how it loomed over the scrub cypress in the moonlight."

Clemmie slowed. "Well, that's poetic. Are you sure? This isn't the only giant oak in Louisiana, ya know."

I scanned the landscape. "Do you see any others

that size? That tree dwarfs everything for miles." I couldn't be positive, but gut instinct said to turn.

Clemmie veered right onto a gravel road. "You're positive this is it."

No. "Ninety-nine percent," I claimed. Not a complete lie. The road Lucy and I took was also *gravel.*

We crept down the lane, scattering birds, armadillos, and a variety of unrecognizable rodents into the brush. My first trip to the cabin came with the benefit of a full moon to light our path. While a bright, afternoon sun offered a different perspective, I still sensed familiarity in the dips, turns, and potholes. "If I'm right, the road should turn, sharply, to the left with the cabin on the immediate right. It's a little hard to spot because of all the overgrown bushes in front."

Minutes later, we made the turn and slowed to a crawl. The weed-covered, rut-filled driveway appeared on the right. Clemmie made no attempt to hide her annoyance. "Seriously? You want me to drive my spotless truck on that?"

I shrugged. "I didn't remember it being so rough. We can park and walk down. Might be best, anyway. If someone is there, they won't hear us coming."

She pulled off the road as far as possible, grumbling about the brush scratching the side of her truck. We stepped onto the muddy road, careful not to slam the doors. Now to navigate the, so-called, drive without surprising a couple of black snakes or worse, cottonmouths.

"Let me try to call Clem, again. It's crucial he knows where we are." She punched speed dial and got an immediate voice message. "Crap. He's not answering." She waited a moment and said, "Hi, honey,

Andi and I are just west of the LaPlace exit on I-10 looking for Stewart Payne. Cell tracking is on. Please call or text when you get this message. Love you." She stepped on the truck running board and flipped open the console. "Okay, the phone is hidden. After you, *Detective Holmes.*"

We hunkered alongside the tall clumps of lemon grass bordering the road, using every square inch of dry ground for stepping stones. The dilapidated shack came into view. "I don't see Lucy's car, or any car," I whispered. "Guess I've taken us on a wild goose chase."

"We're here, Might as well look around," Clemmie said.

I supposed she was right. I'd instigated the trip to the boonies. Why back out, now? We slipped toward the cottage. A couple of beady-eyed crows perched "Hitchcock-like" on the roof peak. *An omen, perhaps?* The window blinds were closed, so we couldn't tell if the place was empty. I stooped down behind a massive elderberry bush on the far side of the porch. Clemmie followed.

"I'm pretty sure the main room has windows in the back. I'll sneak around and see if I spot anyone inside," I whispered. Staying as low to the ground as two bad knees allowed, I snuck around the far side of the cabin. Stilts, on the backside of the structure, offered protection from storms and floods. A rickety set of stairs leading to the deck matched the rotten front porch. Before attempting the climb, I figured my odds about 50-50 to make it to the top without falling through. Since that was the only way to see inside, I took a deep breath and crept slowly, one step at a time.

Another obstacle loomed at the top. Splintered boards that hadn't seen a paint brush or sealer in decades, taunted any and all trespassers. On the bright side, I'd gambled on the stairs and won. Negotiating ten feet to the back windows should be a breeze. Just my luck! The blinds were closed same as the front, except for one small broken section. I crouched to my knees and tested one semi-solid board, then another. *Ow! Damned splinters!* Thanks to my decision to wear capris, heat radiating off the wood burned my shins.

I reached the window with the missing section of blind and eased up to peek over the sill. Scanning the room, I had a decent view of the empty kitchen. The loveseat and easy chair sat vacant. I shifted positions and strained to see the rocking chair on the left side of the room. Yikes! I had no view of an upper body or face but saw blue Sperry Deck shoes with two legs attached. While I couldn't identify the legs, the shoes were identical to the ones Stewart Payne wore during our conversation in the Quarter.

I checked the room, again. No movement, not even from the person in the rocker. In fact, those legs and feet stayed ominously still. Maybe he was asleep. Or, passed out. Or, dead. I shivered with the last conjecture. I had to alert Clemmie. We needed to get inside, ASAP.

I crept down the deck steps and slunk around the side of the cabin. Parked on the far side of a large hedge row was a tan rental car, similar to the one Lucy drove on that first trip. I'd missed it during my first inspection of the yard. Peering around the front, I saw no sign of my partner. Not good. Where could she be? Did she go back to the truck to wait on me? I didn't dare call her name. Back pressed against the windowless side of the house, I slid to the damp ground.

I didn't hear the footsteps until it was too late. "Now, Andi, you don't need to sit out here. Why, you'll get all dirty. Come on in the cabin. I'll bet you and your friend would love a glass of sweet tea."

The smile on Lucy's face appeared anything but welcoming. The sight of her right hand, grasping a giant hunting knife close to Clemmie's throat, was downright horrifying. She gripped the arm of her hostage with the intensity of a prison guard leading a new inmate to her cell. Doubts about her involvement in my kidnapping, or Grace's demise, disappeared in an instant. "Get up. I don't have all day," she snapped. All friendly pretenses disappeared, replaced by tight lips and an icy stare.

I struggled to my feet. Clemmie stayed silent. Fighting the tremor in my voice, I managed a half-credible greeting. "Hi Lucy. We were looking for you. I'd told my friend about this charming little cabin and…"

"Shut up, you insipid girl! And, hand over your cell phones."

I pulled mine from my pocket.

"What about your friend here?"

"I don't have mine," Clemmie answered. "Search, if you don't believe me."

Lucy scoffed, "You have no place to hide a phone in those skinny jeans of yours. Women, these days, have no modesty."

Oh, so now Lucy is the fashion police.

"I will take those truck keys of yours, though." Clemmie pulled the ring from her pocket. Lucy snatched them from her hand and shoved us forward.

"You think I don't know why you're here?" She snarled. "To rescue Grace's poor, grieving widower, right?"

My mouth clamped shut. Reasoning with her was useless. The chill in her voice left no doubt warm feelings between us were long gone. This wasn't the fun-loving Lucy I'd greeted at the agency so many times in the past; the client who had practically skipped out the door, eager to start a new adventure on the ocean, in the mountains, or on some remote island beach. I did not know this woman.

Chapter Twenty-Nine

Lucy shoved us through the front door. The image of Stewart slumped in the rocker, passed out, or worse, made me gasp. I watched for any signs of life. Was the sluggish up and down movement of his chest wishful thinking, or reality? No, I wasn't imagining the slight, but steady rise. Maybe we weren't too late.

My joy was short-lived when the sensation of the sharp blade nudged the back of my cotton shirt between my shoulder blades. "Move it." Lucy motioned to Clemmie. "You, get those ropes and tie her up." Considering one vigorous shove of the knife could puncture my spine, I nodded. Now was not the time to challenge our captor.

Clemmie lifted a handful of white rope off the kitchen counter and stumbled to Lucy's side. "You'd better tie her up, good, or the inside of this shack is the last place either one of you will see," Lucy snapped.

"I've lived on a boat," Clemmie responded, controlled, and with a touch of contempt. "I know how to tie knots."

"Don't tell me. Just do it." I flinched at another threatening poke of the knife. Lucy grabbed my shoulder and moved to my side. *How did she get so freaking strong?* The point of the blade was now positioned in an equally vulnerable spot; just above my waist. I doubted the small muffin-top I'd developed

203

from too many beignets, croissants, and, of course, pralines, would protect my right kidney if Lucy decided to make good on her threat.

Clemmie wasted no time tightly binding my wrists. Lucy checked the knots and motioned toward my feet. "Legs, too. Can't have you running away now, can I?" Her voice, facial expression, and mannerisms indicated a complete departure from reality. I didn't know when or why she fell over the edge, but Lucy was clearly insane, at least temporarily.

She pitched another rope and ordered Clemmie to bind her own ankles. With that accomplished, Lucy stuck the knife between her teeth and quickly tied Clemmie's hands behind her. *If I live to be a hundred, I'll never forget that picture.* My former favorite client clamping down on a ten-inch blade.

"Now you, Andi, sit on the loveseat. Your friend can have the comfy chair," she smirked. "Stewart stays where he is, for the moment." She strolled over to the helpless man, leaned down, and gave him a horrifying kiss on the forehead. Straight out of a Stephen King novel. I wanted—needed—to throw up.

"Now that you're safe and secure, we can relax and have a nice conversation, just like before, right Andi? Oh, we've had dozens of casual talks about friends, family, Daryl." She turned to Clemmie. "He's my rotten, cheating, scrum of an ex-husband, in case you didn't know." Clemmie nodded emphatically, pretending she knew Daryl and agreed with Lucy's assessment. "Now, Stewart is different. Always thoughtful and kind. When the poor dear wakes up, we're traveling to Mexico. There's a lovely little town on a lake about fifty miles from Guadalajara. You know, Andi, I think you gave me the brochure for that piece of paradise. Isn't it funny how life works? If not for you, Stewart and I would've never found our new dream home."

From my perspective, she'd already moved to *La La Land*.

"Speaking of Stewart," I asked, "is he all right? He hasn't moved since we've been here."

Lucy laughed. "Of course, he's resting. Since all this 'Grace dilemma' happened, I thought a relaxing potion would give him some much-needed rest. Fortunately, I have a friend who makes just what the doctor ordered."

Ah-ha! The potion Jules stole from Claudia. If he did steal it for Lucy, where did he fit into the plan? No one, including his boss, had seen him in a couple of days. Come to think of it, Lucy couldn't have possibly managed to drug Stewart and drag him out here on her own. She must have a partner-in-crime. Probably the same one who helped kidnap me...the first time.

Right on cue, Stewart moaned. *Thank God! He's alive!*

Lucy jumped to his side, cradled her cheek with his limp hand. Clemmie rolled her eyes. To our disgust, Lucy had just gotten started. She squeezed onto his lap and rocked the chair back and forth with one foot. If she got any more "chummy" with him, I was outta there! Ropes and all. I didn't care if I had to leap out the door, potato-sack-race style.

As she stroked his cheek and whispered in his ear, his eyes flew open scaring the hell out of us. Lucy leapt from his lap. "Oh, Stewart! You're finally awake. I thought you were going to sleep the clock around, you lazy boy."

Stewart's body lay still, corpse-like, but his eyes moved slowly around the room, obviously still under the effect of the drug. When his lips moved, slightly, I held my breath waiting for him to speak, but all that escaped was a guttural moan. While not familiar with sleeping potions, if this had a paralytic effect, his vocal chords would be affected, too. I didn't need words, however, to interpret the pleading look in his eyes. No, Stewart Payne wasn't there, voluntarily. How could we ever get him away from that crazy woman? How could *we* get away?

Lucy continued playing the leading role in her delusional fairytale, "Stewart and Lucy move to Mexico and live happily ever after." She bounced to the kitchen. "Where are my manners? Who wants dinner? I'm preparing a lovely shrimp etouffe, along with some scrumptious French bread, of course."

Clemmie and I exchanged looks and shrugs. *Is she serious? Dinner?* On the practical side, how did she think we'd eat with our arms shackled? Did she have plans to untie us? Meanwhile, Stewart's eyes darted back and forth, waiting for some direction on how we could all escape. He was becoming more aware of the surroundings, but still in no condition to leave on his own strength.

I faced away from our psychotic chef while Clemmie, with a clear view of the kitchen, watched her every move. She caught my eye and mouthed a message I didn't understand. *Huh? The road? Your home?* What was she trying to tell me? I shrugged.

Her frustration mounted. Finally, she moved sideways, revealing her bound wrists and tilted her head toward mine. *Your ropes?* I mouthed. She nodded as vigorously as she dared without alerting Lucy.

I waited until Clemmie signaled the "all clear" and gave a slight tug on my restraints. Instead of tightening, the rope loosened just enough to let one wrist slip free. I kept my arms behind me and my shoulders still while freeing the other wrist. Now, for the next challenge. Untying my ankles while Lucy was busy coordinating her dinner party. I gave my feet a slight twist and, magically, the ropes fell off! My eyes widened with shock. Clemmie, on the other hand, shrugged. No big deal.

Okay, I was free, but now to get the jump on Lucy and her knife. Displaying the talent of a mind-reader, she called from the kitchen, "Just a few more minutes. I'm almost done mixing the salad. Oh, you're going to love this homemade raspberry vinaigrette dressing. I should bottle and sell it. With all these new online businesses popping up every day, I could make a killing!"

Make a killing? I believe you've already managed that, Lucy.

She continued banging pots and pans, making stirring sounds, humming, off tune. Something was missing from the scene, but I couldn't figure out what.

She trotted into the living room holding a large tray. "Here we are. Oh, I hope you enjoy it!" She placed a plate and salad bowl on the coffee table in front of me. Yep. Plate, bowl, silverware, napkins. *No Food. No cooking smells! That's what's missing.* I'd been in enough New Orleans restaurants to appreciate aromas every bit as heavenly as the food, itself. None here, for sure.

Clemmie and I swapped astonished looks. Even Stewart's eyebrows flashed a bit of life. Lucy went about her business without a hitch, placing the identical setup on the end table beside Clemmie. "Oh, I do hope you enjoy your meal. Daryl, that snake, used to love my gourmet cooking." She looked back and forth between us, seeming to forget Stewart was even in the room. "Well, aren't you going to eat?"

"Uh, we'd love to, Lucy. But did you forget our hands are tied?" I prayed she wouldn't take the hunting knife from her apron pocket and start slashing away.

She looked confused. "Why would I tie your hands? We're all friends. Well, maybe not you." She gave Clemmie a sickly smile. "But, any friend of dear Andi is a friend of mine."

Once again, she paid no attention to Stewart—a fact not lost on the now, semi-conscious man in the rocking chair. For the first time since our forced entry into the cabin, he made eye contact. He was definitely aware of the scene before him, but could he physically react? I couldn't wait. While Lucy's back was turned, I lunged, knocking her to the floor.

"What are you doing?" Rolling onto her back, arms and legs flailing, she screamed at the top of her lungs. I stood over her, ready to pounce if she got to her feet. Stewart struggled to get out of the chair, but his legs crumpled like tissue paper. I had to think fast. I grabbed the knife from Lucy's apron. "Stay down. I don't want to hurt you." And, I didn't. Even with all the horrible things she'd done, or apparently done. I didn't have iron-clad evidence, but her actions and mental state left little doubt she was heavily involved in a serious crime.

I moved around the still-flailing, screaming

woman, acting fast to free Clemmie. I helped my friend to her feet and cut off the leg and arm restraints. Now, to get Stewart out of harm's way. We strained to lift him from the chair. How could someone alive be such dead weight? We stumbled to the front door, eager to leave before Lucy regained her senses, or what was left of them.

I threw open the door.

"Where do you think you're going?" Jules, gun in hand, blocked our escape.

Chapter Thirty

Hanging on to Stewart with my right arm, I lifted my left in surrender; the hunting knife pointed toward the ceiling. Clemmie, supporting Stewart with her left arm, lifted her right. Stewart's arms hung limp at his sides.

"No need to shoot, Jules. We don't want trouble." I loosened my grip on the knife and eased the handle into his out-stretched hand.

"Oh, Jules! Thank God! They tried to kill me!" Lucy struggled to her feet, collapsing, dramatically, into the easy chair.

I swear, for an instant, I saw disdain on his face at the sound of her voice. Momentary, but real. Was he *all-in* with helping Lucy complete her ghastly plan?

He waved the gun toward the main room. "Get back inside. Sit where I can see you and keep those hands up."

Lucy struggled to her feet. Clemmie and I helped Stewart back to the rocker and took our respective seats. "Thought you'd get the jump on me, hmmm?" Lucy smirked. "I don't go anywhere or do anything without backup, right, Jules?"

He said nothing, but a contemptuous look flashed, once again. Definitely no love lost there. In Lucy's delusional state, she didn't appear to notice. Instead, she grabbed the knife from his hand and waved it

210

around with the flair of swashbuckler. If I hadn't been so scared, I would've laughed at the sight.

"C-careful…with that…Lucy," Stewart stammered, surprising us all.

She knelt beside him and patted his hand. "No need to worry, darling. With Jules on guard, this little ol' knife is just for my amusement." Her sickening smile contradicted the vacant look in her eyes.

With no warning, Lucy jumped to her feet; the smile leaving her face. "Enough of this chit-chat. Jules, is everything in place for our exit?"

He nodded with little enthusiasm, a shadow of reluctance in his eyes. During my first kidnapping, Lucy's accomplice had wanted my life spared—even said I'd seemed like a good person. If I'd been right about Jules, I might persuade him to defy Lucy. It was our only hope.

"So, point that gun like you mean it," she snapped. "Let's get this show on the road."

Jules pulled Clemmie to her feet and Lucy tied her arms together in the front. Then it was my turn. He determined we were both securely bound and motioned the gun toward the front door. Once outside, he barked, "Turn left off the porch."

We stumbled through waist-high weeds. Painful thistles stuck to my ankles and thighs. I glanced around long enough to confirm Stewart wasn't part of our procession. He must be alone with Lucy. Poor guy. Hard to believe being led at gun-point by Jules was light-years better than staying cooped up with a knife-wielding, crazy woman. My momentary relief faded as we approached the lake. Jules kept the gun pointed while he slipped the rope from a wooden stake attached to a small boat bobbing just off shore. He pulled our transportation onto the muddy bank and ordered us to get in.

Clemmie hesitated. "Where are you taking us?"

His dark, heavy eyebrows scrunched together. "Guess you'll find out when we get there. Now, climb in the boat and shut up."

The sound of an engine revving in the distance broke the silence of the bayou and surrounding scrub land. Clemmie's eyes widened. "My truck," she whispered.

Pretty smart on Lucy's part. If the police were looking for her, they'd put an APB on her rental car, not Clemmie's truck. Oh, if only Clem got her message! I feared the worst if he was still out in the middle of nowhere with a stalled boat engine.

Jules guided us along the left side of the lake, staying far enough from shore to avoid the tangle of cypress knees and lily pads. I considered whether to jump for freedom, since I was a strong swimmer, but with my wrists tied? *Huh-uh.* The gun, laying inches from his hand, was another deterrent. Not to mention the eight-foot alligator floating past its checkpoint, sizing up three juicy snacks. Dark, slanted eyes followed us from the bank until we were out of sight.

Strange how long you can drift in certain swamps without seeing another human being. I understood why Jules hadn't bothered to put gags on us. Who'd hear our screams? We might surprise a few egrets and pelicans.

It appeared we were heading into the middle of the bayou toward a small island. And, I do mean small! One large cypress and about twenty square feet of land. Jules steered the boat near as possible without dragging on the muddy bottom. "Get out."

I looked at him, then back at the small patch of dirt. "Excuse me? You want us to get out, here?"

"Are you hard of hearing?" He scowled.

He wouldn't make eye contact. Did he regret leaving us there? Or, worse, was he going to shoot us and let the gators dispose of our remains? Whatever the outcome, he controlled our fate. I placed my bound hands on the side of the boat and searched the best place to jump overboard. A forceful shove made my exit faster, but far less graceful than intended. Falling head-first, I struggled to get above water.

Clemmie screamed, "Help her. She's going to drown!"

I thought so, too, until a jerk on the neck of my shirt allowed my flailing feet to contact a shallow strip of rock and mud surrounding the island. I kicked my way onto the tiny bit of land, choking on a mouth full of briny bayou water. Seconds later, I heard another splash. Clemmie's turn. I stuck out one foot. Holding onto my leg, she crawled to safety using her elbows. We lay there, exhausted, coughing and gasping while Jules watched from the boat.

I called out to him. "Please, Jules, don't leave us here. Just get us to land, and you can go. We'll tell the police you helped us escape."

He hesitated. I wasn't close enough to tell whether my plea made a difference. He shook his head, slowly, turned the boat around and sped out of site.

"Are you okay?"

Clemmie rolled to her side facing me. "I think so. Oops, not so much." Her elbows were raw and bloody where she'd cut them getting out of the water. "How about you?"

I thought so until my right shin throbbed. After scraping the side of the boat during my tumble, the skin shredded on my leg leaving a red, angry-looking abrasion. "Good thing I don't have my sister, Georgia's phobia. She'd pass out after the first glimpse of her own blood. Gotta hand it to her, though. She still donates." *For Godsake! Georgia's phobias are the least of our concern.* More urgent was how long it took flesh-eating bacteria to invade an open wound? Two days? Two hours? Two minutes? If we made it back to the mainland, I pictured strong antibiotics in the near future.

Clemmie pushed herself up to a sitting position, careful to protect her elbows. "First thing is to get these ropes off. Lucy's knots shouldn't be much of a challenge. I don't picture her as the outdoorsy type."

"I don't or didn't picture her as a murderer, either," I scoffed. "Hold out your arms." I manipulated my fingers close to her wrists and picked at the knots. She was right. Lucy was no expert. One loop pulled free. I tugged at the second with my thumb and forefinger. Success! She took care of mine in short order.

Now what? Should we try to swim to shore? Since we could barely see land, I'd give myself about a twenty-five percent chance of making it. Even worse, I'd seen enough documentaries to realize it only took seconds for an alligator to drag its prey to the bottom and pin it under a log for later consumption. Nope, I wasn't ready for a swim.

Clemmie rocked back and forth, cradling her sore elbows. "Surely someone will pass by before too long. I'm not familiar with this lake, but it has to feed from somewhere."

"How long can we last here?" The sun glowed red just above the wall of pines in the distance sending new pangs of fear into my stomach.

Clemmie voiced my fear. "We may be here all night. Might as well get comfortable."

Between the mud and soccer-ball-sized rocks, we both had about three-square feet of dry space. Water lapped inches from our feet. *Sure, get comfortable, she says.*

With little else to do, we spent the early evening talking about present and departed family members. "How long have you and Clem been married?" Ellie had never mentioned her relatives, obviously, since I never knew they existed before my trip.

"Fifteen amazing years." She smiled, wistfully. "He's my rock. We're good for each other."

Hmmm. Fifteen years. They obviously married in their early twenties since neither looked older than mid-thirties. In fact, she could pass for late-twenties. I passed for late-thirties in my mid-twenties. *Yep, it's back to the gym for you, Andi, the moment you get back to Miami.* "You mentioned both sets of parents are gone. That's gotta be rough. Guess that's why you two are so close, huh?"

She nodded. "Yep. As I said, earlier, before we were kidnapped and dumped here, Clem made it his mission to get me through school. After losing my dad, I'm not sure I could've done it on my own."

She fell silent so I didn't pursue the conversation. After a long pause she asked, "What about your family?"

"Both my parents are gone, too. I have a sister,

Georgia, who thinks every woman should have a husband, four kids, and no career. As you can imagine, we don't have much in common."

She smiled. "Clem and I wanted kids, but that doesn't seem to be in the cards. Since Ellie and Clyde don't have any either, with none on the horizon, the Clanton tribe has little hope to prevail."

I pictured Clem and Clemmie being the best parents, ever. Ellie? My assistant being responsible for another human being, when she struggled to meet her own personal needs? *Perish the thought!*

Clemmie settled on the ground, arms bent, hands behind her head. "Might as well get comfortable." She turned on her side, a quizzical look on her face. "You know everything about Clem's and my relationship, what about you? Anyone special in your life?"

Even in that miserable heat and humidity, I felt a familiar flush crawl up my neck with thoughts of Manny. "I, uh...well, there is this guy in Cancun." *Guy? Talk about an understatement!*

"And..." Clemmie persisted.

"I met him six months ago when I had to fly to Mexico to get Ruby out of jail."

She sat up. "Whoa! Your stepmother, Ruby? The, uh...eccentric one?"

I nodded. "Yeah, one and the same, but I prefer the term, *ex*-stepmother." *Good! Let's change the subject to Ruby and her exploits.*

Clemmie didn't bat an eye. She wasn't giving up. "How did you meet him?"

I took a deep breath. Maybe it was good to talk, maybe clear up some of my relationship issues. "He was the sheriff overseeing Ruby's arrest."

Clemmie's only response was one raised eyebrow. Clearly, she wasn't surprised by anything, at that point, at least nothing involving dear step-mommy. Instead, she asked, "Aren't you going to describe this sheriff?"

I tried, once more, to divert attention away from my romantic exploits. "You see, Ruby was on this cruise and charged with murdering one of the passengers..."

"So, did she?"

"Huh? Did she, what?"

"Did she murder the passenger?"

"Well, no, but the case was long and involved. I had to fly to Las Vegas..."

Clemmie sighed, impatiently. "So, you cleared her. I get that since she's been wandering about New Orleans, bugging you. Back to this sheriff. Describe him."

I give up. "How do you describe an Aztec God?" My eyebrows danced, provocatively.

She gasped and fell back, faking *a Gone With the Wind* swoon. "Oh, Miss Scarlett. Tell me more!"

Had to admit, once I started, I couldn't stop. Passion and fear had a way of mixing together when you least expected. By the time I stopped to take a breath, Clemmie had the complete visual of Manny— tall, bronze complexion, and deep hazel eyes...the kind you want to fall into and never climb out. I continued with the embarrassing margarita incident. "I'd love to know what he was thinking while he undressed me and put me to bed. Whenever I asked, he smiled and repeated, 'I was a perfect gentleman.' "

She snickered. "You know it's true love when he's seen you at your worst and still comes back for more.

Surely, you're doing everything to keep in touch with this perfect specimen."

"It's sporadic. He's working. I'm working. We're hundreds of miles from each other. He came to Miami to complete the murder investigation, and we had dinner and...dessert." I laughed. Clemmie snorted. "After that, we tried Facetiming at least twice a week. That dropped to once a week and now, we're lucky to talk once a month. I know he's been overrun with cases, so I try not to bother him."

"Oh, Andi." Clemmie shook her head. "Do you want to pursue the relationship?"

I nodded. "More than anything."

"Well, then, get off your butt and call the guy!" She looked around and laughed. "The minute we get off this godforsaken postage stamp!"

"I promise." And, I meant it.

Why had I let the candle burn so low? Like my grandmother used to say, "Andi Anna, when you grab something that makes your heart sing, hang on for dear life."

That's the new plan, Grammy.

We'd talked for so long, the sudden chill in the air took my breath. Shadowy tree outlines replaced the shoreline. With no visibility beyond our noses, cold reality set in. We'd be there for the night.

Our circumstance struck Clemmie at the same time. "Guess we might as well settle in. Fishermen won't be out until early morning, 4:00 a.m. or later."

"If we're lucky," I moaned. "From the looks of it, this bayou isn't a high-traffic area. Probably why Jules, or maybe Lucy, chose to dump us here. I have to be honest, Clemmie. I'm about to lose it." My body shook, uncontrollably.

She scooted over and put her arm over my shoulder. "We'll huddle together to stay warm and get through this night. I've been in worse circumstances and so have you."

I couldn't deny that. *Left for dead in a body's exhibition in Las Vegas. Thrown in the trunk of a car. Trapped in the warehouse.* "I know. I just don't do 'dark, cold, and scary' anymore. Even as a kid, I had a nightlight so werewolves and vampires couldn't slink out of my bedroom closet."

I hadn't thought of that in years.

"Ouch! Damn bites! Just great." I swatted, frantically, at my arms, legs, and neck. "Never fear, Clemmie. You're safe from at least one pest. I'm the mosquito magnet." I smacked at two more stings, real or imagined, took a couple of deep breaths, and tried, again, to summon Georgia's meditation instructions. If I were here, alone, I could scream my lungs out, but having a meltdown wasn't fair to Clemmie. Good, or bad, we were in this together.

Chapter Thirty-One

We lazed on the beach in Cancun. I stretched, provocatively on my lounge chair, taking in the salty air and sunshine. Two mojitos beckoned from the small table separating my chair from his. Manny reached his hand out to mine and softly caressed my fingers. I grabbed my mojito with the other hand. Could I be any happier? Impossible!

He tightened his grip on my hand and pulled on my arm. "Don't be so rough!" I tried to shake off his grasp.

"Andi, you have to wake up!"

"I'm awake," I mumbled. "You're going to make me spill my mojito!"

"Andi, wake up!" Clemmie's hands were on my shoulders shaking me up and down. "We're in danger. Please wake up."

My eyes popped open, and I sprang to my feet. "What's going on?"

She shushed me. "Be quiet. I spotted a set of slanted eyes about twenty feet out."

"Al…alligators?" My voice quivered.

She nodded. "We have to get up high in this tree and hope the gator can't climb."

I searched the wildlife data in my brain. In the many Crocodile Hunter episodes I'd watched, did Steve Irwin—may he rest in peace—ever mention alligators

220

having the ability to climb trees? Oh, why didn't I pay more attention to what he was *saying*, instead of being mesmerized by his Australian accent!

"You first," Clemmie ordered. "That way, I can give you a boost."

Had I not been fully aware of my diminished muscle tone, I would've been insulted. No time for false pride when escaping a curious gator. I settled on a large branch about fifteen feet off the ground. Clemmie balanced on the opposite side, clinging to a smaller one above her head. We waited.

After a half-hour, or so, passed, we relaxed. No more predator sounds or sightings. "Think it's safe to get down?" My backside hurt like the devil and my body trembled when I glanced down at the rippling water. To most people, fifteen feet was nothing. To me, I could've easily been on the ledge of a fifty-story high rise. Add that to an occasional touch of vertigo, and I'd be a goner in no time. "I need to get down."

Clemmie scanned the water on all sides of the tiny island. "Let me go down, first."

Again, I swallowed my pride knowing she was right. When your muscles equal the firmness of a bowl full of ramen noodles, you take all the help you can get.

She jumped to the ground and directed my assent. "Grab onto the small branch just beside you, and swing your left leg around…"

"*Ah…ah…*" The ability to scream, or even speak deserted me. Just feet from Clemmie's legs lay a seven- or eight-foot alligator, mouth opened, widely, revealing razor-sharp teeth. I pointed, frantically, finally forming a single word. "Gator!"

My scream came too late. That swamp monster

clamped onto Clemmie's leg and backpedaled into the lake. She grabbed the top of a cypress knee and held on for dear life. The shock on her face sent me into action. I jumped to the muddy ground and kicked the gator's snout, eyes, any place I could inflict injury or surprise. Probably wondering what hit him, he let go of her leg and charged at me.

No time to think, I grabbed the closest and largest rock I could handle and slammed it down onto the gator's long snout.

I wasn't sure I'd caused any damage to the advancing reptile, but at least it appeared stunned. I spun around and lifted a heavier rock that could inflict more damage. A loud bang sent me sprawling to the ground, paralyzed under the weight of the second rock. The alligator, just inches from my right foot, stared, vacantly; his jaws poised to snap. I gasped at the lifeless form and drew my knees up as close to my body as possible. Clemmie, writhing on the bank clutching her bloody ankle, was oblivious to the life and death struggle. Hearing a splash just a few feet away, I shrieked hoping to scare away a second attack. "Get away, you ugly mother—"

"Whoa, Andi, it's me. I know I ain't too pretty, but no sense calling me names."

I fell to my knees at the glorious sight of Marcel pulling a small boat to shore. "Guess we got him, huh?" He shoved the dead gator with his boot, shotgun ready to fire, again, if needed. He carefully lifted the rock off my chest. "Can you stand?"

I nodded, unable to process the scene before me. Was it a split second, or did it happen over days, weeks, months?

He gently lifted me to my feet. "I feel bad about killing Mother Nature's handiwork, but yours and my granddaughter's lives were on the line."

His granddaughter? Did I hear that right?

He knelt beside her. "Let me look, baby girl." Clemmie threw her arms around him. "Now, 'fore you go hugging on me I need to check out your wound. Appears most of the bleeding has stopped, but we need to get it cleaned. Come here and help me, Andi."

Between us, we positioned Clemmie as comfortably in the boat as possible, wounded leg propped on the seat in front of her. I stepped in, careful to not rock the boat, and rested in the front. Marcel pushed the boat away from shore, jumped in with the agility of a thirty-year-old, and revved the motor. He smiled at Clemmie. "Didn't I say *Grand-père* would always take care of you?"

She managed a nod and a weak smile.

He turned his attention to me. "Now, young lady. That leg of yours needs tending, too." He circled around and sped towards land. Once underway, he shouted over the sound of the motor, "I 'spect you have a few questions."

"To say the least." I yelled back. "My wound is superficial, and the questions can wait." Clemmie's safety came first.

We sped across the lake. Clemmie, becoming more alert, gestured toward the back of the boat. "Andi, meet my grandfather, Marcel Dupree."

"Otherwise known as Mudbug." He winked. "Sorry to keep you in the dark, Andi, but when Clem and Clementine found out you were coming to town, they asked me to pick you up at the airport and keep an

223

eye on you." He shook his finger at Clemmie. "I just didn't know I had to worry about my granddaughter, too."

Clemmie lowered her eyes. "Sorry, Paw Paw."

Nothing, so far, cleared up my confusion. "But, why you? Ellie never mentioned anyone but her cousin and his wife."

Marcel shrugged, but Clemmie answered for him. "My grandfather was one of New Orleans' finest private detectives in the day. Back in the 70s and 80s, he worked with the NOPD to solve cases from extortion to robbery to murder. He even collared a few corrupt politicians during his career."

"Collateral damage." He chuckled. "When Clem said you were here investigating a client's disappearance, we weren't sure about the safety of a snoopy travel agent. 'Specially with all the unsolved murders in the last couple a months."

I was poised to object to that "snoopy" tag when Clemmie asked, "Anything new on that, Paw Paw?"

He gazed into the distance and shook his head. "'Fraid not, baby girl. "Carey keeps me up to speed. Every parish law enforcement agency, within a hundred miles of here, is taking leads, but it's got the whole state stumped. One thing no one can agree on, is this the work of a serial killer or just random crimes."

I sympathized with the relatives of all the recent victims, even though they didn't hit home like Grace's death. Stewart! How could I believe for one moment he had anything to do with the crime? *Being a cantankerous old buzzard didn't make him a murderer.* "I hope they catch up with Jules and Lucy," I added. "Clemmie and I can give our statements, but until they're caught, it's just our word against theirs."

We'd traveled about halfway across the lake when Marcel got a text. He read it and smiled. "Your hubby is waiting for us on shore, Clemmie. An ambulance is on the way, too."

For the first time in almost twenty-four hours, her face relaxed. Tears slid down her sunburned cheeks. I reached over and grabbed her hand. "We're okay, now."

Chapter Thirty-Two

Relief on Clem's face was replaced by alarm when he saw Clemmie's lower leg. The bleeding had slowed to an ooze, but shredded skin and exposed ankle bone left no doubt that gator had meant business.

Marcel filled him in on the reptile's demise. "Andi hit him on his sensitive snout, where it hurt most. Her blow probably did him in. If not, the next one would've. I shot to make one hundred percent sure he was a goner."

The ambulance arrived minutes after we got Clemmie on dry land. The EMTs cleaned the wound, thoroughly. After a discussion with the patient concerning allergies, they administered an antibiotic. "We'll still have to monitor you for thirty-six to forty-eight hours for infection," a sandy-haired young woman ordered with authority well beyond her years. "A gator bite is nothing to take lightly."

"I'll follow you," Clem confirmed and kissed his wife on the forehead. He turned to Marcel. "Will you see Andi gets to the hospital? I'll call ahead and fill them in on what happened."

The old man nodded. "I will. You let me know how my granddaughter is doing, y-hear?"

Clem smiled. "She'd never let me hear the end of it if I didn't." He stopped and pulled a phone out of his pocket. "We found yours beside the front porch. Just

226

lucky I called your cell when I got here and heard the ring tone. Otherwise, it might've been buried under the weeds, forever. This place hasn't seen a mower or weed-eater in years."

"Never thought I'd see this again, thanks. Clemmie left hers in the console before we entered the cabin. Lucy must have it, since she stole the truck."

We watched the ambulance slowly pull onto the main road with Clem trailing close behind on Bertha. Marcel turned to me. "Are you sure you're okay, Andi? I think Clem's right. You need to be checked out."

I examined the scratches on my shin. Compared to Clemmie's wound, mine was equal to a paper cut. "I just need a first aid kit. Is this a good time to ask a couple of questions for the sake of my scrambled brain?"

He threw back his head and let loose with a hearty laugh. "Of course, you can. Mine could use some unscrambling, too. Tell you what. Why don't we have a casual conversation on the way back to the city?"

Marcel must've noticed my surprise at seeing the same limo that picked me up at the airport. "I'd just dropped off a client when I got Clem's SOS. Didn't have time to go back home and get the old caddy. I live east a ways, all the way over in Slidell. Besides, Maggie May sometimes forgets to start."

"Maggie May? Does everyone around here name their modes of transportation?"

Marcel opened the front passenger door for me, walked around and slid into the driver's seat. "There's a story behind it."

Isn't there always?

He backed the limo out of the drive and headed,

slowly, toward the highway. "Yessiree. It was the early 70s. I'd just gotten my baby blue Cadillac DeVille. Oh, it wasn't brand new, but to me I might as well be behind the wheel of a high-priced mansion. I was in my late twenties and none of my friends owned anything close to my beloved Caddy. That first night, I drove around and picked up...let's see," He tapped his cheek with his index finger. "Freddie Mac, Jimbo, Dougie, and Bennie Tee. We drove down Canal Street, radio blaring. Rod Stewart's *Maggie May* came on and we all sang at the top of our lungs." He chuckled and shook his head. "Such memorable times. I believe the name was unanimous. That *sweet ride* would, forever after, be known as Maggie May. All the old gang is gone except Dougie. He's living in Red Stick, uh-Baton Rouge, with his daughter."

His voice trailed off. I squirmed with impatience. As endearing as he was, I wanted to talk about the present, not reminisce. We were halfway back to town, and I still hadn't gotten any answers. "I'm sure you miss the old days, but do you have any word on Jules or Lucy? Does anyone know where they are?"

He shook his head. "Sorry, but the police are looking for them now. Clem told them Lucy had taken off in Clemmie's truck. Who knows where Jules is. He could stay lost in the bayou for weeks."

Well, that wasn't much comfort. *Crap!*

****

Carey was waiting outside the station when we pulled up. She opened my door and helped me out. "Wow! You look terrible! Are you okay? Should you go to the hospital?"

"Maybe one of these days, you'll greet me with,

'Hey, Andi. You look spectacular! Just get back from a spa vacation?' I probably feel better than I look, but thanks for letting me know what a mess I am," I chuckled. "Seriously, I am okay, but worried sick about Clemmie."

Marcel got out of the car and confronted the young detective. "I'm worried too. Have you heard anything, Carey?"

"Let's go inside." She motioned. "I was just about to check on her but wanted to wait until you got here."

We settled in one of the private offices. Before I let loose with a barrage of questions, an EMT cleaned my leg with a strong antiseptic, applied antibiotic, and wrapped a huge bandage with gauze around my shin.

"What about Lucy? Have they found her or the truck? Is someone hunting for Jules? What about Stewart? She kidnapped him, you know!"

Phone in hand, Carey assured me, "I'll answer all your questions after I find out about Clemmie." Then spoke in her phone, "Yes, this is detective Giles with the NOPD. I'm calling about a patient who was just brought in with a severe alligator wound. Yes, Clementine Clanton." She put her hand over the mouthpiece. "They're checking, now," she whispered. "Yes, I'm here. No surgery required? That's good news. Thanks, we'll be in touch."

She put down the phone and smiled. "She's doing okay. No permanent damage, although they want to observe the wound for forty-eight hours before releasing her. From what the E.R nurse said, she's very lucky"

Marcel heaved a sigh. "Thank the good Lord. And, thank you, Andi, for your quick thinking. How did you know to smash his nose?"

Instead of going into boring detail about my love of TV nature episodes, I said, "Just lucky, I guess."

Carey laid her phone on the desk. "Thank goodness you got to them in time, Marcel."

"About that," I interrupted. "How did you know where to find us?"

"We had an anonymous call come in just after midnight," she explained. "A muffled voice saying two people were spotted in the middle of Seaux Swamp. The dispatcher was still searching for the exact location when Clem called in. He'd just gotten cell service, called Marcel, and was headed your way. Clemmie's text and our mystery caller helped pinpoint your location."

Mystery caller? I'd bet money it wasn't Lucy. Not in her state of mind. Jules, maybe?

"Marcel reached us in the nick of time." A mental snapshot of Clemmie being dragged into the water sent me into a full-body shiver.

Carey noticed and called for a blanket. "Here, wrap up in this before you pass out, again. Still say you're okay? I'll load you in the car, turn on the siren and get you to the hospital in minutes."

I took three deep breaths and exhaled. The blanket provided warmth and protection. "I'm relieved now that I know Clemmie's okay."

For the first time since Marcel brought me in, Carey sat down and relaxed. "Okay, I need to hear exactly what happened. Clem gave me a *Reader's Digest* on the way to the hospital, but, naturally, his main concern was Clemmie. So, are you ready?"

I nodded.

Carey tapped *record* and I spilled my account of the past twenty-four hours, starting with my hair-brained idea to go to the cabin to look for Stewart, and being caught by Lucy.

"Just when we thought she was incapacitated, and we could escape, there was Jules, standing outside the door pointing a gun."

I described hearing Clemmie's truck start as we were forced into the boat, and Jules dumping us on the tiny island. "I can't believe he failed to carry out Lucy's orders. She definitely wanted us dead. Our hands were tied, already. He could've easily tied our feet and dumped us into the middle of the swamp. But he left us on dry land, instead."

"Puzzles me, too," Carey conceded. "So, you don't believe he was going to kill you?"

"I don't know. I'd like to think Lucy didn't want us dead, either, but she did try to kill me, once. At least she gave it a good try! If she ordered Jules to get rid of us, he couldn't, at least not directly. I don't think murder is in his DNA. I heard him ask to spare me during the first kidnapping. Maybe, by taking us to such a desolated spot in the lake, he figured nature would take its course, and he wouldn't be wholly responsible if or when we died."

Carey wrote a couple of notes on a scratch pad and asked for more detail about Stewart's condition when we got to the cabin.

I'd started to answer when we heard shouting coming from the main lobby.

"You think you can steal from me? I took you in and gave you a job when no one else would even talk to you." A high-pitched scream shattered the previous quiet of the station.

"Wait here," Carey ordered.

Marcel and I exchanged quizzical looks but stayed silent so we could listen to the commotion coming from outside the room. Finally, a calming voice, probably Carey's, got control and normal speaking tones prevailed.

"Darn! I wish they'd talk louder," I complained.

A few minutes later, Carey returned, looking satisfied. "Well, it appears one of our fugitives is in custody. Jules was caught sneaking into Claudia's House of Magic as he searched her desk for his passport. Said she'd kept it as collateral for weeks of pay advances she'd given him. A couple of patrol officers brought him in after Claudia ran into the street, flagged them down, and led them to an unconscious man, lying on the floor of her office. According to Claudia, the perp dropped like a rock when she banged him over the head with a wooden fertility statue."

I couldn't help but laugh. "Whatever works. But what was all the commotion out front?"

Carey shook her head. "Guess she followed him into the station, still attempting to bop him on the head."

"Did he confess?"

She nodded. "They're booking him right now for theft. He didn't put up much fuss. We'll get the rest out of him. The officers who brought him in are taking him to the clinic around the corner for concussion protocol. After that, we'll find out what he knows about Lucy's plan, her whereabouts, and if he did steal the sleeping potion used on Stewart."

"What's this about a sleeping potion?" Marcel

asked.

I told him what I knew. "Claudia claimed he stole a potion made by a witch-friend of hers."

Marcel's eyes widened raising both abundantly, gray eyebrows. "You mean, Giselle?"

"Yes, do you know her?" It was my turn to be surprised.

"Didn't Clem mention her? She's the great-great-granddaughter of his ancestor, Marie Josephe. Guess Marie created quite a stir in her time. Folks swear she turned men into frogs and fed them to the gators around her place." He laughed at my horrified expression. "Don't take that seriously. I suspect most of her exploits were either made up or embellished throughout the years."

Elbows on the table, I cupped my face in the palms of my hands. "Let me get this straight. You're Clemmie's grandfather. Now, I find out the witch, er, uh, chemist who makes potions for Claudia, is related to Clem and Ellie. It's no wonder Ellie gets along with her goat-cooking neighbor."

Marcel sat back, pleased at my grasp of the complicated situation. "I believe Giselle is his third cousin, twice removed."

Carey looked as stunned as I. "All those years I've heard stories about Marie Josephe, the Swamp Witch, I never suspected she was Clem's ancestor."

"He'd prefer to keep it that way. His logical brain refuses to buy into voo-doo or witchcraft. Clemmie, now, loved to visit Claudia's shop as a child. Used to beg me to take her when I picked up a poultice for my rheumatism."

"Clemmie and I stopped by, yesterday, or was it

the day before?" I couldn't remember one day from the next. "Anyway, Claudia was thrilled to see her and talked, fondly, about you."

Did Marcel just blush? "Aw, pshaw. We're just old friends."

Hmmm. Mentioning old friends doesn't usually make your face turn beet-red.

Eager to change the subject he pushed back his chair. "Carey, if you don't need us anymore, I'm going to take Andi back to her hotel so she can get some rest."

"Good idea, Marcel," Carey affirmed. "But, with Lucy still on the run, I want to send an officer to guard her."

Marcel shook his head. "No need, Carey. I'll do that, myself."

He stood, extending his six-foot frame, arms spread like wings. My "guardian angel" lifted me to my feet and guided me toward the door. "I'll stay as long as I'm needed. Call me if you get any leads."

Chapter Thirty-Three

Exhaustion crushed me with the weight of a steel blanket the moment my head hit the pillow. Marcel, bless his heart, had pulled a courtyard chair up to my door and parked his 70-plus year-old body. "I'll be right here guarding the door. Now, you get some rest."

I woke around 8:00 p.m. when my cell buzzed. It was Ruby. *Just what I need.* Clearing my throat, I summoned strength from my better angels. "Hey Ruby. What's up?"

"Well, now, sugar, I could ask you the same thing! Where on *God's green earth* have you been?"

"It's a long story." Knowing her impatience to listen to anyone but herself, I wasn't surprised when she blurted out, "Oh, honey, I'd love to hear it, but the girls and I are signed up for a ghost tour. Isn't that exciting?"

"Exciting, Ruby. Have fun."

"I have a super idea, Andi. Why don't you come along? The tour begins at 9:00 p.m. so you have time to meet us. Why, I'll even spring for your ticket. Well…technically, Dougie will." Her piercing laugh jeopardized what remained of my eardrum.

"Wish I could, but I'm leaving tomorrow evening and need to tie up some loose ends before I go. You know, with the police and Grace. I also want to say goodbye to Ellie's cousins and Clementine's grandfather. But I appreciate the offer."

235

"Well, if you change your mind, it's the Double Spirits Ghost Tour. Get it? Along with hunting spirits, we get to drink to them before and after the tour."

"I get it. Just watch how many spirits you consume. Have a good trip home. I'll see you in Miami."

"You bet, sugar. We're flying out day after tomorrow. Bye-bye."

I flopped back on the pillow. How could I wake up feeling refreshed and let one phone call sap all my energy? Ruby had that uncanny knack. Needing to check on Marcel, I staggered to the window and pulled back the drapes. Yep, he was still sitting there, sipping on a cup of coffee.

I stuck my head out the door. "How are you doing?"

"Well, good to see you up and at 'em. Want a coffee or espresso. I swear this stuff will keep a body upright for days."

"No thanks. I have too much on the agenda tomorrow to be up all night. C'mon in and sit in the recliner," I motioned. "You can put your feet up."

He stood and rested both palms on his low back. "I don't know how I can stiffen up in all this humidity, but I sure do. Knees don't work too well, either. Old age ain't for sissies, Andi."

Middle age ain't either. After clearing yesterday morning's clothes off the recliner so he could sit, I pulled out the straight back desk chair across from him. "Have you gotten any news from the police about Lucy? Did they interview Jules?"

"Let me check." He paged through his messages. "Here's something from Carey. Wants me to call her." He hit redial and waited for the detective to answer.

"Hey, Carey, you called?" He paused. "Ah-ha! She thought she'd get away with that? Uh-huh...uh huh. You don't say! If you ask me, she's a couple sandwiches short of a picnic for six. Yeah, she's right here. I'll tell her." He nodded and disconnected the call.

"Well! What did she say?"

He settled back in the recliner appearing to gather his thoughts. "That client of yours is one desperate lady. First, let me assure you she's off the streets."

The *whoosh* of air expelled from my lungs managed to flutter sweat-soaked bangs on my forehead. For the first time in days, my shoulders relaxed. "Details," I pleaded.

"Seems Lucy Minor, and her drugged captive, Mister Payne, were caught all the way down in Terrebonne Parish trying to charter a boat to take them to the Yucatan. Oh, and the best part...she tried to trade Clemmie's truck to pay for it."

"Mexico? She thought she could get to Mexico? And, with Stewart in tow?" After all the evidence, Lucy's behavior simply didn't add up. Maybe my ego was too bruised from being so wrong about someone I'd considered a friend.

"The pair is being transported back to Orleans Parish. I assume Stewart will go straight to the hospital and Missus Minor, straight to jail. Oh, and Carey asked that you be available in case they need more information."

"Is Stewart going to be all right?"

"Seems his kidnapper gave him a second dose of Giselle's sleeping potion, but Carey said he was conscious and talking to the EMT's. So, that's a good sign."

Indeed, it was. Imagine two clients. One I'd practically considered a mother-figure. The other, a client I'd previously considered my worst nightmare. My concern had switched sides.

"Did they get any more information from Jules?"

Marcel shook his head. "Not much. The only thing he expressed was regret. So, maybe you were right about him. After that, he clammed up, said he'd wait on his lawyer, whoever that might be."

I noticed Marcel's droopy eyelids and tired demeanor. Clear signs of exhaustion. Hell, I was exhausted at more than half his age! "Why don't you go on home? With Lucy and Jules in custody, I'm safe. Besides that, I need to get some sound sleep. If I know you're sitting outside all night, I'll never close my eyes."

He reluctantly agreed. "Only if you promise to bolt this door behind me. I don't care if Harry Connick, Jr. comes knocking, dragging his piano behind him, keep this door shut. Ya hear?"

I had to smile picturing that marvelously ridiculous scene. "But what if he promises to dedicate a song to me?"

Marcel gave me one of those looks your parents gave when you'd pushed their unconditional love a little too far. "You call me first thing in the morning, young lady."

"Yes, sir." I knew when to comply.

After he left, but not before one final stern look, I stumbled to the bathroom, splashed luke-warm water on my face (there is no such thing as cold water in New Orleans in the summer), gave my teeth a hasty brush, and grabbed a clean T-shirt from the bottom of my bag.

"Hmmph. Fitting message." *Trust but verify*. A birthday gift from my left-brained sister.

I crawled into bed wondering how in the world I'd ever shut off *my* brain. The last thing I heard were the haunting notes of a saxophone, floating somewhere in The Quarter.

****

I might've slept all day if not for the persistent commotion in the courtyard from hearty souls who stayed up all night, or began their day at the crack of...

"Ten o'clock?" I jumped out of bed. Late enough to feel refreshed after a good night's sleep, but too early to accurately organize my thoughts. A giant mug of coffee was in order before any attempt to think logically.

Barely presentable, I slipped into the café, ordered my usual extra-large coffee, and managed to creep back to my room before concerned citizens called hotel security on the frizzy-haired vagrant. For once, I was glad Manny was hundreds of miles away. Sure, he'd seen me at my worst after my margarita binge, but I'd been barely conscious; unaware of any reason to be embarrassed.

I'd hide under a hibiscus bush before I'd let him see me now!

Back in the safety of my room, I propped my iPad on the table and flipped through the latest news. *Politicians butting heads over...* Hmmm, surprise, surprise.

Hedge-fund heir kills father after allowance cut off. Dude, seriously?

Deadly shark attacks continue to escalate. I'm sticking to the condo pool.

239

Same tragic headlines. Couldn't something good happen?

Then I came upon some positive local news. *Florida woman captures apparent New Orleans-area serial killer.*

A vacationing North Miami Beach woman was credited with the capture of the man police suspect in the murder of four women over the past six months. Senior citizen, Ruby Jones, incapacitated the suspect until police arrived. "Why, I had no idea he was dangerous," Mrs. Jones related to the Times-Picayune last night. "But, he was extremely rude!"

I read it again...and again. I might've brushed it off as a weird name coincidence if not for the "extremely rude" statement. That had to be my Ruby. I paged down to the most recent link.

"Oh, for the love of Pete." A full-page photo of my stepmother—posed with a bright red shoe in hand—jumped, mockingly, off the screen. Captioned: *Don't mess with a lady and her six-inch spikes.*

I took a giant swig of coffee and continued reading.

"The Florida woman credited with capturing the suspect told reporters, "At first, he acted like a gentleman. Otherwise, I never would've consented to have a drink with him in his hotel suite. I kinda got suspicious when he tied my arms behind my back and pretended it was all in fun. The kicker was...oh, I made a joke, didn't I? Anyway, when he tore the strap off one of my new Ferragamos, I got royally pissed, er-uh, mad. That's when I gave him a swift kick in the ear with the other shoe."

I slumped back against the headboard, took another shot of coffee, and read on.

According to Mrs. Jones, the alleged killer fell over immediately, but was revived after police arrived. The suspect was arrested when items belonging to all four murder victims, were found in a brief case and hotel dresser. The as-yet-unnamed, fifty-three-year-old male is being held without bond.

My tablet clattered on the table. How could this be? I must still be asleep and having one whale of a dream!

A persistent banging on my hotel door and subsequent, "Yoo-hoo, Andi? Are you in there?" turned what might've been a dream into a nightmare. Ruby pushed past me the moment I cracked the door.

"You're not going to believe what happened! Oh, you're just not going to believe it, Andi. Maybe you better sit down, sugar."

I remained standing. "You hit a serial killer in the ear with your shoe." Oh, I knew it was mean and petty to steal her thunder but, old habits die hard.

She flopped down on the corner of the unmade bed; mouth agape, surprise written all over her make-up laden face. "How did you know? Oh, was it in the newspapers this morning? Was there a picture of me?" She bounced up and down. "Some photographer was there snapping one photo after another of me holding my 'weapon'." She snickered.

I handed her the tablet. "I read it here, and yes, there is a full-size photo of you and your *weapon*."

She huffed when she saw her picture. "Oh, dear. That's such a bad angle." With the back of her hand, she patted the underside of her face. "Why, for goodness sakes, in this picture you'd think I had a double chin!"

I bent over, laughing. "Oh, Ruby. Only you could capture a serial killer and worry about the photogenics."

I wonder what she'll think about the "senior citizen" label?

I gave her an uncharacteristic hug. "I'm relieved you're okay. That had to scare the daylights out of you."

Her shoulders slumped. "Well, now that you mention it. I've been on such a high since last night, I guess the danger hasn't sunk in. Do you know I've been contacted by every newspaper and TV station in South Florida? Not to mention several around here!"

I sat on the bed beside her. "So, did the police release you, or do you have more interviews or statements to give?"

She fiddled with the diamond tennis bracelet Dougie gave her before the trip, even though she'd never stepped foot on a tennis court to actually play.

"They want me to come to the station one more time, this afternoon. Oh, Andi, could you come with me?"

"If I can still make my 6:00 p.m. flight to Miami."

She patted my knee. "Oh, goodie! I'll tell that sergeant to pick me up, here! Meanwhile, we can grab lunch and do some shopping." She jumped off the bed and gave me the once-over. "You are taking a shower and doing something with that hair, right? So, how was your night? Better than mine, I hope."

"Not much, Ruby. Not much. We can talk about it, later." I gathered clean underwear and clothes and headed to the bathroom. Maybe I'd get sucked into a bathtub portal and end up in another state, or country, or planet. I could hope.

242

Chapter Thirty-Four

Ruby's interview with Sergeant Le Blanc went better than expected. In fact, she was almost reserved. *Almost.* I also got additional information on Lucy.

"She's nuttier than a fruit cake," he asserted. "When we brought her in, she had on that matching pendant you described. She swore to the arresting officer, it was the only piece in existence and that her husband, Stewart, had given it to her for their wedding anniversary."

Oh, Lucy. I should've felt vindicated, but sadness overwhelmed me. "Will she go to prison, or a psychiatric hospital?"

"Too early to speculate," Le Blanc indicated. "My guess is a combination; a prison/psych institution."

"Did she give a reason for killing Grace, other than wanting her out of the way?"

"No specific reason from her, but Jules indicated she was bitter over her divorce and needed someone, other than herself, to blame. Turns out that pendant Stewart gave to his wife, was the tipping point."

"Why? She was jealous of a piece of jewelry?"

"Lucy talked, non-stop, during moments of lucidity, according to Jules. Apparently, she'd spotted the pendant in a specialty craft shop and had begged her husband to buy it for her. Instead, he led her outside and announced he was leaving. Her ego wouldn't let her believe anything other than another woman was the cause. Coincidentally, shortly after Lucy's husband, uh..."

"Darryl," I cut in. "Darryl, the Snake, to be exact."

"Of course, he is," the sergeant chuckled.

What'd'ya know? Andre Le Blanc almost laughed!

"Anyway, coincidentally," he continued, "Stewart bought that same piece for Grace. The first time Lucy spotted her wearing it, I guess her mind snapped. According to Jules, she was convinced Darryl left her for Grace and had given it to her."

"Why did Lucy get the identical piece of jewelry?" I didn't get the connection.

Andre shook his head. "That, I don't know. We can speculate, but—"

"Maybe she talked herself into believing Stewart bought it for her," Marcel said.

"Very well could be," the sergeant added. "I suspect once she'd eliminated her competition, the pendant would forever link her to Grace's widower."

"What about Jules?"

"That's a little tricky, Miss Jones. He did give us valuable information on Lucy. Specifically, a location, motive to eliminate the competition, and plan to take Stewart out of the country. We wrongly suspected Jules had killed Grace, but Lucy was the mastermind all along. From Jules' account, Lucy met her victim at the airport on the pretense of taking her to the hotel. Instead, she managed to strangle Grace to death before leaving the body for Jules to dispose in the bayou. While he's innocent of murder, he's an accessory and also guilty of helping kidnap you. I'm certain immunity is out of the question, but his cooperation may lighten the sentence."

I was, unexpectedly, relieved. Jules was a victim of greed, but that wouldn't lessen my nightmares, thanks to his role. And thanks, mainly, to Lucy. "I know Lucy is mentally unstable—"

Andre scoffed, "Putting it mildly."

"Didn't it occur to Lucy that Stewart might not be on board with the living arrangements?" I struggled with grasping her complete mental breakdown.

"Maybe she planned to keep him drugged the rest of his life. She is that delusional." He stood abruptly—a standard Andre signal the interview was over. "We have your deposition, and I seriously doubt this will go to trial. When I know more, I'll let you know.

"Before we're dismissed, I'm happy to offer my services, if the need arises." Ruby had been so quiet, for the past hour, I jumped at the sound of her voice! My relief, she hadn't caused a scene or mentioned her "stay" in the Cancun jail, dangled precariously.

Oh, Ruby, please don't say something to get us both locked up!

She stood as close as possible to the sergeant without stepping on his shoes, straightened his tie, patted him on the chest, and offered one final piece of advice. "Now, Sugar, if you have any more trouble in your city, you know who to call. Ruby Jones! Day or night, I'm always available for the men in blue." She turned on her high heels, blew a kiss and waved. "Bye, y-all!"

I cringed at the dazed look on Sergeant Le Blanc's face and grabbed her elbow. "Let's go, Ruby."

"Was that necessary?" I asked on the way back to the hotel.

She sniffed. "Well, I did catch a dangerous criminal for them, didn't I? Who knows, this may be the beginning of another career."

Another career? I didn't know you had a first.

She waved her hand across the sky as if painting a marquee. "Jones Private Investigating."

****

Back at the hotel, we said our goodbyes. "Are you sure you can't stay another day, Andi," she pleaded. "We could take that ghost tour I was supposed to go on last night. Cloris and Doris said it was horrific!"

"Much as I'd like to, Ellie needs me back at the agency." While I needed to call and thank her for overnighting my replacement ID for the plane trip home, I dreaded talking to my assistant. While checking my phone at the police station, I'd noticed eighteen text messages from her—the last three marked S.O.S. Another message from Clem said he'd filled her in about the latest on Lucy's arrest, so her frantic calls must be work-related. "Besides," I added, "after your altercation with a serial killer, are you up to staying another day?"

She gave me another hug and opened the door. "Sweet of you to worry, but Cloris and Doris have signed on as my bodyguards." After a giggle and a flip of her hand, she scurried across the courtyard, out of sight.

Finally, back in my room, I collapsed on the bed for some down-time before I had to pack. Clemmie had arranged for Marcel to pick me up at 4:00 p.m. "No charge, Andi. You've been through enough," she'd insisted. *I agree with you there, sister.* I planned to call Manny once I got to the airport. As far as I knew, he'd heard nothing about my dramatic, danger-filled week. He'd texted before I left for Louisiana that he had to fly to Mexico City for a few days, but he must be back, by now.

But, before my attention turned to Cancun, I had one more crucial call to make before leaving for the airport. "Hi, Clemmie."

"Hey, Andi. Sure is good to hear your voice."

"I'm so relieved to hear yours. How are you doing?"

"Oh, don't worry about me. I'm good and I have the best nurse a girl could ask for."

I laughed. "So, Clem's right there, huh?" He must've been listening in because I heard, "She's a rotten patient, Andi. You need to stay a few more days."

I smiled. *Big talker*. I couldn't picture his leaving her side until she completely healed. "You keep me posted. Just because I'm in Florida doesn't mean I can't fly back at a moment's notice."

Clemmie chuckled. "You take care of business there. And I don't just mean travel business."

"Yes, ma'am. I'll give your best to Ellie." I cringed at the thought of the cross-examination my assistant would inflict the moment I stepped into the agency. That reminded me. Better check those S.O.S. texts.

"Where are the coffee filters?!" *Good grief, Ellie*. "Beside the coffee pot!" I answered.

"Did we order passport apps?" *Yes! Filed under P!*

"Never-mind. found 'em"

To think I was worried about Ellie being on her own for a week dealing with coffee filters and passport applications. Try spending the week fleeing kidnappers

247

and murderers!

****

I stood on the airport sidewalk and hugged Marcel. "I don't know what I would've done without you, Clem, and Clemmie. Matter of fact, I'd probably be dead." I placed my hand on his forearm. "Oh, and Bonnie. I never got the chance to thank her."

"I'll tell her how grateful you are, Andi. I enlisted her help the minute you came to town. She's been my extra set of eyes and ears for a few years, now. That girl knows the goings-on in the Quarter like the back of her hand."

"I wondered how she knew my name." Only fitting my dad would have a hand in my introduction to Bonnie. *Sorry, Dad, but you're on your own when it comes to loving sazeracs.* After my experience in the alley behind the bar, I didn't plan on drinking another one.

"Clem and Clemmie promised to visit in the near future. I hope you'll come, too."

"You can count on it, Andi. I think of you as a second granddaughter. I couldn't forget you if I tried." He leaned down and kissed me on the forehead. "Safe travels and let us know when you get home."

Stepping through the automatic doors, I turned and waved to the gentleman who was the first to welcome me to The Big Easy and the last to wish safe travels back to Miami.

Wonder how long it would take to switch mental gears for the trip back.

Passenger traffic was surprisingly light for that time of the day. Tourists had probably taken early flights and business travelers were few and far between.

I checked in and hunted for a quiet spot to call Manny. A gate on the other side had just loaded passengers for a non-stop flight to Chicago. I found a soft seat in a corner. Heart pounding, I hit # 1 on speed dial. Four rings. No answer. I was prepared to leave a message when a smoky voice answered. "Andi, *mi amor*."

I choked back tears. "Oh, Manny. You don't know how good it is to hear your voice. I've missed you, so much."

"What's troubling you, Andi? Are you alright?"

Where do I begin? Was it fair to spill the whole story over the phone, sitting at an airport gate? How would he react when I described being almost killed…twice? "Manny, are you back in Cancun?

"*Si.*"

"Anything major coming up in the next few days?"

"Work wise? I don't believe anything out of the ordinary," he answered. "Why do you ask?"

"Uh, could I call you back in a few minutes?"

"Sure, please don't be too long, though. I've missed talking to you." In a softer voice, he added, "I've missed all of you, Andi Anna Jones."

My heart skipped a beat. "No need for concern. If my plan works, we'll be able to talk, and more." I disconnected and immediately called the airline. "Yes, this is Andi Anna Jones. I'm scheduled on your 6:00 p.m. flight to Miami. Yes, I'm here at the airport, but need to change the destination. Is that possible? Great! Please book me on your next available flight to Cancun."

My next call?

"Hey, El. I have some good news and some bad news."

249

A word about the author…

Author, Mary Cunningham grew up on the northern side of the Ohio River in Corydon, Indiana. Her first memories are of her dad's original bedtime stories that no doubt inspired imagination and love of a well-spun "yarn".

Through the author's horrifying stint as a travel agent, protagonist Andi Anna Jones, travel agent and amateur sleuth, sprang to life. The adult/mystery series gives extra meaning to the phrase, "Write what you know."

Cunningham also has a published biography depicting a military brat, college and professional basketball player, along with a five-book, middle-grade fantasy series.

She is a member of Sisters in Crime, Sisters in Crime, Atlanta Chapter, International Thriller Writers, Inc., and the Carrollton Writers Guild.

When she gives her fingers a break from the keyboard, she enjoys golf, swimming, and exploring the mountains of West Georgia where she makes her home with her husband.

http://www.marycunninghambooks.com

Thank you for purchasing
this publication of The Wild Rose Press, Inc.

For questions or more information
contact us at
info@thewildrosepress.com.

The Wild Rose Press, Inc.
www.thewildrosepress.com